THE INVISIBLE CHAINS

A CHILLING SCOTTISH CRIME THRILLER

L E HILL

TIDE END PRESS

This book is for those affected by gender-based violence.

COPYRIGHT

First published in 2021 by Tide End Press

ISBN 978-1-8381243-4-2
Ebook ISBN 978 1 83812 433 5

Cover design by Emmet MacIntyre & cover photograph

PROLOGUE

***Daily Post*, 2 February 2016**

Police are appealing for the public's help to identify a young woman found dead in the River Clyde. The body was discovered by a member of the public on Monday morning. The death is being treated as unexplained. The young woman is believed to be of African descent and thought to be aged between 15 and 21. She is 5ft 6in and of slim build. She was wearing black leggings, a black T-shirt and no shoes. A Police Scotland spokeswoman said: "We're currently conducting a number of inquiries as part of our efforts to identify this person and trace her family. We're appealing for the public's help and urge anyone who may recognise her description to get in touch with us as soon as possible." The spokeswoman added that an investigation was underway to establish the full circumstances surrounding the woman's death.

1

Glasgow, May 2016

THE PEW WAS hard against the back of Megan's legs, the air cold and slightly sour. Sitting alone at the front of the crematorium, she watched the morning sunlight trickle through the A-frame window overlooking the Garden of Remembrance. It was strewn with cellophane wrappers and dead flowers. Glancing at her watch, she shivered, pulling her coat tighter around her shoulders. Megan had been to enough paupers' funerals to know this wouldn't take long. She was desperate for a caffeine fix. She breathed out a whoosh of air, let her shoulders sag and closed her eyes, trying to savour the peace and stillness of the crematorium chapel - of death. Her brain ached at the jumble of thoughts racing through it. She became aware of soft footsteps walking down the aisle. It was probably someone from the council, or someone like her, there to show support for the poor friendless soul about to be trundled into the furnace. She stretched her neck slowly from side to side, then heard a rasping cough behind her. A heavy hand pressed down on her shoulder.

'No need to move, darlin',' said a vaguely familiar voice.

Megan frowned, trying to place it.

'Fancy seeing you here.'

'Sam Martin!' Megan turned to look at the small man sitting behind her. His hair was thinning, he had a wispy moustache and he wore a brown leather jacket. 'Bloody hell. You gave me some fright there. See you're still wearing that bloody jacket.'

'Lovely to see you too,' said the man, smiling sardonically. In fact, despite her words, Megan was genuinely pleased to see Sam, not just as a familiar face but as an important figure from the beginning of her career as a journalist.

'What are you doing here?'

'The same thing as you.'

'Old tricks never die, eh? Paupers' funerals. You never know what you might find.'

'Aye,' agreed Sam. 'Old friends for a start. I did hear you were back through in the west. I've been waiting for your call.'

'Shh,' said Megan as the minister and a couple of other well-wishers filed down the aisle. 'I'll fill you in later.' She turned to face the front and traced her fingers over the Bible stowed in the chair in front of her while she processed the coincidence. What were the chances of her bumping into him at this crematorium at this particular time? Unless he'd been following her. She wouldn't put it past him. They'd worked together in Aberdeen when Megan was a trainee. Sam was a tabloid journalist; Megan had opted for the broadsheets. But he'd taken her under his wing and kept an eye on her when they'd been out on jobs. He was fearless, obnoxious and arrogant, which had made him an ideal reporter.

When the service finished, Megan stood up. Sam followed her out into the car park, watching as the next contingent of mourners circled in their cars looking for a space.

'Well,' said Megan, 'I think you and I must be the only hacks to hang about funerals. That was one of the first things you taught me.'

'Glad you remembered. Aye, well, it has given me some good stories over the years,' said Sam, stroking his moustache. 'Not today though.'

Megan glanced at her watch.

'You in a hurry?'

'Yes, I am actually,' she said, pulling out her phone. 'I wanted to go and see the First Minister's press conference. Just going to call a cab.'

'Where is it?'

'Concert Hall. Have you got your car?'

'Sure do,' he said, pointing at a grubby little white Honda. 'Lucky, that, eh? Come on. I'll give you a lift. We can catch up on the way.'

'So, it's true then?' said Sam as he reversed at speed out of the parking space.

'What's that?' Megan was scrolling through the messages on her phone.

'You're working in Glasgow permanently now?'

'Yip,' said Megan, without looking up.

'Interesting move. Have you had enough of Edinburgh then?'

'Something like that,' she said, glancing down at her screen. Then, to divert attention away, she switched tack. 'Anyway, how are you? Are you still at the *Sunday Tribune*?'

'Aye, well . . . no, not any more. I'm freelancing. Doing shifts here and there, you know.'

'Why, what happened?' she asked. 'Did you get sacked?'

'No.' His eyes were fixed on the road. 'I took voluntary redundancy. All these cutbacks, you know. Digital is the way forward.'

'I know. I don't know many who're still surviving,' Megan agreed. 'It's getting harder and harder to make a decent living in newspapers.'

'What's new with you then apart from the job? How are you?'

'I'm good, thanks,' said Megan, shrugging.

'You look well.'

Megan rolled her eyes. Her long hair no longer had blonde highlights, it was now a dull brown, and she had given up on her regular Pilates sessions. Some days she felt about ninety. She glanced over at Sam. He'd also aged since she last saw him; his hair was definitely receding and he'd developed quite the pot belly. 'You too,' she said.

'Liar.' He laughed. 'Anyway, I'm surprised you didn't end up in the jail. You know how careful you have to be these days if you have too many police contacts.'

Megan was looking out of the window in disbelief at the number of Aldis and Lidls they were passing. How many supermarkets did one city need? 'Look, it wasn't me that had a reputation for entertaining the cops and putting it on my expenses bill.'

'Ouch,' he said. 'I know. The good old days, eh?'

Megan glanced at the balled-up crisp packet and empty water bottles on the floor. 'You on a health kick?' she said, pointing at them.

'Aye, something like that. Decided it was probably a good idea to give up the fizzy juice.' Then, pulling over, 'I'll drop you here. Then I'll park the wagon and see you in there. Wouldn't mind having a wee sniff around. Free coffee at the very least.'

Megan was glad she'd worn her thick coat as she walked up Buchanan Street towards Glasgow's Royal Concert Hall. Didn't matter that it was spring, it was still freezing and damp. It was so very damp. She looked at the grey blobs of chewing gum studding the rose-coloured pavement slabs, then glanced up at the buildings around her. It had been a while since she'd been here, and, for as long as she could remember, ugly scaffolding had been a constant fixture. But now she noticed the metal structures were finally gone and the architecture was on show. As she passed the statue of Donald Dewar, Scotland's first First Minister and the architect of devolution, she stifled a laugh. Someone had wrapped a Partick Thistle football scarf around his neck. Music blared into the empty street from Topshop and there was a dull hum from the buses trundling down West Nile Street. Walking up the steps to the concert hall, which reminded her of the tiers of a wedding cake, she began to mentally scroll through her to-do list. Pulling open the heavy door, she headed over to the registration table and decided the matter of caffeine was most pressing.

The floppy-fringed man behind the table greeted her with a nod. 'Name and publication?'

'Megan Ross. *Sunday Edition*.'

He casually flicked a finger over his tablet, glanced up and smiled.

'Here you are, Ms Ross.' He handed her a laminated badge and a press pack. 'If you just go through to the restaurant area, coffee and pastries are being served.'

She strode across the lobby towards the waiter who stood beside a table draped with a thick white linen cloth. Pouring her a cup from a cafetiere, he offered her a platter of mini croissants.

'Thank you,' she said, popping one in her mouth. She surveyed the small assembled group of hacks who looked like they had an average age of seventeen. Taking a sip from her cup, she tried to make eye contact with anyone who was willing, but they were all glued to their phones. Hunched shoulders and dipped heads, furiously tapping and swiping. A lot had happened to Megan since she'd moved to Edinburgh four years ago after working briefly in Glasgow. She thought she should have, in that time, managed to reinvent herself. But being back now felt alien. A sliver of doubt crept into her head.

'At least you raise the average age in here quite significantly,' said Sam, appearing at her side. 'Even at the ripe old age of what? Twenty-nine?'

'And there was me thinking it was actually quite nice to see you,' retorted Megan. There had been plenty of times when she would have happily emptied her cup over his head.

'Aye. You still haven't told me why you wanted to come back to Weegieland.'

'It seemed like a good idea. Richard asked and I fancied a change.' Richard was the editor of the *Sunday Edition*, the popular weekly tabloid. 'Mind you,' she added, with a shiver, 'it's a bit dreich.'

'You turned all posh after a few years in the capital?' teased Sam.

'No, just got used to the drier climate. Looks like it's time for the First Minister. Come on.' She walked towards the auditorium.

'By the way, how's your sister?'

Megan was focused on securing a seat at the front, staring at the stage where Rachel Thompson was about to appear. She took a few deep breaths and then turned around. 'She's great, thanks. I'm staying with her for a bit until I get settled.'

'Right,' said Sam. 'And what about your love life? Are you still with that bloke of yours?'

Megan sighed. 'I'll tell you another time.' She sat down and stared numbly ahead.

~

*T*HE GIRL HAD LIVED *in the small village in Edo for all of her sixteen years. She shared a mud-walled house with her mother and two brothers. At night she lay on her mattress, too hot to sleep, listening to the wind rattling the corrugated metal panels on the roof. Sometimes the girl would sell tomatoes at the market. But her younger brothers were growing up fast and she noticed her mother's face was getting thinner, her spine more curved. She knew the family needed money. The girl had been thinking of going to Italy to get a job selling tomatoes. Her auntie Angelika had lived there for several years and made a good living. She came back to the village to visit at times and was treated like royalty. One day when she returned from market, Auntie was at her house. The girl ran across and hugged her. She wore a beautiful red dress and smelt of sweet cherries. The girl's mother was slumped on a seat, her hands trembling. Auntie's eyes were shining. She said she had good news. She said a friend had a job for the girl in London: household duties and babysitting in return for a small allowance each week. Mother gasped when Auntie told them how much. You work in England a month. You send your mother more money than you earn in a year selling tomatoes in the market, said Auntie. That wasn't all. There would be a chance for the girl to go to college. The girl glanced at Mother, but her eyes were fixed on the ground. She looked over at Auntie, who smiled reassuringly. The girl went to her mother and knelt beside her, clasping her wizened hands. She told Mother everything would be fine. The job offer was great news, she said. Gently tilting Mother's head up from the ground, she thought she saw a look flicker across her eyes. Was it regret or fear? It will all be okay, the girl told her mother. This will be good for the family. I can earn a wage for you and the boys and get an education too, she said. A ripple of excitement began to flutter in her stomach. It doesn't need to be for ever, she said. Auntie bobbed her head enthusiastically and clapped her* *hands. She told Mother it was for the best and if the girl's father had still been alive he would have agreed. Auntie stared at Mother, long and hard. It was the right thing to do, she said. The flights were booked and she would personally escort the girl to London and make sure she was settled.*

That night the girl hummed as she helped Mother prepare the green stew. She felt a glimmer of hope about what lay ahead for her now. She was going to see the world. She was going to earn lots of money for her family. Suddenly she felt very grown up. It was time for her to leave home. She was going to work and study hard and make Mother proud.

2

After the press conference, Megan decided to head straight back to the flat. Monday was supposed to be her day off. However, she thought it best to keep herself busy as she wasn't yet used to being alone on her days off. She knew she would have to explain to Joanna at some point what had happened with Johnny but the thought made her feel increasingly anxious. She and Joanna had drifted apart over the past couple of years, which was largely down to Johnny. Pressing her trembling hands together, she tried to focus on the red blur of the traffic lights through the taxi's rain-lashed windscreen. Normally she didn't mind taking the train back to her sister's flat in the West End, but she'd forgotten how changeable the weather in Glasgow could be. She knew she would get soaked in the short walk up the road from the train station. She made a mental note to make sure she always remembered to put an umbrella in her bag. Megan searched for something to say to the driver, anything at all, but the inside of her mind felt like a mass of wool. *Why* was she starting to feel worried now? In his compartment in the front, the driver chuckled to himself as he listened to the radio. He must have been the only cabbie in Glasgow who didn't want to talk to his passenger. The rhythm of the windscreen wipers had a hypnotic effect. For a moment, she allowed her mind to drift. Was it really just a month ago that she was living in Edinburgh in her own flat and flicking through wedding magazines? Had she made a mistake? She pulled her phone from her bag and scrolled through the missed calls. Then, setting her mouth determinedly, she hit call.

'Hello, Natasha,' she said, her voice cautious. 'It's me, Megan. Can you talk?' She knew Natasha's job in the Justice Ministry was highly pressured and full of back-to-back meetings and she didn't want to be a nuisance.

'Megan! At last! I thought you must've left the planet, or at least gone into a witness protection programme or something. Where have you been? Why haven't you answered my calls?'

'I'm really sorry,' said Megan, immediately feeling guilty that she'd been blanking Natasha's calls. 'Things have been . . . difficult.'

'I know. And a wee birdie told me you've moved to the west.'

'Yes,' said Megan sheepishly. 'And I'm sorry. I meant to call and let you know.'

'That was kind of sudden, wasn't it?'

'Er, yes and no. Just fancied a change of scene, you know. And my sister needed me,' she said, her face flushing.

'Mmm, And what about Johnny? What's he saying about all of this?'

Megan didn't reply. This was why she'd been avoiding everyone. She just couldn't face talking about it.

'Listen, we need to meet up. I've missed you. And I can't believe you've left Edinburgh. Is it for good?'

'Well, I'm working in the Glasgow office now. So, yes, I'm looking on it as permanent,' said Megan.

'Let's get together and you can tell me all about it,' said Natasha. 'Aside from that, I need to talk to you. I have a proposition.'

Megan could feel anticipation start to swirl in her stomach. 'Um, how urgent is it?'

'It can wait. Though not for too long,' said Natasha. 'We're working on a draft bill and I want to run some of it by you. Thought it might make a good investigation in your paper . . . Sorry, hold on a minute.'

Megan listened as she heard Natasha's hand fumbling over the phone. She could picture her sitting in a huge swivel chair with her feet on the desk. Natasha was a press officer for the Justice Minister, though Megan knew she probably ran the department.

'Sorry about that. Bloody civil servants. Another meeting to go to.'

'What's the bill you're working on?'

'I'll tell you when I see you,' said Natasha. 'Better to keep you guessing, otherwise you might stand me up.'

'As if I'd do that,' said Megan, now intrigued to know what Natasha wanted to tell her. 'I'll get in touch a.s.a.p.'

'How about we go surfing soon? This weekend? You're off on Sunday, aren't you?' Megan heard her typing something into her computer. 'Fab. Looks like there will be plenty of swell. And the forecast is good. Usual place? Eight o'clock?' She paused for a second but not long enough to allow Megan to answer. 'I'd better run to this meeting. Talk soon and see you Sunday.'

Megan was smiling despite her previous mood,as she pushed the phone to the bottom of the bag and leaned forward to tap the glass screen. 'Just anywhere here, please.'

'No problem, hen. I'll pull over here.'

As she stepped from the taxi, she gasped as the cold air hit her cheeks. She slid the door shut behind her and managed to dodge the puddles in the gutters. The wind tugged at her hair and she ran to take shelter in the doorway of a delicatessen. She stood for a moment. Joanna had refused to take any rent from Megan and, although Megan did try to bring groceries home when she remembered, she still felt guilty that she wasn't contributing enough. She opened the door and walked into the shop. Her eyes flicked over the chocolate-chip shortbread, then the flavoured coffee, and she walked across the terracotta-tiled floor to the basket of flowers. She decided on the roses and the coffee. Both were luxuries she knew Joanna wouldn't buy for herself. It looked as though the rain was going off, so she started walking down the slope of Clarence Drive towards Falkland Street. Turning into the street, she quickly scanned the numbers on the red sandstone tenements flanking either side of the road. She continued walking, looking at the carefully pruned hedges and the Charles Rennie Mackintosh stained-glass doors. Some of the buildings weren't quite so well maintained: the brickwork was crumbling, and the tiny front gardens were strewn with shiny packaging, soggy newspapers and poly bags. Her sister's building was one of the more well-kept properties. Walking up the freshly weeded path to the duck-egg blue front door, she read the brass name plates next to each buzzer. *Ross.* Pausing for a moment, she pressed her forefinger into the brass bell and waited.

'Hello?' said a tired voice over the intercom. 'Hello?' said the voice again, this time sounding more impatient.

'Joanna. It's me. It's Megan.'

There was a moment's silence, then the door clicked open. Megan pushed it open and walked in. Her footsteps echoed as she padded along the corridor and up the worn marble steps. She was slightly breathless when she arrived at Joanna's door, two flights up. Joanna stood in the hallway, wrapped in a soft grey silk gown with her hair scraped back in a ponytail. Her arms were folded, her head cocked to the side. 'Forget your keys, did you?'

'Yes, I'm sorry. I'll make sure to keep them in my bag from now on,' said Megan.

Megan thrust the roses and coffee at Joanna. 'Here you are.'

'Thanks,' Joanna said, 'they're lovely. But you need to stop bringing me stuff.'

'Yeah, I would, but since you won't let me pay rent, or even housekeeping, what else can I do? Come on, Joanna, I'd feel a lot better about pushing myself on you like this if I could pay my way. Who knows when I'll find a place of my own?'

'OK, we can talk about that later,' said Joanna equably, leading the way through to the living room.

'Where's George?' Megan sat down on a pink-upholstered chair in the bay window. Her sister sat on the sofa opposite, tucking her feet underneath her.

'He's at after school club until five.'

'I forgot,' said Megan. 'Of course he is. Did I get you up?'

'Aye, but don't worry. It was time I was getting up anyway.'

'Oh,' said Megan, not really knowing what else to say.

Joanna worked at the women's refuge in Dumbarton Road. Since Megan had come to stay, she had been able to take on some night shifts while Megan looked after George.

Megan scratched her head and looked at her sister. She was only three years older than her but she looked so different to Megan. She had a few more lines around her eyes, and looked older. There always used to be an air of vulnerability around her, but now she seemed stronger, somehow less fragile, although she was still very slim, and looked quite delicate the way she sat curled up on the sofa. There was a coolness in her eyes, which looked like two large pale-blue marbles. She had grey around her temples now but it suited her, made her look quite distinguished. Megan caught sight of her sister's feet, noticing her toenails were painted a gunmetal grey.

Joanna noticed. 'Do you like them? I got them done last night.' She smiled. 'One of the perks of the job. A girl comes in and offers to do wee treatments for the women. That's if they want them done. Some of them don't want to be touched. But some welcome a wee bit pampering time.'

'They look good,' said Megan. 'The colour suits you.'

'Och well, sometimes it just makes the time pass a bit more quickly, you know. And if I offer to get mine done then sometimes some of the women take my lead.'

Megan rolled her neck back and forth to try to loosen the tension which was making her feel so stiff. She jumped when she heard the bang of the main door and the echo of footsteps pounding up the stairs in the close outside.

'It's just the kids below. They don't know the meaning of shutting it quietly. You get used to it. They're just kids.'

Her words hung in the air for a moment, so awkwardly that Megan wanted to reach out, pluck them and put them in her pocket.

'Look, I don't know about you, but I fancy a cuppa. Or actually some of that fancy coffee you brought. Shall I put the kettle on?'

'Yes, please. That would be lovely.' While she was gone, Megan looked about the bright and airy room.

'What are you back so early for?' said Joanna, walking back into the living room carrying a tray with a cafetiere, two mugs and a couple of Kit-Kats on a tray.

Megan was sitting with her coat still on and her bag on her lap.

'You can take that off if you want, if you're staying for a bit,' said her sister with a laugh.

Megan shrugged it off and tried to make a joke. 'Yes, I'll stay. I don't fancy hanging about outside in this weather.' She felt the start of a horrid sensation gnawing in her stomach and she clasped her hands together. 'And . . . well, I'm wondering if I've made a mistake.' Fat tears began to slide down her cheeks.

'Oh, Megan, it's okay. Of course you'll be wondering if you did the right thing. It's only natural and it must still feel very raw for you.'

Megan waved her hand in the air. 'I know. I know. I just hate feeling like this. My head has been all over the place.' Her stomach started to gurgle.

'Eat your biscuit. You look like you could do with one.' Joanna paused to let Megan take a bite of the chocolate-coated finger. She poured some coffee into a mug and handed it to Megan. 'Are you missing him?'

Megan didn't respond immediately. 'Kind of. It's been so busy though, there's not been much time. But yes, I do.'

Joanna moved nearer Megan and awkwardly patted her knee. 'You'll be okay, you know. You're stronger than you think.'

'I don't know if I am,' said Megan.

'Yes, Megan, you are.' Joanna ran her fingers through her hair and Megan noticed that her nails were painted to match her toes. 'You'll get there. As long as you're sure you did the right thing for you.'

Megan nodded. It had been her decision to break off her engagement to Johnny, the man who everyone else thought was perfect. It had been her choice to walk away from the flat they shared in Edinburgh and the life they had planned together. And she had done it for reasons which she wasn't prepared to share with anyone just now. Especially not her sister who had been devastated when Megan had told her about their broken engagement. She wasn't ready to tell Joanna the full story yet.

'Oh, look,' said Megan, glancing at her phone. It had been on silent and she realised she had fifteen missed calls. She stood up abruptly. 'I'd better answer these.'

'Okay. Well, remember and speak to me if you need me. And next time take your keys.'

Megan felt a smile cross her lips. 'I promise.'

The day before leaving for London, the girl was taken to the village priest. Auntie said it was important for her to go. The priest would invoke the protection of her guardian spirit. It would keep her safe in London. His room was dark and cool. The girl began trembling when he told her to remove all her clothes. Auntie told her to do as she was told and then left the room. The girl peeled off her pink cotton sundress and white pants, leaving them neatly folded on top of her sandals. She felt a knot in her stomach, but she knew she had to do this. She gulped when the priest raised his hand and she saw a glint of steel. Pulling her to him, she flinched as the itchy material of his cloak scratched against her skin. She stared down at his feet. He wore bright blue Nike trainers. The priest spoke slowly in a clipped voice, using words she didn't recognise. Then he started cutting into her. Small, stinging incisions in her breasts, then her stomach, then her buttocks. Her torso began to burn but she knew she had to fight through the pain. It was all part of the experience. It was for her own good. The priest moved down her legs and then onto her feet, cutting between her toes. Then she watched as he tipped chalky dust from a small dish and rubbed it into all the cuts he'd just made.

He walked towards a table in the corner of the room where a chicken was lying. It gave a final flutter of protest, then the priest cut its throat. Blood poured out, sticking to its feathers. The girl felt bile rise from her stomach as she watched him cut out its heart. He cradled the sticky, glistening red sac of veins and arteries in his hands then put it on the table and began to slice into it. Walking towards the girl, with a piece of it in his hand, he held it out and told her to eat.

Forcing the gristly tissue into her mouth, she tried to chew. It felt fatty and oily in her mouth. He handed her a glass of liquid which she sloshed into her mouth, not caring that it had a foul taste. She just wanted her mouth to be empty and clean of the rubbery flesh. Wiping her mouth, she watched as the priest came towards her with scissors. He grabbed her hands and cut her fingernails. Then he knelt down in front of her to clip at her smattering of pubic hair. He tipped the cuttings into a clay pot then took it over to the collection of dishes and pots in the corner of the room. The girl saw the shrine. She shivered, desperate now to put her clothes back on and go back out into the warm sunshine.

The priest stared at her and spoke slowly. The gods know who you are. They know your name. They will know if you disobey.

3

Megan was in the office attempting to read the morning papers. Rubbing her eyes, she sat back in her seat. The rest of the team weren't due in for another hour or so but Megan had come straight to work after walking her nephew George to school. She smiled as she thought of the way he'd held her hand to cross the busy main road, without complaint, even though he was now aged ten and in Primary Five. It had been nice getting to know him properly these past few weeks after four years when she'd hardly seen him. Initially her friendly approaches had been met with indifferent, monosyllabic replies. Then she'd accidentally had a breakthrough when she'd made him laugh by upsetting a panful of baked beans all over the kitchen floor. The façade cracked a little bit, and after that he started asking her for help with his homework – testing his spelling, listening to him reading aloud and so on. Then, one day when they were both at home - he with a cold, she on her day off - desperate to find something to amuse him other than TV, she'd fished out her pocket versions of Mastermind and Othello. Dismissive at first, now he often played with Megan in the evening before he went to bed. She enjoyed that special time they had together. It felt nice to be appreciated, and she realised how enjoyable a simple thin like a game could be. She'd also developed even more respect for her sister who'd been a single mother to George since he was born. She couldn't believe how seamlessly Joanna seemed to juggle life as a mum as well as working in the refuge.

Chewing her bottom lip, she opened the file of pictures they had chosen to use with the feature on domestic abuse she'd been working on. There were a couple of stock images – rear views of anonymous women - and a couple of Rachel Thompson at the press conference. She thought about the Minister's hard-hitting initiative to crack down on domestic abuse. Two strikes and the perpetrator of domestic abuse, male or female, would find themselves serving time. While Rachel had smashed the glass ceiling for aspiring politicians in Scotland, Megan wondered just how much had really changed. She'd thought a lot about coercive control since Rachel had mentioned it during the press conference. The thing was: how on earth did you prove it? She scratched her head.

She decided that a blast of fresh air and some coffee might help wake her up and clear her head. As she reached for her coat, the phone rang. She glanced at the clock – it was a bit early for calls.

'Hello? *Sunday Edition.*'

Nobody spoke.

'Hello?' she said impatiently.

'Megan Ross?' said a muffled voice.

'Speaking.'

'That prostitute they found . . . the one in the river . . .'

Megan's heartbeat quickened. She flicked the call onto speakerphone, then hit the record app on her mobile. 'Can you tell me who I am talking to?'

'It doesn't matter.' The voice sounded tinny and distorted.

'Okay. So what can you tell me?' Automatically, she reached for a pen.

'There's another one.'

'What do you mean another one? Another what?'

A silence.

'Hello?' Megan clutched the phone. 'Are you still there?'

'There's another body,' whispered the voice.

'Another body?'

'In the River Kelvin.'

'Right, okay.' Megan's voice was breathless, despite her best efforts to remain calm. 'What else can you tell me?'

'It's in the Botanics. By the bridge. You know, that shiny one.'

'Okay, and can you tell me your name?'

The caller had hung up. Megan sat for a moment, staring in disbelief at the phone. Could it have been a crank call? Why would the caller have asked for her by name? Was it Sam trying to have a laugh now he knew she was back? She wouldn't put it past him. Pressing 'play' on her mobile, she listened to the conversation again. Then she snatched her bag and ran out the door to the street below.

There was no point in calling in the police quite yet, she told herself. She would look like a prize buffoon, which was probably exactly what Sam wanted. Megan half expected to see him hanging around in the bushes waiting to see if she'd fall for his bait. It wouldn't have been the first time she'd been duped by him. She jabbed out a text, just in case, as she hurried up Byres Road, dodging people running into the subway, clutching their cups of coffee.

She focused on the click of her shoes on the pavement. This wouldn't take long, she reasoned to herself; she would return to the warm office with her own coffee and an almond croissant. The green man lit up and she ran across Great Western Road. The bushes and trees in the Botanics were heavy with blossom which trailed over the railings. The gates were open, but she followed the curve of the road onto the bridge which gleamed red in the early morning sun. Megan berated herself. This had to be Sam, or else one of those random calls that would turn out to be a wind up. There was no way somebody would have dumped a body here, in such a public place. It was the West End of Glasgow for God's sake. She stopped to peer over the bridge, the water sparkling in the sun beneath her as crisp packets and plastic bottles bobbed past.

She retraced her steps, going through the gates and stepping out of the way of a couple of runners, then walked briskly along the path lined with blooming daffodils. The morning was still: no breeze, no buzz of traffic, no people. Just her, in an empty city park, surrounded by bushes. She wondered if anyone would come to help her should she suddenly scream. Now she was standing on the path directly beneath the bridge, looking down at the muddy water and the sandwich wrappers, juice cartons, stray branches and reeds. There was no body, no limb protruding from the water. She scanned left and right, shrugged and was about to turn away when something caught her eye. She hoisted herself over the railing to get closer to the edge. Crouching down, she grabbed a stick to poke the bin bag she could see in the water. Well, Sam could at least have a good laugh at her when she told him this story. She wished she hadn't just sent him a text telling him what she was up to.

'I need a coffee,' she said to a bird hopping about on the path. She was about to stand up when she saw it. There, poking out of the bag, tangled in the reeds. Was she imagining things? She leaned in closer, peering at what looked like dark flesh. Nails. Bright, pretty and perfect, a foot was sticking out of the bin bag - with glossy, pink nails.

On her last night at home, the girl packed her belongings into the small suitcase Auntie had given her. She'd told the girl not to pack too much as they would be able to buy new, more suitable clothes in London. The girl knew it was cold there and often wet. As she folded her favourite blanket to put in the case, she idly wondered what kind of clothes she would wear. Her brothers started to play catch with her hairbrush and cheekily asked if they could come to London with her. The girl laughed and shooed them away. They were annoying, but she would miss them.

She hummed to herself as she thought considered what to take. She chose some underwear, a few dresses, sandals, hairbrush, toothbrush and Bingo, her favourite teddy. Mother clutched the girl to her chest, then insisted she take the beads from round her neck. The girl refused. She knew how important they were to her mother. They'd been a gift from her father. But her mother insisted. The girl wrapped them around her hand, feeling the smooth sensation of the beads, then tucked them in at the back of her suitcase.

Auntie had arranged for a car to take them to the airport in Lagos in the morning. She couldn't believe she was leaving her village for the very first time. And she was going to England! She wondered if she would miss the hot sun at home and the dust which stuck to her tongue. What would another country, a city, be like? She was excited but nervous about going on a plane, but Auntie kept reassuring her and telling her not to worry. Everything was going to be okay, she said. She just had to remember what the priest had said and to never, ever forget the oath she had sworn. The girl smiled and nodded her head. She shuddered as she remembered the priest in his deep red robes. She would never forget what he had said.

When she lay in her bed for the final time she thought about her next room. What would it be like? Would the bed be the same? Would there be a window with a view over Big Ben? Auntie said the family she was going to were nice. They lived in a big house in London near the Queen.

Mother was quiet, and concentrated on clearing the supper dishes away. The girl knew her mother would miss her. But it wouldn't be for ever.

4

'Megan,' shouted Sam, just as she stood up and wiped her mouth.

She watched him stride towards her, his mouth in a tight line. 'How did you get here so fast? Are you some kind of superhero?'

'Don't touch anything.' His voice was low and urgent.

Megan shrugged. 'It's a bit late for that.'

'Jeez. Megan.' He threw his hands up in the air. 'What is it? What did you find?'

She pointed to the water. 'There. A foot. In a bin bag.' Her voice trembled.

He gave her a puzzled look. 'But, Megan, I told you not to do anything. I told you to wait for me.'

Megan was trying to bite back the tears. He must have texted her back and she hadn't noticed. 'It could have been a false alarm though. All I did was have a look. It's there, sticking out. Anyone could have seen it.'

'Did you touch it?'

'No. Not the foot. Just the bag . . .'

'Megan, don't you get it? Your DNA will be all over the place now.'

Megan covered her mouth with her hands. 'But I didn't touch it, I used a stick.'

'Don't move. Don't touch anything else. I'd better call the cops.' He glared at her and turned away.

Just then, sirens blared as police screeched to a halt o the bridge.

'I've done that already.' She watched as several officers ran onto the footpath. Sam directed them to the bag.

After that, things seemed to pass in a blur. Megan was asked several times to tell the officers what time she had arrived on the scene and exactly what she had seen. For some reason, though, the image of a woman, struggling on all fours, eventually slumping in a corner, was the only picture in her mind. She wondered if the rest of her body was in the bag or if it was just a foot and maybe a bit of leg. She watched Sam talking to a policeman as he ducked under the police cordon and started making his way towards her. A wide circle had now formed around the crime scene with police crawling over every inch of the path. The large white forensic tent, which had been erected over the remains, reminded Megan of a marquee at a wedding. Several years ago, she had been at a wedding in these gardens and now she was part of a crime scene.

'You okay?' said the policeman, not looking directly at her or waiting for an answer. 'Jesus. It's not a pretty sight.'

The air felt heavy, smelt sour. Megan was shaking now. 'Was the rest of her there?'

He ignored her question and looked at Sam who'd appeared at Megan's side.

'Jim meet Megan, a friend of mine,' said Sam.

Jim nodded at her.

'Looks pretty fresh,' said Sam. 'Think she must have been dumped in the last few hours. But they'll get a better idea once forensics have done their stuff.' He looked over at the white tent that had appeared by the water. 'She's black too, like the other one.'

'You trying to do my job?' said Jim.

Just then a young officer ran under the police cordon and retched.

'Must be his first murder,' said Jim. 'Yours too I'm guessing?'

Sam placed a hand on Megan's shoulder, squeezing it awkwardly. 'What a morning. You all right?'

'Oh,super,' she said drily. 'Look, here are the tourists.' She pointed up to the bridge where a small cluster of people had stopped to gawk.

'Mathis,' shouted Jim, 'get up there and tell them to beat it.'

The young officer raced off to deal with them.

'We're going to want to talk to you again,' he said. 'You'll need to make a statement.'

'Why? I didn't do anything. I just found the body.'

'Yes, I think I can safely say you've been eliminated from the inquiry. But we'll need to ask you about the phone call, get a copy of the recording off your mobile. Have you thought about why someone would have called you? Asked for you by name?'

Megan paused for a moment. 'I'm a journalist. I get tip-offs. It's part of the job.'

'Anything odd about it?'

'I want to help you, but the voice was muffled.' She shrugged. 'Maybe just a bad line.' She pulled her mobile from her pocket. There were ten missed calls. 'Shit. Is it okay if I go now? I really need to get back to the office.'

'Okay. We'll be in touch.' The police officer headed back towards the tent.

Sam frowned at her. 'Surely you want to go home?'

'Back to the flat? And do what, Sam? Mope about feeling sorry for myself? Go and soak in a hot bath?'

'No.' He took a step towards her. 'I meant just give yourself a bit of time. You've had a shock.'

'I have had a shock but I'll be fine. I've a job to do.' She pointed at the tent. 'It's not me that's in bits in a bag in the river. There's no point in wallowing.'

'Okay, well, if you're sure.'

'I am sure,' she said stepping back from him. 'I just need a coffee. Anyway, how did you get here so quick?'

'I was out and about anyway.' He rubbed at his eyes.

'Right. Look, I need to go. My head's pounding. I need to get back. I'll speak to you later.' She turned and walked away, leaving Sam staring after her.

~

Before she left, her brothers hugged her. The little one, Osato, clung to her like a limpet. Then his brother, Dmiklo, peeled him away and told him to go and play football with the other boys in the field. The girl kissed them both on each cheek and shooed them away. They ran, giggling and waving. She turned to her mother who stood beside the car, crying silently, salty tears flowing down her cheeks. The girl buried herself in her arms, breathing in the fruity scent of her skin and looping her hands tightly around her waist. Mother held the girl, squeezing her hard, and then, she pulled away.

She turned to Auntie and said, you look after her. I trust her with you. Your brother would have too. Then she grabbed the girl and held her one last time.

Come now, said Auntie briskly.

Mother turned to go back into the house. The girl called after her and started to follow her but Auntie grasped her arm. Leave her, she said. She will be fine. We need to go now.

The girl stared after her mother and hesitated. It would be so easy to run after her and stay at home with all that she had ever known.

Your new life begins now, said Auntie. Good times ahead. Now come, she said opening the car door. Auntie waited for the girl to get in, then slid in next to her.

The girl stared out of the window and waved to her mother who stood watching. She rested her head against the glass. Her mind was jumbled. Then she began to weep. But as Auntie started to tell her what an adventure she was going to have, butterflies started to dance around the girl's stomach. She was doing this for her family, Auntie reminded her. They needed money and she could earn it for them. The girl would get to see the world, see the sights of London!

Big Ben, Buckingham Palace, the London Eye.

Auntie passed the girl a tissue. The girl felt reassured as she wiped away the tears. She couldn't wait.

5

'Sorry I'm late, everyone,' said Megan, walking into the office. 'I've brought coffee though, and croissants,' she continued, holding up the cup carrier and paper bag.

'You okay, Megan? We were wondering if we should send out a search party for you,' said Ronnie. 'You're looking a wee bit peely-wally.' Designer Ronnie was tall, slender and always in jeans and a bright shirt.

'I'm fine.' Megan shrugged. 'In fact, if I told you I don't think you'd believe me.'

Ronnie's dark eyes flashed and he just about managed to raise an eyebrow in his botox-injected forehead. 'Try me,' he challenged.

'Coffee first,' she said, hanging her coat on the back of her seat and smiling at Katherine, the administrator. She was on the phone, but gave Megan a small wave.

The office was based on the ground floor of a Victorian town-house off Byres Road. The location had been an added bonus of the job for Megan. The room had high ceilings with ornate cornicing, polished wooden floors and a bay window overlooking a lush green park. Yet she was two minutes' walk from a murder scene.

'Did you steal Emma's coffees?' Ronnie pointed at the scrawled name on the cups.

Megan laughed. 'I'm being Emma today. Easier to say and easier to spell. Keeps the queue moving without folk behind you sighing and moaning that you're having to spell out your name.'

Katherine walked across to her, carrying a bundle of envelopes. 'Here you go – some mail for you.'

'Thanks. So how's everyone this morning?'

Ronnie was staring at Megan, desperate to hear what had happened. Sunita, the picture editor, gave her the thumbs-up sign. 'Sunita, in case I forget, can you remind me to ask you about the images of Rachel Thompson on that spread, please. I need your advice.'

'Of course.' Sunita turned back towards her screen.

'What happened to your shoes?' asked Katherine as she picked up a coffee from the tray.

Megan looked down at her black suede shoes, which were smeared with mud and grass. Her trouser hems filthy too. Then she looked up at Katherine, who was dressed immaculately, as always, in a grey woollen dress with expensive, polished boots.

'Oh dear. I'm a bit of a mess.'

'You just need a wee tidy-up.' Katherine went back to her desk, reached into her drawer and pulled out some wipes. 'Here - you might want to use some of these.'

'Thanks.' Megan bent down to scrape the dirt from her shoes. It was no use. They were manky.

'So where have you been? Come on Megan.' Ronnie had now scooted his chair over towards her and was helping himself to a pastry.

Megan took a sip of her coffee. 'It's a long story . . . I found a body.'

'You what?'

'A body. I found a body.'

'Where?' said Sunita, perching herself on the edge of Megan's desk. She was petite and had cropped hair which framed her almond-shaped eyes.

'The Botanics.'

'Bloody hell. You okay?' Ronnie broke off a piece of croissant and shoved it in his mouth.

'Do you know what?' said Megan. 'It's weird but I feel fine. Maybe I'm still in shock.'

'So, who was it? Where was it?' Ronnie's mouth was now full of croissant.

'In the river. In a bin bag. And don't talk with your mouth full.'

He quickly swallowed. 'What did you see?'

'A foot sticking out of it.'

'A real foot?' said Ronnie, now helping himself to a *pain au chocolat*.

'A real foot, Ronnie, with nail varnish and everything.'

'Jesus.'

'What about the rest of the body? Was it there?'

'I'm not sure. They didn't tell me.' Megan felt suddenly tired. She sat back in her chair, clasping her cup.

'So, it was a woman then?' asked Sunita.

'Yes. That's all I know.'

'Fuck a duck.' It was Sunita's turn to look horrified.

'Maybe there's a serial killer on the loose,' said Ronnie. 'The tabloids will have a field day with this, won't they?'

'One body hardly means a serial killer, you daft prick,' Sunita said.

'It's not just the one body though, is it?' Ronnie leant back against Megan's desk and scowled. 'What about that body pulled from the Clyde last year? They still haven't found out who did that.'

Megan turned to her computer, typed quickly then clicked on a link.

Daily Post, February 2, 2015

Police are appealing for the public's help to identify a young woman found dead in the River Clyde.

The body was discovered by a member of the public on Monday morning. The death is being treated as unexplained.

The teenager or young woman is believed to be of African descent and thought to be aged between 15 and 21, 5ft 6in and of slim build. She was wearing black leggings, a black T-shirt and no shoes.

A Police Scotland spokeswoman said: "We're currently conducting a number of enquiries as part of our efforts to identify this young woman and trace her family. We're appealing for the public's help and urge anyone who may recognise her description to get in touch with us as soon as possible." The spokeswoman added that an investigation was underway to establish the full circumstances surrounding the woman's death.

'Or even who she was.' Megan spoke quietly as she remembered that the caller, earlier, had made the link to the other body.

'And then there have been all those prostitutes done in over the years. Maybe there's a madman on the loose. There must be.'

'Ronnie, will you shut up. You're not Columbo.'

'There's no need to be like that. I'm just trying to piece it together,' he said.

'Aye, you're putting two and two together and coming up with eight. Leave it to the professionals.' Sunita wagged a finger at him.

'What colour was the nail varnish?' asked Ronnie.

'The nail varnish?' Megan frowned, closing her eyes for a moment. She could see the toenails on the small, slender foot.

'Aye, on the foot.'

'Why do you want to know that, you sicko?' said Sunita.

'Just do,' he said.

'It was pink.' Megan's voice was quiet. 'Cerise pink . . .'

Katherine looked up from her desk. 'You don't look that great, Megan. A bit pale. You should go and freshen up.'

'You know, I think I will,' said Megan, rubbing her temples. The enormity of what had happened this morning was starting to press down on her. She needed some fresh air and to be alone for an hour. 'If you don't mind, will you let Richard know what's happened?'

'I'll get you a cab.' Katherine picked up the phone and started to dial.

Ronnie and Sunita had skulked back to their desks, clearly not talking to one another.

'Well, good morning, troops,' said Richard, the editor, striding into the office. 'How are we all on this fine day?' He hung his coat on the stand by the door and then caught side of Megan. 'Bloody hell. What happened to you? Have you been out playing extreme golf?'

Megan's face flushed. 'Um, no. Not quite. Just been involved in a bit of an incident.'

Ronnie looked up. 'There's been a murder, boss.' He paused for a minute and smirked. 'You have no idea how long I've wanted to say that.'

Richard threw him a withering look. 'Are you not too young to have watched *Taggart*? Anyway, what's happened? Who's dead?'

'A woman. I got a call,' started Megan. 'A body at the Botanics.'

'Jeez. Can't believe I've missed this. I've been stuck at the dentist,' he said, his tongue rolling across his teeth.

'I'm just away to get showered and changed. Then I'll be back,' said Megan.

'Good idea,' he said.

Katherine pointed out the window. 'That's your cab.'

Megan pulled on her coat and grabbed her bag. 'I'll be as quick as I can.'

Richard shrugged his shoulders. 'Shame we're not a daily, otherwise you could have written about it. Would have made a great first-person piece.' Then he clicked his fingers. 'Sod it,' he said, pointing at Megan. 'Do the first person-piece anyway. We'll get it up online. Well, some of it . . . as a teaser. We can print the rest on Sunday.'

'Okay,' said Megan, looking down at her clothes. 'Can I still go and get changed?'

'Yes,' he said, 'but hurry.'

When the plane began its descent into London, the girl strained in her seat to look out of the window. She was desperate to see one of the sights Auntie had talked about. All she could see was blackness. Auntie told her to stay

where she was and wait as the other passengers around them rushed to the front. The girl was looking forward to stretching her legs. It felt like she had been sitting for hours. It had been good fun though. She had enjoyed playing with the headset and flicking through the channels. The best bit was when they were brought a meal to their seat. She excitedly opened the foil container and tried her best to eat the beef stroganoff with the plastic cutlery. She'd never tasted anything like it before.

At last, she followed Auntie's lead and walked down the aisle towards the exit. The first thing she noticed was the whoosh of cool air as she descended the steps onto the tarmac. It smelt different too. Fresher, sharper. Not the dry heat of home. The girl saw a white neon sign, with black letters, as they hurried up the steps into the terminal building. She was confused. She didn't understand why the sign said Milan. The air stewards had said they were landing in Milan too. Maybe it was just the name of the airport in London. She didn't mind that Auntie was a bit grumpy and kept telling her to hurry up. She was trying her best to keep up but her feet were sore and rubbing against her shoes. She kept her head down like she'd been told. They might send her back home if she made eye contact with anyone. Auntie had warned her about this constantly during the flight. She said she would take care of everything. Auntie had her passport and travel documents in her bag. The girl knew that was best. She would hate to lose them. The girl hobbled alongside Auntie and watched as she handed tickets to a lady wearing a black suit. She didn't ask why they were boarding another plane. Maybe that was what happened in London. Perhaps they were flying to another part of the city. She was thirsty. When she asked Auntie how long it would take before they got to their destination, the woman glared at her. You stop asking questions. I do the talking, she said in a harsh voice. The girl felt as though she had been slapped. No one in her entire life had spoken harshly to her. She looked at Auntie's chipped nails and her lipstick, which was smudged across two of her top teeth. The girl said nothing as they sat down and fastened their seatbelts. Her ears ached as the plane took off, and she sat clenching her hands, willing the shooting pains to go away. After a few moments, her ears popped and the pain disappeared. She daren't ask where they were going now and she couldn't understand what the stewards were saying. The girl felt as though they had been in the sky for ages, and she began to fidget with her seatbelt. She squirmed in her seat. She needed to use the toilet. Auntie put a warning hand on her knee and held her firm. Almost there, she said. Her breath was hot and smelly in the girl's ear.

6

Megan couldn't sleep. When she closed her eyes all she could see was mottled flesh and a decaying corpse. She longed to turn the clock back. She wished she was still in Edinburgh sleeping in her old bed, with his arms around her. Then she immediately felt guilty for being so pathetic. She got out of bed and crept as quietly as she could through to the kitchen. She stood there, sipping tea and thinking. She was onto her second cup when she heard the sound of the key in the front door.

'Joanna, it's just me,' she said, opening the kitchen door as her sister came through the hallway.

'Oh, hi,' said Joanna, her voice groggy. 'You okay? Is George okay?'

'He's fine. Don't worry,' she said, glancing across at his door. 'I just couldn't sleep.'

'What's up?' said Joanna, taking off her coat and hanging it in the cupboard by the door.

'Just stuff.'

'Go and make me a cup of tea while I nip to the loo. Then you can tell me all about it.'

'Thanks,' said Megan and paused. 'If that's okay. I could do with a chat.'

She made her sister's tea and took both mugs through to the living room. She opened the curtains. The sky had clouded over and spots of rain were starting to fall. But at least it was growing light. Joanna lived in a top-floor flat and Megan loved the view of the tenement-lined street: the cherry blossom was starting to bud on the trees below.

'So, are you going to tell me what's up?' Joanna plonked herself on the sofa, curling her legs neatly beneath her.

Perching on the edge of the seat, Megan's eyes darted around until they fixed on the picture of George on the mantelpiece. 'Joanna, it was just horrible.' A fat tear plopped onto her cheek.

Joanna leant forward, resting her elbows on her knees and clasping her hands together. 'What was horrible?'

Megan rubbed her chin with her thumb. 'A body. Joanna, I found a body. A young girl. Stuffed in a bin bag and dumped in the river. Like a piece of shit in a bag.'

Joanna looked at Megan blankly. 'What do you mean? What are you talking about?'

'Just what I said. I found a body. A body in a bag.'

Joanna's eyes widened. 'Where? How?'

Megan's stomach began to rumble and it dawned on her that she hadn't eaten since yesterday. Was it dinner last night? She couldn't even remember having any. She cleared her throat to cover the sound. 'I got a call about it. Assumed it was a wind-up but thought I should check it out just in case. Happens more often than you would think.' She paused, and the ripple of bubbles in her stomach filled the silence. 'Though this is the first time it's been a dead body.'

Joanna sat back. 'Is it that story that was on the news last night?'

Megan nodded.

'What are the cops saying?'

'Murder. Obviously. But not much more.' Rubbing her eyes and puffing out her cheeks with a sigh, she said, 'We're wondering if it's maybe linked to that other girl who was pulled from the river last year.'

Joanna stared at the wall beyond her. 'Jesus. Poor, poor soul.'

Megan watched her sister across the room. She was saying all the right things but didn't look particularly shocked by this. 'You look calmer than me, Joanna. Have you seen a body before?'

Joanna laughed drily. 'Apart from Dad? No.'

'Oh, Joanna. Me and my stupid mouth. Sorry.'

'It's okay, Megan. Don't get your knickers in a knot. That was a bit different.'

Megan bit her tongue. What the hell was wrong with her? She sat staring at the dots on the carpet. Megan hadn't wanted to see their dad when he died. She wanted to remember him how he had always been to her. Both had been too young when their mum had died and they weren't given the option of viewing the body.

'Look, don't worry. I know what you were getting at. So no - other than Dad, no I haven't seen a real body. But I may as well have. I've seen women come to us with their teeth hanging by threads or knocked out completely. I've seen them with their faces completely smashed in. We even had a woman with an axe sticking out her head.' Joanna leant towards Megan. 'And I'm getting on. But nothing really surprises me any more.'

'Who would do that though? In the middle of Glasgow?'

'Yes, I know. But it's been around for ever. It's not going to disappear overnight just because of a few government initiatives or free legal advice.'

'I know. And I should be more hard-nosed than this, Joanna. I mean I've been to war zones and interviewed child prostitutes on the other side of the world. I think. . .'

Joanna put up her palm. 'You've always been a softie,' she said and smiled.

A tear escaped Megan's eye as she remembered again the pathos of that foot with its gaily painted nails. Who had she been? What was her life like? Megan had a horrible feeling it had not been a happy one. 'I'm not sure that I like it . . .'

'Rubbish. It makes you a better person, Megan.'

'It doesn't feel like that,' she said, wiping her eyes. 'I just want to be able to focus and get the job done. I want to tell this girl's story.

Find out who she was and who was responsible for doing that to her.'

Joanna stood up. 'And you still can. But you're human, Megan. Let yourself have a bloody cry. And then get on with your job. You're good at it. Don't forget that. Now let me go and make you something to eat. You sound like you could do with it.'

'Okay. You're right. Thanks.'

'And Megan - I think you should give yourself a break. Go off and do something fun. You're always working. Or babysitting. Be selfish for a change and do something good for *you*.'

Megan nodded and thought about Natasha's suggestion for the weekend. Maybe it wasn't such a bad idea after all.

When they eventually got off the plane, the girl was tired. She walked slowly behind Auntie, who had applied a fresh coat of lipstick and dabbed some perfume behind her ears as the plane taxied down the runway. Auntie scanned the waiting crowd in the arrivals hall. It was noisy. Lots of people were shouting and the girl felt overwhelmed by all the faces staring and leering at her. Hurry, said Auntie. Hurry up. The girl looked up in confusion as she felt Auntie's hand in the small of her back, pushing her towards a tall, bald-headed man. He was African and the girl wondered if Auntie knew him. Here she is, said Auntie, passing him an envelope. He rubbed his hands together and snaked his arm out towards the girl, pulling her to his chest. His black leather jacket was tatty and she screwed up her nose at its musty scent. Yes. You are a beauty. You will do nicely, he said.

The girl was confused. She didn't like this man. He didn't seem to be a friend. She felt a knot of anxiety forming in the pit of her stomach. I don't feel well, Auntie. Can I go to the toilet?

The woman sighed. Silly girl. We will be right back, she said to the man

Just make sure you are. No funny business, he said.

She raised an eyebrow. As if. I have a plane to catch. And you have something to give me, I believe.

The man laughed.

Hurry up, said Auntie, steering the girl towards the toilets. Stay close to me, and no nonsense, okay?

In the cubicle, the girl sat with her trousers at her ankles, frowning in confusion. What was going on? Who was the man? And what was wrong with Auntie? She was different now, behaving weirdly. The girl didn't have a good feeling about any of it.

Come on. Hurry, shouted Auntie, who was tapping her foot outside the door.

The girl swung it open and walked out slowly. Where are we going now, Auntie? When will I go to my new home? And what about the job? Are we in London?

Auntie dismissed her questions with a wave of her hand. My friend will take you there, she said.

I thought you were doing that? said the girl. You told Mother you would look after me. You said you would make sure I was okay. You promised.

Auntie slapped the girl hard across the cheek. Stop! Enough!

The girl was speechless. You always did ask too many questions, said Auntie. Even as a little girl. But that is enough now. You're staying here. And I'm going home.

7

Megan gasped as she toppled back and her head smacked off the water. She was tumbling through the icy waves, gulping mouthfuls of salty water. Breathe, she said to herself. Just keep calm and breathe. But as the North Sea sloshed around her, and a swell tugged at her legs, she began to panic. She focused on slicing her arms up through the water and then for a moment allowed herself just to drift with the current. It felt peaceful beneath and she briefly wondered if this was what it felt like to drown. Then a hand grabbed her and pulled her back above the waves.

'You okay?' said Natasha. 'You gave me a fright.'

Megan nodded. Natasha was staring anxiously at her, a black hood moulded over her skull and water dripping from her face.

'I'm fine.' She grabbed her board. 'In fact, do you know what. I love this. Best fun I've had for ages.' She gave Natasha a huge grin of sheer excitement and happiness.

Natasha smiled back. 'See, I told you this would do you the world of good. Come on.' She jerked her head towards the shore and slipped onto her board. Megan copied, paddling behind her.

It was just after nine on Sunday morning and, apart from one or two dog walkers, they had the Dunbar beach completely to themselves. After talking to Joanna, Megan had decided that her sister was right. She needed to do something for herself, something that would help her forget work for a while. So she'd asked Joanna if she could borrow her car for the day, promising that she'd return it with a full tank of petrol. That was another thing she needed to sort. Although Glasgow had a good public transport system, Megan had been used to having a car. She and Johnny had shared one but it had been registered in his name. It was another part of her old life that she had left behind. Joanna's car was an old Renault Clio her modest income meant she couldn't afford much – but to Megan it felt like the best car in the world. Just being behind the steering wheel made her feel liberated, and she felt quite carefree when she left Glasgow early in order to make the drive to East Lothian. She pulled into the car park just after eight. Natasha was already there waiting with her wetsuit on.

Megan had known Natasha for about five years. They'd met through work, when Natasha was a political reporter. However, Natasha had quickly decided that journalism wasn't for her and set her sights on the corridors of power at Holyrood. She'd started as a press officer, quickly been promoted to the role of senior press officer, and had told Megan that her next goal was to become a special adviser. One night, in a bar tucked in a close off the Royal Mile, drinking red wine and putting the world to rights, they discovered they each had an ambition to learn to surf. And since neither of them planned to move to Hawaii or the Gold Coast any time soon, they'd decided to bite the bullet and brave the surf of the North Sea.

Megan pulled her board from the sea and headed for the dunes, where she collapsed in a heap.

'I'm exhausted,' said Natasha. 'But that was *amazing.*'

'I know. But I really need some food,' said Megan. 'Quick refuel session and head out again?'

'Sounds good to me.'

Megan reached into her bag and pulled out a towel which she dabbed over her face. She shivered. 'Right, fancy a coffee?'

Natasha looked at the flask she'd produced. 'Oh, Megan. You are just the perfect friend to hang out with. You're always so organised.'

Megan smiled as she handed her a mug of coffee. 'Black and strong. The way you like it.' She paused and turned back to her bag. 'Roll? There's cheese and tomato or peanut butter and banana.'

'Peanut butter and banana, thanks.' Natasha sank her teeth into the white bap.

Neither of them spoke as they gazed out at the white curls of the waves.

Megan took another bite of her roll and then sighed.

'Are you going to tell me what's going on?' asked Natasha.

'What do you mean?' said Megan, her voice sheepish.

'I mean you disappeared from Edinburgh pretty quick to take this job in Glasgow. I didn't realise you were looking for a move.'

'Um, well, I wasn't really,' said Megan. She gave a dry laugh then exhaled through her mouth. 'Maybe something stronger would have been a good idea,' she suggested. 'A wee nip of whisky?'

Natasha nodded, but didn't take her gaze off her friend. 'Has something happened?'

'Well yes . . . I've left him. I've left Johnny and the wedding's definitely off.'

Natasha gasped. 'Since when?'

'A few weeks ago. I spoke to work about a transfer and they agreed. So I packed up my things and left two weeks ago.'

'Where are you staying?'

'With Joanna and George. Just until I can get a place of my own.'

'And how are you feeling about it all?' said Natasha.

Megan shrugged. 'Okay sometimes. Not okay other times.' She brushed away a tear.

'What happened?' said Natasha. 'Is there someone else?'

Megan shook her head. 'No. No one else. Things just changed.'

Natasha raised an eyebrow. 'But what changed? I always thought you were meant to be. With the plans for the wedding and everything.'

Megan couldn't respond. There was so much she *could* say. But where could she even start? 'Anyway, tell me how you are. How has work been?'

Natasha snorted. 'I know what you're trying to do Megan. But we're not quite finished. Come on, I want to know more.'

'I don't want to talk about it just now. It's just going to bring me down – we're meant to be here having fun.'

Natasha squeezed her hand.

'Entertain me with one of your work stories,' said Megan.

'Okay, if you insist,' she said, smiling. 'Well, there's a new "energy performance consultant" currently doing the rounds. God knows how much he's getting paid. Or what his job title even means. He seems to like talking about Key Performance Indicators and strategic plans. But he's quite easy on the eye, so I don't mind too much.' She batted her eyelids in a comical, exaggerated way that made Megan laugh.

'Have you asked him out yet?' She wouldn't put it past Natasha to already have been out with him for several dates.

'Of course,' she said. 'You know me. We've even shared breakfast.'

Megan spat her coffee into the sand. 'Oh for God's sake, Natasha! You haven't changed a bit.' She was envious of Natasha's relaxed approach to life and wished she could be more like her.

'But enough about that. I'm worried about you. And Johnny. How's he doing?'

'He's fine. Doing okay,' Megan croaked. She stood up, brushing the sand off her legs. 'Come on,' she said, pointing out to sea. 'Let's get back out there while we can.'

~

The girl couldn't allow herself to have any bad thoughts. The gods wouldn't like it. Auntie had disappeared and left her with the creepy man.

He ordered her to follow him, pulling her close and moving her along. As they walked outside, she shivered.

Haha, don't worry, I will soon warm you up, my little one, he said. Pushing her towards the car park, he unlocked a dark blue saloon car and shoved her in the back.

She looked around frantically, wondering if she should make a dash for it, if she should run back towards the terminal. But just as she tried to grab the door, he clicked the locks shut.

Don't fucking think about it, he said, turning round and glaring at her

. Where are we going? asked the girl.

I'm taking you home. To meet your new family, he said.

But, but I thought I was going to school in London, she said.

Your new boss is a very rich man. You will clean his house and look after him.

What was he talking about? New family, new job? I want to go home. To my village. Please take me there, she said and started to cry.

Sshht. That's enough of that. This is your new home.

She stared out of the window and watched as the illuminated buildings flashed by. Then gradually everything became pitch black. She felt a dull ache in the pit of her stomach again, and tension in the muscles at the bottom of her back. Maybe this was a dream? Where was her mother? Then her shoulders began to shudder and she sobbed.

The car stopped abruptly and the man jumped out. The door swung open, and the man hauled her out of the car, pushing her to the ground. She could feel the damp soil through her jeans, then she heard a zip.

Stop that, he shouted, leaning close to her face. Enough of the snivelling and tears.

She stared in horror at his pock-marked face leering down at her.

Any more fucking noise and your mother and your brothers get it, he said, slicing his hand across his throat. Is that what you want?

She gasped.

You should be enjoying this bit. Sitting down in the car having a rest. Because this will be the best bit of it. This is like a fucking holiday. You wait and see. Now get back in the fucking car.

The girl did as she was told and he slammed the door behind her. He didn't get in the car immediately. She waited, not daring to look out and see what he was doing. Then suddenly he jumped back in the driver's seat, roughly started the ignition and the car roared off.

She felt a warm sensation between her legs and realised she'd wet herself.

8

Megan woke up with a start. She rubbed her eyes, then tried to stretch her neck. 'Ouch,' she said with a groan. She must really get back into some sort of fitness routine. The day of surfing had left her feeing so achy. She'd clicked on The Body Coach's Instagram links a few times but got no further than watching his workouts. That was no way to get herself fit, though. She reached for her phone to check the time. It was only just past six. There was still plenty of time before she needed to wake George for school but she just couldn't get comfortable. She was grateful to Joanna for letting her stay, but Megan knew this couldn't go on indefinitely. Especially when she was sleeping on a mattress on her sister's bedroom floor. Joanna was on nightshift and had left last night just as Megan had arrived home. It didn't matter though that Megan was in the room alone. It just didn't feel like home. Forcing herself to get up, she padded across the wooden floors, feeling the dust cling to her feet and some crumbs stick to her toes. She really should hoover, do something practical to help out around the flat. Maybe she could do that after work. Reaching for her laptop, she perched on the end of Joanna's bed. She'd been giving a lot of thought to the dead girl. Could she be a victim of human trafficking? She'd read the reports of the Vietnamese workers trafficked to the UK to work in cannabis farms and the women brought over to work in nail salons and brothels. An image of a pink toenail flashed through her mind and she shuddered. It just seemed too horrifying to think that it could be happening on her doorstep, in the West End of Glasgow. Then she remembered a colleague she'd worked with in Aberdeen who had since moved to London. She had a vague memory of a feature she'd written. She typed her name into Google and in seconds a list of features appeared. It took Megan a while to scroll through them but she clicked on the one she was looking for.

The Daily Standard, London, April 4, 2011

Modern Day Slavery: The Truth About Human Trafficking

Julie Wilson, Chief Reporter

Anastasia refuses to make eye contact with me for more than a second or two. Her eyes flit between the door and the floor and she constantly rubs her thumb and forefinger together.

'If you tell anyone, if you speak to anyone about this we will hurt you and your family. The police won't believe you. You are nothing. That is what they said to me. Every day,' she says in a quiet voice.

Anastasia (not her real name) is from Moldova. She came to London two years ago after being promised a nannying job by a friend of the family. When she arrived at Stansted Airport the family friend gave her to another man. A pimp. Within a day of leaving her home and family life in Moldova she was being held hostage in a dirty flat.

She wipes away a tear as she starts to tell me what happened to her. 'I tried to ask to go home. Said I wanted to leave. That man, he beat me. The . . . then he rape me.'

The beatings and rape continued for months. Sometimes Anastasia would be forced to have sex with up to ten men a day. The pimp taunted her and told her she couldn't leave.

'He said to me you have no ID. You will be sent back. You have debts to pay back before we give you back your passport. You keep working.'

One day she was beaten so badly her arm was wrenched from its socket and she had internal bleeding. Her pimp panicked and dumped her at Accident & Emergency at the local hospital.

'The hospital, they called the police. The police, they want to know where my passport was. Where my visa was. I told them I didn't know. I told them I didn't have it.'

After hospital treatment Anastasia was then taken to Yarl's Wood detention centre and locked up. 'I thought I would be helped. I realised I was silly to ask for help. Other women were there like me. They told me the police wouldn't help me.'

Anastasia remained there for two months, confused as to what her crime was. 'I was told I needed visa. I told them the man had it. It was like they thought I made it all up. Why would I make any of it up?'

Anastasia was released thanks to the Poppy Project, an organisation set up to help victims of trafficking. It was then she finally realised what had happened to her; she had been trafficked.

She is now trying to rebuild her life though says she is constantly scared. 'I keep thinking the man will come back. That he will get me and make me do that stuff again and again.'

Anastasia is just one of the estimated thousands of victims of trafficking in the UK. Human trafficking is a hidden crime and so it is impossible to assess accurately how many are affected.

The UK Government will publish its Human Trafficking Strategy next month. When asked what she hopes this will do for victims like her, Anastasia speaks slowly, saying: 'I do not know what this means for people like me. I do not understand. Will it mean girls like me stop being raped and hurt? Can it save their lives?'

Megan shut down the page on her screen. She would email Julie later and ask her about the report. She thought about Anastasia and wondered where she was now and what she was doing. Had she managed to forget what had happened? Had she been able to move on and rebuild her life? She knew that Julie's article would only have scratched the surface of what had happened to her. She must also put a call into the TARA Project, the charity that worked to help trafficked women in Scotland. Perhaps they could shed some light on what was going on. When she realised the time, she closed the laptop and leapt off the bed.

When she reached George's door she rested her hand on the door handle. It felt cool against her clammy skin. 'George,' she called. 'George, are you up?' The spring sunshine was streaming through the windows and she squinted in its glare. She took a tentative step into the room and looked around. A Partick Thistle FC poster was on one wall, and a Star Wars poster on the other. A light layer of dust had settled on his desk, which was scattered with sheets of paper. His empty bed was made. 'George?' she said, turning to walk back into the hall. Perhaps he was in the bathroom. But it was empty too. 'George?' she called. He wasn't in the kitchen. She started to panic. Where was he? She ran into the living room and saw him sitting staring out the window. 'There you are,' she said. 'You had me worried for a minute.'

He looked up at her. 'Morning, Auntie Megan. I've been up for ages.'

Megan took a step towards him. He looked so small, sitting in the armchair by the window. He was dressed for school and his face was sticky with tears. 'What's the matter?'

He didn't answer. Instead he wiped his nose with the back of his hand and stood up.

'I wondered how you felt about scrambled eggs for breakfast?' Megan asked casually.

He chewed his bottom lip for a moment while he thought about it.

'I think there may even be some bagels in the cupboard.'

He raised an eyebrow. 'What about some smoked salmon?'

Megan laughed. 'Hey, don't push your luck, chum. I'm already being extra nice to you.' She held out a hand and George grasped it. 'There might be some tinned tuna though – never tried it with eggs before, but there's always a first time.'

He threw her a dubious look.

'Or maybe at the weekend I could take you out for breakfast and we can find a café that will do it for us. How does that sound?'

'Sure,' he said and followed her into the kitchen. Megan asked George to crack some eggs into it and beat them up in a bowl. Then she told him to add some salt and pepper. While he stirred the eggs around, she sliced two bagels and popped them in the toaster.

'Is everything okay buddy?' she said, her back to him. She heard him sigh.

'I was just wishing I had a dad, Auntie Megan,' he said in a small voice. 'I can't say it to Mum - it would just upset her.'

Megan took the bowl from him and poured the mixture into the pan. She kept stirring the eggs, wondering what to say. She had wondered when this might become an issue for him. 'I know, sweetheart,' she began. 'But the thing is you *did* have a dad. But now you have a very special mum. And an auntie Megan.' She heard the bagels pop up and glanced over her shoulder to check what he was doing. He was looking thoughtfully at her as he buttered them. She lifted the pan and started to spoon the eggs onto the plates. 'Has this bothered you before?'

He shrugged. 'Yes. No. Not really. It's just sometimes I feel left out. When my friends are talking about their dads. I mean I know not everyone has a dad. A girl in my class has two dads and another has two mums. But . . . well, sometimes I think it might be good to have a dad to play football with.'

Megan made a mental note to speak to Joanna later. Joanna didn't keep in touch with George's father after he'd left her when she was pregnant. But she wondered when he'd last been in touch. Surely Joanna would have mentioned if she had heard from him? 'Well, George, you know what? Some dads are rubbish at football. My dad, your granddad, couldn't play football at all. Even when you were little, you could still beat him.'

George giggled. 'I don't really remember him that much. He died and went to heaven too soon. That's what Mum said.'

Megan felt her tears well up. 'I know. It's not fair. Your granny and granddad did go to heaven too soon. But at least you got to know your granddad a bit. And at least they're together . . . and do you know what else?'

'What?' said George, his brown eyes wide.

'I bet they still keep an eye on you from Heaven, to see how you're doing. And I bet they're very proud of you.'

George managed another smile.

'Now, come on, wee guy. Let's eat up our breakfast. And then we'll make a plan,' said Megan, carrying the plates across to the table.

'A plan?' said George, looking confused.

'Yes, a plan. It's not everyone that has an Auntie Megan. And it's not everyone that has an auntie who can teach them how to surf.'

George gasped. 'Really?'

'Yes, really. How does that sound?'

He beamed at her. 'That sounds like a great idea. I don't know anyone else in my class who can surf.' He sat down and started tucking into his eggs.

Megan watched him. If only she could wave a magic wand for him and make everything okay.

'Are you not hungry?' he said when he realised she was watching him.

'Yes. Yes, of course I am.' She picked up her fork and started to eat.

When the car eventually slid to a stop outside a barn, the girl gazed out into the darkness. Then the man ushered her out of the backseat and towards the building ahead. As her eyes adjusted, she made out a red-brick house about twenty metres away, and the smell of woodsmoke crept up her nose. The man gripped her arm, slung her bag over his shoulder and hauled her towards the door. Her feet skidded in the slush. She tried her hardest to pull her sweater down over her soiled jeans. Then the door opened and a fat, olive-skinned man, with gold capped teeth, opened the door. Behind him stood a small, scrawny woman with brassy yellow hair pulled back tightly in a high ponytail. The girl could see her pale scalp.

The man pushed her forward to the couple and had a brief, staccato conversation in another language. The girl hung her head and kept her eyes fixed on the floor, but she knew the woman was staring at her. Then the door slammed shut behind her and she heard her captor crunching over the gravel back to the car. He really was leaving her.

Come. This way, said the woman. We show you your room.

The girl had no choice but to follow the woman through a small door in the hallway and down a set of damp concrete stairs. She knew the man with the gold teeth was behind her, watching and waiting. The girl shuddered. She focused on the stairs beneath her as she descended into a darkened room. The woman switched on a light and the girl squinted as she took in her surroundings. The walls were roughly plastered, the ceiling low and the floor bare and grey. There was a narrow bed with a flat grey pillow, a yellowing sheet and a moss-green blanket. The woman's eyes narrowed and she pointed at another door in the wall. The toilet, she said.

Thank you, the girl managed to say. Though she wasn't sure what for.

Clean yourself up, said the woman, flicking her gaze over the girl's crotch, then come upstairs and I will show you the kitchen. Knock twice and I will fetch you.

The girl looked up and could see the silhouette of the man against the door. The woman walked up the stairs slowly, then shut the door behind her, bolting it shut. The girl stood for a moment in the silence. The room was sparse and col,d and she screwed up her nose at the unpleasant stench in the air. Walking over to the toilet door, her heart sank as she realised the smell was coming from there. It wasn't a proper bathroom or even toilet. It was just a cupboard with two buckets and a cloth.

9

The next day, Megan sat drumming her fingers on the desk. The office was noisy with phones ringing and constant chatter. She'd been glued to the phone all morning without stopping for her usual coffee so she felt more irritable than usual. She picked up a biro and chewed on the end as she thought about the discussion she had just had with Julie Wilson. The article had been drastically cut, much to Julie's fury, because the features editor thought it was 'too depressing'. He'd told Julie that people wanted good news stories and not to be reminded of the darker side of life. She'd tried yelling at him to tell that to Anastasia and all the other girls, but he'd just licked the foam from his cappuccino and gone back to playing Candy Crush on his phone.

'Charming, eh?' she said. 'Let me know if I can help, once you have more of an idea of what you're dealing with.'

Megan then tried the police press office, but they were saying very little even though she said she told them she'd been the one who found the girl.

She felt a tap on her shoulder from behind.

'Hello, stranger,' said a voice. 'Admiring the view?'

She spun her chair round and laughed as she saw Craig James, one of the photographers they used, standing behind her. He pulled over a chair and put his camera down.

'What's happening with you? I haven't seen you for ages. Been avoiding me?' He had a few days' stubble on his chin and shadows under his eyes. Megan thought his shirt looked rather crumpled and she noticed that his trainers were muddy.

'Nah. Don't be daft,' said Megan. 'Why would I be avoiding you? I've just been busy.'

He grinned at her. 'But it's only Tuesday. There's not a lot happening. Shouldn't you be swanning about and having lunch with some of your contacts?'

'Very funny. What have you been up to?'

'Apart from my usual hectic social life, you mean? I was away on a watch job. Been on it all night. Waste of time. The usual. How about you? Where've you been hiding?'

Megan sighed and leaned back in her chair. She rested her feet on the stack of books sitting on the floor.

'Just been busy with stuff, you know. And I'm working here permanently now.'

'I heard,' he said.

Megan was trying to avoid holding his gaze for too long. He was looking at her intensely, his head cocked to the side and a smile still on his lips.

She shrugged and turned back to her screen.

'Are you too busy to have a drink later?'

Megan blushed. 'Eh . . . well I don't know.'

'Don't worry, it's okay, if you're too busy. Just thought you might like a local to show you the nightspots.' He stood up and tucked the chair back under the desk.

Megan looked up at him. 'It's just . . . I've got this big story on. There's some stuff going on . . .'

'It's okay. Another time.'

Megan shrugged again.

'Look,' he said, his voice gentle now. 'It's okay. Just let me know when is a good time. See you.'

Megan wanted to scream out in frustration and call him back. She watched as he disappeared over to the other side of the office to speak to Sunita at the picture desk. Sighing, she rubbed her eyes and swivelled her gaze back to her computer.

But she couldn't focus now on the screen. She needed a drink so she grabbed some coins lying loose in her in-tray and made her way towards the vending machine which sat by the lifts.

'Megan, a word please,' said a nasal voice behind her.

Her heart plummeted. It was Paul, the crime editor of their sister daily paper. He was shuffling towards her, his cheeks flushed and in his long leather coat as usual. He looked like an angry pimp.

'What are you working on?' he demanded.

'Getting a bottle of water,' she said.

'Don't play the smart arse. I want to know what you're working on. I hear you've been making some calls to the police.' He waited for her to respond.

'Well, Paul,' she said as calmly as she could, 'If you have a wee look at our website you might see the first-person piece I wrote last week. Maybe a bit of a giveaway?'

'Well, just watch you're not treading on any toes, okay?'

Megan blinked. *Really?* 'Treading on toes?' she said.

'Aye, you're making calls on my territory,' he said.

'Your *territory*? What are you? A cat?'

'You know fine you're treading on my patch.'

'Oh, right. So now saying we all have to ask your permission before we call the police?'

He glared at her, his pinched expression making him look constipated. 'Just you stick to your wee features, honey.'

'Is that right, Paul? I think of myself as a proper journalist. Perhaps you should try it sometime.' She shoved her coins angrily into the slot and waited for the bottle of water to fall from its perch. It slammed to the bottom of the machine.

'Now, now, children,' said Richard, Megan's editor, who had just stepped out of the lift. 'I hope you're not giving away our list of potential splashes this weekend to the rivals.'

'Of course not, Richard,' said Megan.

'Rivals,' said Paul in disgust. 'We work for the same bloody company.'

Richard gave a dry laugh. 'Yes. Exactly my point, actually.'

'Anyway, I need to go. I don't have time for this. In fact I'm off to see a contact right now,' he snapped and walked off in the direction of the toilets.

Richard and Megan turned to watch him go.

'Looks to me like he's off to the toilet. Maybe that's where his *conta*ct is.'

Megan giggled.

'Something really needs to be done about that man's coat,' he said. 'So, Megan, let's walk and talk.' He strode towards the office. 'What have you got for me this week? Any more on the girl?'

'Um, a few things on the go,' lied Megan. 'Nothing too firm. But I'll let you know.'

'Well . . . soon as you can. Slim pickings so far this week.'

'No pressure then,' she said.

'None at all.' He glanced at his watch. 'I'd better go. Let me know how you get on.' He paused to speak to Katherine briefly then jogged back the way he'd come.

Megan's phone rang just as she reached her desk. 'Hello, Megan Ross,' she said.

'I saw your piece in the paper last week. About finding the girl.'

Megan grabbed her pen and sat down. 'Who is this?'

'I've got information for you. Off the record. Can we meet?'

Megan's heart was now racing. 'Yes. Tell me where and when.'

'Tonight at five. Do you know the Haymarket pub by the station?'

'By the rail station?' said Megan, her heart sinking at the thought of going to Edinburgh.

'Yes. I'll see you there.'

'Wait. How will I know who you are?'

'Don't worry. I'll find you,' said the man before hanging up.

Megan glanced around the newsroom and smiled as she felt the welcome surge of adrenaline. It had been a while since she'd felt excited about anything. Perhaps she would have something for Richard after all.

They expected her to clean the whole house and make all their meals under their watchful gaze. For the first week or so, the girl had managed to keep track of the days. But then they all began to merge into a mass of drudgery and nothingness. She slept scrunched up in a ball, rocking herself to sleep. During the night she would frequently wake shivering, and pull the blanket tighter around heself. It didn't matter that she slept in almost all of the clothes she had,, she was still cold. She would be woken at six o'clock by the shrill bell on the alarm they had put beside her bed. How she longed for a warm bath and to wash her hair properly under hot running water. Just before half six, she had to stand by the door, waiting for the bolt to be slid open. Then she would empty her bucket in the toilet, scrub her hands and go to the kitchen to prepare breakfast. Then scrub the floors, the walls and do whatever list of tasks was thrust upon her. Their bathroom was filthy. It didn't matter that she cleaned it every day. Each morning it looked the same. Towels balled up on the floor, skid marks in the toilet, pools of piss on the rim, black pubic hairs clogging up the plughole. And every morning she had to swallow down the vomit in her mouth.

She would scrub, wipe, chop, fry, wash, iron and fold throughout the day, until her eyelids were drooping. Surely her mother must have told the police that she was missing? Surely someone would be out looking for her now? The skinny woman kept a watchful gaze on her as she chopped the onions for the evening meal. She was preparing a stew and she tried to focus on slicing and dicing the knife through the onions knowing she was being monitored. She couldn't help the tears springing from her eyes as she chopped the onions, it always happened to her at home. And for a moment she could hear her mother singing in their kitchen at home, cooking and moving around, humming a lullaby. The tears started to fall harder. Then as she wiped her tears away, out of the corner of her eye she saw the woman pull the belt from her trousers and flick it in the air. The stinging thrash of the hard leather across her back winded her and she choked back a sob. She could feel the skin swell under her thin T-shirt, and knew that a welt would appear, snaking its way across her shoulders. The woman stood there, eyes sparkling, watching the girl trying to compose herself.

10

Typically, the train to Haymarket was running late, and when it finally pulled into the station it was after 5 p.m. Megan jumped off as soon as the doors opened and pushed against the incoming swell of passengers who were desperate to clamber on the carriage. She clutched her bag close to her shoulder and forced her way through the throng and to the exit. The pub was diagonally opposite the station and although she had walked past it loads of times, she had never been inside. She glanced around. It was unlikely she would bump into anyone she knew here. Stockbridge had been her local area when she lived in the city.

As she stood at the bar waiting to be served, hoping the mysterious caller was still there, she froze when she felt a hand on her shoulder.

'Megan Ross?' A man, in his mid-thirties with dark hair, was standing next to her. He wore a suit, with an open-necked shirt.

'Have a seat and I'll get you a drink,' he said and pointed towards a booth in the corner.

'And you are?' said Megan, annoyed at his directness.

'My name's Jamie.'

'Well ,let me buy *you* the drink, Jamie,' she said. 'What are you having?'

He looked slightly taken aback. 'I'll have a pint of Best, please.' His dark eyes darted around the bar before he settled his gaze on Megan again. 'Gin and tonic for you? That's what hacks normally drink, isn't it?'

'Actually, I'll stick to a mineral water, please,' she said to the barman.

Jamie took the drinks and Megan followed him to the booth. He sat down and said, 'Before I go any further, I want to make sure this is off the record.'

'Are you going to tell me who you are?' asked Megan.

He frowned. 'Look, love. All you need to know is that I'm in the police. And if any of this gets, I'll get my arse kicked. So no funny business, okay?'

'Of course,' said Megan.

'And that means none of this,' he said as he slipped his hand into her pocket and pulled out her phone. He switched it off, put it on the table and glared at her.

Megan was grateful for the dim lighting. Her cheeks were burning.

Then he shook his head. 'I'm not stupid. I know what you lot are like.'

She clasped her hand around her drink and took a calm sip. 'So, what do you want to talk to me for if you know what we're like?'

'Look, I know you've been calling and asking questions about the women who've been found. And I saw your piece last week.'

'Right,' said Megan. 'I'm just doing my job, trying to find out what's happening.'

Jamie took a glug from his pint. 'You know that girl that was pulled from the Clyde? The young black girl. Well, we can't identify her. Even through the publicity appeals.'

Megan nodded. 'Yes, I know.'

'Look,' he said. 'I'm taking a big risk talking to you. But I know you found the other girl. Plus, I'm told you're good at your job. And I'm getting frustrated at how slow this is moving.'

'Then do something about it,' said Megan. She took a sip of water, avoiding the slice of cucumber floating in her glass.

'If I could I would. I'm not that senior - yet. Budget cuts, staff cuts and lack of resources . . . nothing is moving quickly these days. And they're so bloody obsessed with statistics at the moment and solving things. Let's just say that these two women are not exactly a priority.'

'Why?' said Megan.

'Because we don't know who they are and we don't have the resources to fly a team to Africa to investigate it. Therefore it's unlikely we can solve it.'

'Okay,' said Megan slowly. 'What is it you want me to do then? How can I help?'

Jamie eyed her for a moment. 'I thought maybe if you could write something about the girls then it would focus the attention of the bosses, you know? Maybe something would actually be done about this before it happens again.'

'Again?' said Megan.

Jamie nodded. 'And it might just sound off a warning to the folk behind all of this.'

'Okay,' said Megan. 'So tell me what you know.'

'We think it's linked to human trafficking.'

'The girls were trafficked?'

'Yes. We think they could both be from somewhere in Africa. We've contacts in the immigrant community, in Glasgow, but nobody has been reported missing locally. Obviously, if she's been trafficked into the country then she's a nobody, isn't she?'

'*Somebody* must know who she is,' she said, watching him as he scratched his chin.

He shrugged. 'There are all sorts of rumours. Depends who you talk to. But, yes, trafficking seems the mostly likely explanation.'

Megan thought about her call to the TARA Project earlier. The woman she had spoken to had confirmed that Nigerian women had consistently been the largest nationality group for the charity over the years. She was about to say something when her attention suddenly switched to the door.

'You okay?' said Jamie. 'You've gone really pale.'

'Yes,' said Megan, frowning. 'I'm fine.' She gripped her glass in both hands and tried to look anywhere but in the direction of her ex-fiancee, who was now standing at the bar.

Jamie raised an eyebrow but Megan dismissed him with a flick of her hand. 'These girls. Nobody's reported anyone missing? And nobody's coming forward to claim them?'

'That's right,' he said. 'It's a total blank.'

'Do you know how they died?'

He nodded. 'Well, certainly with the first one. Still waiting for all the other test results to come.'

'Let me guess . . . asphyxiation?'

He shook his head.

'Stabbed?'

'No and I'm not sure you want to know,' he said in a clipped voice.

Megan noticed the dark circles under his eyes. 'It's okay. I'm sure I've heard it all before.'

'Mmm, I wouldn't count on it,' he said. 'She died of a heart attack . . .'

Megan frowned. 'A heart attack? A young girl? That's quite unusual, Isurely?'

He nodded. 'Aye. She was covered in bruises. All over. All the signs of sexual abuse were there . . . forensics are wondering if she had the heart attack in sheer terror of what was happening to her.'

Megan covered her mouth. 'Jesus. Poor kid.'

Jamie didn't speak for a minute. 'There's not much that shocks me, you know, but this has. Her body was a mess. I just want to get the bastards who did this,' he said, his voice thick and hoarse, 'before it happens again. She was just a young girl.'

'And I can use this i,' she said, looking again at the bar.

'Yes. You can. But it has to be off the record.'

He was about to stand up when Megan grabbed his arm. 'Please, can you sit down for a minute?'

He looked puzzled. 'Are you okay?'

Megan's hands were trembling. 'I'm fine. There's just someone at the bar I'd rather avoid.'

'Okay,' he said, glancing over. 'Boyfriend trouble?'

'Something like that,' she said.

Neither of them spoke, and Megan couldn't help but glance at the wedding band on his finger. He noticed, and his cheeks flushed.

Megan looked up. 'It's okay. He's gone to the toilet. Come on, let's go.' She quickly gathered her things together and they left.

'Give me a call if you want to have another chat once you've thought about what I said.' As they walked across to the station, he reached inside his jacket and took out a piece of paper. 'Here's my number.'

Megan stashed it in her handbag. 'Okay. Thanks. I'll be in touch.'

'And remember, you didn't hear this stuff from me, okay?' He watched her as she nervously looked back at the pub. 'You sure you're okay?'

'Yes, yes. I'm fine. Thanks. I'd better go. By the way how did you know it was me?'

'What do you mean?' he asked.

'In the pub.'

'Your photo in the paper,' he said and then smiled. 'Doesn't do you justice though. See you.'

'Thanks,' she called after him, desperately trying not to blush. She checked the departures board and saw there was a train to Glasgow in three minutes. She pushed her ticket through the barrier and walked quickly towards the steps.

'Megan!' she heard someone shout after her. It was him. It was Johnny.

She heard the train's arrival being announced and stood for a second, unable to move. Then she raced down the stairs, heart hammering, and jumped into a carriage. Only when the doors closed did she sit down and start to breathe more easily.

It was always going to be just a matter of time. The man was a constant presence, waiting and watching. Lingering in the background, staring in anticipation. All the doors were padlocked shut. Where would she go anyway? The gods would be furious if she disobeyed. They would harm her mother and her brothers. She thought of little Osato. How she longed to hear his chuckle. She had been there, she thought, for almost a week when the woman told her that she stank. You need a bath, she said, grabbing her hair and sniffing it. Ugh, it's disgusting. You are smelly. Like an animal. The girl couldn't disagree. She was embarrassed that she smelt so bad. The thought of a bath gave her a small glimmer of hope.

Come, said the woman, roughly pulling her. I run you bath.

The girl followed her into the bathroom, which she had cleaned that morning. Sitting amongst the bubbles, in the bath, was the gold-toothed man.

Get in, said the woman, slamming the door shut. Don't be afraid, said the man, putting his hands behind his head. His stomach was pale and flabby, and the hairs on his chest floated in the water like tendrils of seaweed. You know you must obey me. You have sworn an oath of obedience to the gods, he said, moving his hands under the water. No, get clothes off and get in.

The girl bent down awkwardly to fumble with the clasps on her sandals. For as long as possible she stared down at the floor she'd earlier mopped. The faint smell of bleach started to work its way up her nostrils, and she tried to hold back the tears. She stood up, feeling a trickle of warm liquid between her legs, and pressed herself against the wall. Her heart was beating erratically, her eyes on the locked door.

I said, get clothes off and get in. Now.

She pulled off her T-shirt and let her trousers and pants slide to her ankles. His eyes flicked over her rigid body and he held out his hand to her. She stepped into the tepid water. Her mouth was dry and she gulped when he grabbed her. She tried to focus on the water sloshing up and down the sides of the bath like waves.

11

Natasha stood outside the restaurant in Nelson Mandela Square, her phone clamped to her ear. Petite, with a sharp brown bob, she was never seen without her trademark brightly coloured heels. Today she was wearing pink shoes, teamed with a navy-blue trouser suit. On anyone else the ensemble would have looked ridiculous, but somehow Natasha managed to carry it off. Rolling her eyes at Megan, she gestured at her friend to go inside.

Amarone was an Italian restaurant close to Queen Street station. Megan was shown to a table at the back and while she was waiting, checked her phone messages. She'd changed her mobile number since the split and closed her Facebook account. But she had forgotten that Johnny could still get at her through her work email. She saw a message from him which she deleted without opening. She made a mental note to add him to Blocked Senders.

'Sorry about that. How are you?' Natasha strode towards Megan. 'Feels like it's been ages since we last saw each other!' She hugged Megan. 'How were you feeling by the way on Monday? I was soooo stiff.'

'Me too,' said Megan, smiling as she remembered trying to play

Twister with George. He had laughed at her for being so 'unflexible' and told her she was getting old.

'So how's things?' Natasha helped herself to a piece of bread from the basket on the table. 'Are you really autonomous from the Edinburgh office and allowed to do what you want? Fancy a glass of wine? Sod it, let's have prosecco.' She signalled to the waiter. 'By the way that feature on women and sectarianism last weekend was brilliant.'

'Thanks,' said Megan. 'I thought it was time it was covered properly, and the woman at the Glasgow Women's Library told me about the launch of their film ages ago. Thought it would be a good hook for it.'

'Well, it certainly seems to have gone down well with some of the West Coast ladies,' said Natasha. 'Though some of the usual suspects are moaning about it.'

'The same ones who think it's a good idea to reintroduce regular Old Firm games and drinking at matches now that Rangers are no longer relegated?'

'The very ones,' said Natasha. 'Sectarianism's all just a bit of banter to that lot. Just a bit of fun.'

Megan rolled her eyes. 'Like the arseholes I used to work with years ago, who thought squeezing your arse was a laugh. Or asked if an interviewee was "fuckable".'

'Unbelievable,' said Natasha. 'Can you imagine the stick you'd have got if you'd said something about the size of their man wands?'

Megan laughed as the waiter set down two glasses of prosecco on the table. 'Well, cheers.' Natasha clinked her glass against Megan's. 'Congratulations on the new job and the move to Glasgow. I hope it all works out.'

'Cheers. It's good to be here. Anyway, tell me how things are with you? How are the corridors of power?'

Natasha groaned. 'Okay . . . Actually, that's a lie. Things are good. Much better now that Rachel is in charge. At least she actually gets things done rather than just talking about it.'

'And what about your boss? Karen?'

'Well, she's all right.' Natasha shrugged. 'As a Justice Minister she's okay. She's just a bit . . . serious. Talking of which, I read your piece about finding that girl. Megan why on earth didn't you say anything when we were at the beach?'

Megan tried not to let her voice falter. 'I know . . . I should have. But I just wanted to forget it.'

Natasha swirled some prosecco around her mouth, then swallowed. 'Wonder if she's linked to the other one.'

'I suppose we'll find out soon enough,' said Megan, thinking about her conversation with Jamie.

'It must have been grim?'

Megan sat back, an image of the dead woman's foot suddenly flashed into her mind. 'It was.' She was still reeling from Sam's call to her earlier. There was no CCTV footage; apparently the cameras hadn't been working for a while. Budget cuts had struck again. Jamie had been right. Megan eyed Natasha, wondering if she should say anything to her about him. But she didn't get the chance. Natasha had an agenda to fulfil.

'Right, get your pen and pad out,' she said.

'Oh, okay, is this the thing you wanted to talk to me about?' Megan reached down to slip a notebook from her bag. 'Anything exclusive? Specifically for us?'

Natasha tapped her nails on the table and nodded. 'Yes.' She glanced around and lowered her voice as the waiter returned. 'Megan, do you know what you would like?'

Megan quickly scanned the menu. 'The salmon, please.'

'The same for me, and a large bottle of sparkling water, please.'

The moment the waiter stepped out of earshot Megan leaned forward, pen clasped between her fingers. 'So what can you tell me?'

'Well,' said Natasha, 'this all actually ties in quite nicely with these women. Have you heard about the Human Trafficking and Exploitation Bill? We've got traffickers facing life imprisonment and no punishments for the victims forced into committing the crimes . . .'

'Yes,' said Megan.

'Well, what I think the government is planning,' said Natasha smoothly, 'is to bring in the Nordic model. I think if we follow that then we can reduce the levels of human trafficking. And exploitation through prostitution. But I'm coming up against resistance.'

'Yes, I saw that,' said Megan. 'So it's not going into that Bill then?'

'No. But I'm looking at suggesting another one.'

'What, specifically legislation for criminalising prostitution?'

'Yes. And so . . . this is where you come in.' Natasha smiled. 'How do you fancy a trip to Sweden? International trafficking conference next month in Stockholm . . . Karen will be announcing the legislation there.' She took another sip. 'If you can work something into your investigation about the Nordic model and its success rates, then it may just keep the pressure on.'

'A bit contrived, no?' Megan jabbed her pen at the pad.

'Not if I get you some case studies and an exclusive interview with the new Lord Advocate. A proper sit-down chat with her - the first she'll do in her new post. She's keen to make sure Scotland leads the way with this legislation and we're already getting international interest. This will just cement the Scottish position.' Natasha took another sip from her glass. 'Think about it. Your marketing department will love it too. They'll get loads of positive PR for the paper, they'll be able to syndicate the interview and it raises your profile.'

Megan could see a smile twitching at the corners of Natasha's mouth. She laughed wryly and raised an eyebrow. 'A win-win situation all round then? You should really become a spin doctor. You're better than Alastair Campbell.'

'Ugh, please don't compare me to *him*,' she said and sat back, smirking.

Megan felt a surge of adrenaline. If she could get the exclusive on the Justice Minister's trip to Sweden plus an exclusive with the Lord Advocate, packaged with a piece on the rising number of trafficking victims in Scotland with a wee bit help from Jamie and perhaps a couple of real case studies too, it was a guaranteed cover story.

'Salmon, ladies.' The waiter placed their plates on the table.

Megan was now desperate to eat so she could get back to the office and start planning. She watched Natasha check a text message and grin.

'Secret admirer?'

Natasha laughed. 'Maybe. I'll let you know if it comes to anything.'

'What about the consultant chap?' said Megan, remembering their conversation from the other day.

'Oh no. That was a fling. All done and dusted.'

'Life's never dull, eh?'

Natasha chewed thoughtfully on her salmon. 'How about you?'

'Since I saw you last, no, I don't have any man news to report.' She had tried to push all thoughts of Johnny yelling after her at Haymarket to the back of her mind. Once again, regret, bewilderment and guilt smacked her in the gut. She was desperate to tell someone about it all and also about her attraction to Jamie. 'Work keeps me out of all kinds of mischief,' she said. 'Natasha, do you think the police are doing enough to identify these women?'

Natasha wiped her mouth with her napkin. 'I don't know. I suppose it depends on their resources, doesn't it? And their priorities?'

'So why bring in the legislation if there aren't enough resources to police the problem then?

'That's tricky,' said Natasha, sighing. 'This legislation is ground-breaking. We're ahead of the rest of the UK with it and . . . well, it sends out a message, doesn't it?'

'A message?' asked Megan.

'Yes. That trafficking won't be tolerated here. That we're taking it seriously. Which hopefully takes the pressure off the police.'

Megan decided to say nothing else for the moment. She laid her pen on the table,

Natasha forked some noodles into her mouth. 'How's the boss?'

'He's fine - still fairly mellow.'

'I always had a soft spot for him.'

Megan raised an eyebrow. 'Really?'

'Really.' Natasha smiled. 'So are you up for Sweden then?'

'Definitely,' said Megan. 'Well, once I've cleared it with the boss.'

*T*HE GIRL HAD ALWAYS TRUSTED *other women. But now she knew that women could be worse than men. That night she was in the kitchen washing dishes at the sink. She'd felt a crack on the back of her legs and fallen to the floor. She tried to grab onto the cupboard as she fell, but her hands were soapy. Before she was able to stand up, the woman kicked her again. Then again. The girl tried to curl herself up into a ball but the woman grabbed a fistful of her hair, kicked her again in the stomach then casually walked out of the room. The girl didn't dare move. She couldn't. She lay there whimpering until she heard footsteps and her muscles tensed. You take this, said the woman in a rasping voice. The girl managed to turn her head to see the woman holding something out in her hand.*

Get up, she said, yanking at her hair and hauling her up onto her knees. The girl tried so hard not to scream out in agony. You take this now. Take it. Swallow. The woman lunged at her again, pushing the girl's head back and forcing her mouth open. The girl felt something in her mouth, a dry lump, and she retched. The woman poured water into her mouth and hissed in her face. You take this. You swallow. The girl thrashed her head from side to side, desperately trying to spit the tablet out, but the woman forced her fingers down the girl's throat, pushing it further and further down. Drink. You drink this. The girl swallowed the water and the woman finally stood back, arms crossed, eyes hard. You done now. You go down there, she said, pointing at the girl's door. Now. The girl, wincing with every step, shuffled towards her room.

12

'What's wrong?' Megan was walking through Dowanhill towards Hyndland Road. Her hand was clamped around her phone, her heart fluttering as she tried her best to push down the anxiety which was threatening to gush to the surface. 'Right. I see. Yes. Okay.' She chewed her lip as she listened. 'What? I don't know. Right, I'll do something about that then.'

Sitting down abruptly on a bench, she rested her elbows on her knees and held her head in her hands. Her clammy hands felt cool against the heat of her cheeks. Johnny had been trying to reach her for days, his mother told her. Her tone was accusing and Megan felt nothing but guilt, even though it was particularly shitty of him to get his mother to call her. And how had he got hold of her new mobile number?

Looking up, she saw a young woman pushing a designer buggy. 'Hiya,' she said.

Megan glanced at the baby, chewing on a dummy. The woman was walking with purpose, and for a moment Megan let the strange feeling of rootlessness settle over her. Where did she belong? She felt like a coward. She'd failed everyone. Johnny's mother had berated her about how upset her son was. Didn't she realise what a mistake she'd made? Didn't she realise that she would *never* find another man as good as her son? And what was she going to do about letting everyone know about the wedding? It was all *very* embarrassing, she said. Megan rooted around in her bag for a piece of gum. There was no sense of empathy or concern or support from the woman. Nothing, despite the fact she'd gone out with Johnny for five years. Just a perfunctory phone call to inform her she was very disappointed and worried sick about her son. The image of Johnny weighed down on Megan and she felt the burden of responsibility grow heavier. She knew the best thing for her mind was the distraction of work, so she called Jamie for an update.

He answered his phone after just one ring. 'Hello. Megan?'

'How did you know it was me?'

'I've got your number in my phone,' he said.

'And here was me thinking it was a private number. Now every Dick and Jamie has it.'

He laughed.

'So, I was thinking that, yes, I could do an investigation into trafficking. Give it some exposure. What do you think?' Megan could imagine him sitting at his desk, his shirt sleeves rolled up, a pen behind his ear and his feet on the desk.

'Okay. Glad to hear it.'

'So what else can you tell me?'

He paused. 'Megan, where are you just now? Are you in the office?'

'No. I'm out and about.'

'Look, are you sure you want to do this over the phone? Or would you rather meet up?'

'Probably over the phone would be better,' said Megan. 'I don't fancy another trip to Edinburgh, thanks.'

'I could come and meet you?'

'I don't mind.' Megan felt an unexpected rush of sadness wash over her.

'Megan, is everything okay?'

For a moment she couldn't speak. 'Yes, I'm fine. Just busy.'

'Where are you?' asked Jamie.

She looked at her watch. 'I'm in Hyndland just now.'

'Do you know Epicures?'

'Yes,' she said.

'Meet me there. I'm in Glasgow today anyway. I'll be with you the back of five.'

'Okay.' She stood up, rolled her shoulders and started walking. Her thoughts began to flicker between work, Johnny, Jamie and back to work again.

An hour later, Megan sat alone in Epicures nursing a large hot chocolate, wishing George was there to enjoy one alongside her. It was nice just to sit at the window and watch life pass by against the backdrop of the red sandstone tenements opposite. She saw a famous actor sauntering past with his plastic bag of groceries and a couple of school kids giggling and pointing at him. She scrolled through her emails idly looking for anything of interest. An email had dropped confirming sweeping cuts to the Scottish Fire and Rescue Service. Richard had mentioned something about it earlier in the week. She knew he would probably want feedback from some fire fighters. Perhaps she could suggest a first-person piece to him. She knew someone who worked in the trade union and he was always happy to oblige if it meant positive publicity for his colleagues.

'That looks good.' Jamie sat down opposite her, several days of stubble shadowing his face.

She looked up. 'Oh, hi, Jamie.'

'Same again, please,' he said to the waitress. 'Sorry, have I interrupted you?'

'No, no,' she said, slipping her phone back into her bag. She was annoyed with herself. Why was her heart starting to race in his presence?

'So, anything new to report?'

'Not really. We're still waiting to get all the tests back from forensics. Think we'll do a press conference later in the week to try and get something. Still getting nowhere with the IDs.'

'So that's two women now with no names?' Megan took a sip from her cup.

'Aye. Two young black girls. We think they've both been sex workers. And the chief thinks they may or may not have been trafficked. Doesn't give us much to go on, does it?'

'They're not really prostitutes though, are they, if they've been trafficked here?' said Megan.

'Well, if you want to get down to the nitty-gritty of it, no. But for our purposes they are.'

Megan pulled a face. 'But surely that's the whole point? They're not. They're not *choosing* to sell themselves, are they? Someone else is forcing them to do it.'

Jamie sighed. 'Regardless of the specifics, Megan, we're trying to gather intelligence from our usual sources. But coming up with nothing. We just need a wee break so we can get some movement on this. At the moment nobody seems to know anything.'

'I agree. If they *are* victims of trafficking, then maybe we need to raise awareness of it as an issue here and let people know that this is happening in their neighbourhoods.'

'Yes, exactly. But you'll need to tread carefully, Megan.'

'Okay. But I'll need something,' she pointed out, 'something to link these girls to a trafficking ring.'

He lowered his voice and moved nearer. 'Though what is interesting is that we have a link between both bodies.'

Megan's eyes widened. 'What?'

'We think that both of them may be from the same area of Nigeria. just awaiting confirmation.'

'Right ... and how do you know that?'

'It can be done by tracing minerals in their bones.'

'Are you making that widely known?'

'No, not at the moment. The tests are complex. They take time.'

Megan thought about her contact who was an expert in African ritual crimes. She'd get in touch with her and ask if she had any insights. 'Anything else?'

'Just heard this afternoon that both victims had bleach inserted in their arses.'

'Eh? I don't understand.'

'It means that they've had unprotected sex. And someone has tried to cover their tracks.'

Megan let out a low whistle and sat back, staring at the grim look on Jamie's face. Her hot chocolate was no longer appealing.

THE GIRL CURLED *up in the foetal position on her bed and drifted into sleep. She was dreaming of Mother, humming that same tune in the kitchen, and she was trying to reach out and tug at her yellow flowery skirt. She could smell Mother's soapy scent and hear the laughter and chatter of her brothers outside. Then she saw the village priest, standing with the chicken and the knife, and she smelt the blood and saw it dripping onto the floor. She could hear him talking to her, reminding her of her bond, and what she had promised. She could feel the rubbery chicken's heart in her mouth and she woke up gagging, her heart racing. She tried to uncurl her body but her stomach was clenched in agonising spasms. Clutching the bed covers around her, she squeezed her eyes shut and rocked back and forth to help ease the pain. She lay, eyes wide open, for a while until the urge to pee forced her up. Gingerly, she stood up and limped to the corner where she squatted over the bucket. The girl had no idea of the time, but there was a little light in the room which had crept under the door, so she thought it could be early morning. Glancing down, she saw blood dripping from between her legs into the bucket. Her breath quickened in panic and she began to feel queasy. She started to wipe herself, but there was blood smeared on every piece of tissue and she didn't have much left to use. She padded her knickers as best as she could and crept back to bed. She must have been in a deep sleep because she was woken abruptly by the woman jabbing her fingers into her arm. You. Get up, she said. She kept prodding at the girl until she stood up. Then the woman reached up under the girl's night dress and yanked her knickers down. The girl yelped. The woman's eyes shone when she saw the blood and she clapped her hands together.*

13

Megan had just arrived at work when her phone buzzed.

'Megan, it's Gina.' Gina was an old college friend of Megan's who had left the seedy world of journalism behind and moved up through the ranks of corporate communications in Police Scotland. She had been a useful friend and contact on more than one occasion. 'I'm just calling to let you know there's a press conference scheduled this morning. All a bit last minute. It's due to start at ten at Stewart Street.

'Is it about the girls?'

'Yes,' said Gina. 'I just wanted to give you a heads-up.'

Megan waved at Katherine and walked out the door. 'The dailies are going to be all over it. Is there anything you can tell me?'

'I'm sorry, love. No can do. It's a live inquiry and we need help. We need to put out an appeal.'

'Okay.'

'Maybe see you there?'

'Yes. See you then.' She used to think that having a friend in the police's media department would be quite helpful. However, everyone was so paranoid these days about information leaking out that they might as well have been discussing the weather.

She saw a Facebook message from Sam and was about to click on it when her online calendar buzzed to remind her about the editorial meeting at ten. Scowling, she ignored it. She was going to the press conference; that took priority. Yes, she she could watch it on *Sky News* but she wanted to be there in person. She simply could not just sit there waiting when she knew that she might be a step ahead of the police. She picked up the phone to call Richard's line and leave a message. 'Hi there. It's Megan. Just to say something's cropped up with the trafficking stuff. There's a police press conference on. I'll let you know how it goes. Oh ... and I've been promised a chat with a firefighter on the cuts. No holds barred.' Then she emailed Katherine to let her know she had been called out on urgent business, grabbed her bag, and headed to the door, almost colliding with Katherine.

'Sorry to run again,' she apologised. 'I've just emailed you to say I've been called out.'

'But the editorial meeting?' Katherine said crisply.

Megan noticed that her face was drawn. 'It's okay. All taken care of . . . I let Richard know . . . are you okay? You look a bit tired.'

'Fine, fine. Just a wee bit under the weather.' Katherine walked back to her desk.

'Okay, well, if you're sure. I'll see you when I get back.'

Katherine smoothed her hands over her dress as she sat down. 'Okay.' She grimaced as her buttocks made contact with the seat.

'Are you sure you're okay?'

Katherine's shoulders tensed. 'Yes. I'm fine. Honestly. It must have been the new Zumba class I went to last night. I'm obviously not used to it.'

'Good for you,' said Megan. 'The most exercise I get these days is walking up and down these stairs. I should really get back out running again.'

Katherine's attempt at a smile failed to reach her eyes. Maybe she's just having an off day, thought Megan. God knows I have enough of them.

The venue for the press conference was near Cowcaddens in the centre of town. Megan decided she would take the subway, aware that her taxi usage was verging on the ridiculous. When she arrived, she was ushered to a small, windowless room. She quickly scanned the place, smiling to acknowledge a few hacks she knew, looking for other useful potential sources of information. She headed to the back row, trying to avoid tripping over one of the many bodies from the BBC. Glancing over her shoulder, she saw Paul from the *News* standing near the door, looking around shiftily. She glanced at the Messenger icon on her phone and clicked it open.

Fancy a drink soon? Sam

'Thanks for coming, ladies and gentlemen,' said Detective Superintendent Michael Henderson. 'As you know, the body of a young woman was found in the Botanic Gardens last week. We are appealing to the local community for anyone who knows anything about this woman to come forward. Someone somewhere knows who she is, and possibly what happened to her.' He took a sip of water. 'We'd also like to make the same appeal to anyone who may know anything about the woman who was recovered from the River Clyde last year to come forward. Her body was found opposite the Riverside Museum and Tall Ship under suspicious circumstances. Despite extensive inquiries, we have been unable to trace next of kin for either of these women. If anyone was in the vicinity at the time or thinks they may have information that could help us with our investigation please get in touch.'

Megan sat quietly, thinking the statement added nothing to what she already knew. She noticed Jamie standing in a and tried to catch his eye. Why was he in Glasgow again? He avoided looking at her.

'Now, if anyone wants to ask any questions?' Gina had swept in to join the DS.

'Is there anything to link these two girls together?' asked one of the daily reporters.

'Not at this present time,' said the DS, 'though obviously we are keeping an open mind.'

Megan raised an eyebrow.

'Any leads at all?' asked another.

'We are working on a few lines of inquiry. But we need more

information from the public. Who are these girls? Does anyone know them? What were they doing?'

'Do you think they were trafficked here?' The room turned to look at Megan.

DS Henderson looked at her as though she had whipped a rattlesnake out of her bag and waved it in his face. 'We do not wish to speculate at this present time.'

'Why not?' said Megan, unable to stop herself.

DS Henderson cleared his throat. 'We do not think it would be helpful to speculate on this at the moment.'

'Now, if anyone wants to do a one-to-one then DS Smith would be happy to do a piece to camera.' Gina caught Megan's eye and gave her a curt nod.

Megan let the throng of reporters push ahead for their interviews and headed towards Jamie. But he was too quick for he; he'd disappeared by the time she got to the door.

'Hanging around again, I see?' Paul appeared at her side, a smirk on his face.

Megan smiled. 'Yip. Just doing my job. Reminding myself what the dailies do when you're on the road. Very little, if this is anything to go by. The questions weren't exactly probing, were they?' Her phone beeped. Glancing at it, she saw an urgent email had dropped. 'Excuse me a minute Paul, need to sort this out.'

'New lead?' he said. 'Or an offer for Viagra.'

'Yes, that's it. Shall I forward it to you?'

He laughed. 'I heard it's drug-related.'

'In what way?'

'The girls were finished off after someone didn't pay a drug debt.'

'Is that right?' Megan asked.

'Aye,' he said, tapping his nose.

She turned away. Finding a quiet corner in the corridor she quickly read the email and took in a sharp breath. She felt a spike of adrenaline surge through her as the story began to develop in front of her very eyes. Megan's contact had confirmed her suspicions. The injuries on the bodies of the girls did seem to be very similar, and her initial thoughts were that if the women were from Nigeria then they could be dealing with witchcraft.

TODAY YOU GO. *You go away, said the woman. The girl shrugged and frowned, unable to understand what the woman meant. You go, hissed the woman. poking her finger at her. Go. She thrust a shabby grey holdall at the girl. Your stuff.*

The girl thought briefly about the suitcase she had left home with. It was her only reminder of her family. It had contained her mother's precious beads. She hadn't seen it since that first journey when the man had taken it from her. Where are my things? My suitcase? she asked. There, said the woman pointing at the bag. You don't need anything else where you are going. She sniggered and walked away. The man with the gold tooth appeared and ordered her to follow him. It was dark outside and he shoved her into the back seat of the car. She sat there, trembling and chewing her lip. Maybe she was going home? Maybe it was over and she was being taken back to the airport to meet Auntie? The man didn't talk to her and she didn't dare say a word. She sat quietly for an hour, maybe more, and then the car stopped suddenly. She could see flashlights flickering in the darkness. The man opened and slammed the door and she could hear voices. She sat, frozen, wiling herself not to shake, and felt the mucus from her nose dribble down her chin. Then her door was abruptly opened, a hand grabbed her shoulder and she was hauled out. The man with the gold tooth didn't give her another glance. The man gripping her arm was dressed in a black suit and a heavy overcoat. The girl managed a sidelong glance at him and saw he had a scar running down his cheek. He pulled her over to another black car, opened the door and shoved her in. She didn't dare speak. Maybe he was taking her to the airport. She closed her eyes and prayed that she was going home. The man turned to her, his eyes steel. He thrust a bottle of juice at her. Drink this, he said. She hesitated and he grabbed her wrist, clutching it tightly. She reached out, took it and drank.

14

It was after lunchtime when she got back into the office, and only Ronnie was there. He raised an eyebrow when he saw her.

'What?' she said.

'We missed you at the meeting,' he said.

She grinned. 'Aw, missed you too.' She scrolled through the news wires and read what the dailies had on their sites. They had all taken the same line from the press conference: that police were baffled by the discovery of these nameless women and were begging the public for help. Megan was excited at the thought of sitting on a scoop. As it stood, she seemed to have more information than the police. She just didn't know how long she could wait, though, without telling them what her source had revealed. After Tricia's email had dropped she'd called her to verify a few of the facts. Tricia was an expert in ritual crime, who had given evidence at a child-abuse case Megan had covered at the Old Bailey a couple of years ago. That was in the glory days when Scottish papers had big enough budgets to fly their reporters to London to cover stories. Nowadays they just used agency copy. Megan and Tricia had kept in touch, occasionally meeting for a drink whenever Tricia had been in Edinburgh. Tricia did not want to be quoted on the record yet as she was giving evidence in another case down south. But she had given Megan enough of a background to run with. Megan typed 'Nigerian trafficking victims UK' into Google and had pulled up several news stories. The reports went on and on. A story was formulating in Megan's mind, and she felt her heartbeat quicken as she realised that she now had a very strong hook. She picked up the phone and called her contact at the city morgue, who confirmed again that the two women had similar scars on their bodies.

'We think they may have been tortured. Or perhaps they self-harmed,' he said.

'On their feet?' asked Megan.

'Aye. That's right.'

'What about something else? Like a ritual killing or something like that?'

He gave a snort. 'Think you've been watching too much *CSI*, love.'

'It's a possibility though?'

He exhaled loudly. 'We'd need to get a specialist to look into it and we've not been given any special instructions by the cops. Tight budgets and all that - you know how it is.'

'But surely it's worth mentioning?'

'Who to?'

'The cops.' Megan felt tears of frustration prick her eyes.

'It might just complicate things. We're trying to establish where the women are from. We've flagged up the presence of the cuts to them, that's all we can do. Up to them to join the dots together. Or put the dots there in the first place.'

'For fuck's sake.'

'Tell me about it. Look, I need to go. It's going like a bloody fair in here.'

'Okay . . . Listen, one last thing, have the blood tests come back yet?'

'No, we're still waiting. There's a backlog in the labs.' He coughed and said something to someone else in the room.

'Will you let me know if anything odd comes up?'

'Aye, love. Look, I really need to go. I'm needed in the lab.'

'Thanks.' Megan hung up and jabbed a message into her phone.

Dinner? Tonight?

A few moments later her phone buzzed.

Okay. Take-away at mine. 6ish?

Stretching her legs out, she circled her feet and rolled her shoulders back. She needed to talk to someone else about this and get a fresh perspective. Her stomach grumbled and she felt in her bag for the chocolate bar she'd bought for George. She tore off the wrapper and sank her teeth into it.

'Come in, come in,' said Sam, opening the door and letting her in. 'Well, what do you fancy? Indian or Chinese?'

'Indian from the Ashoka, please. Been dreaming about it all week.'

'Okay. I'll order it. What do you want?'

Megan rubbed her eyes. 'Anything. Pakora, chicken Chasni, naan bread.'

'Okay.' Sam laughed. 'Just give me a minute.'

'Fancy some wine?' Megan pulled a bottle of red from her bag.

'Sure. Do you want to get the glasses?' He gestured towards the kitchen.

Megan took the wine through and paused for a moment as she noticed the tidy worktops and pristine surfaces. Nothing had been left out and even the tea towel was hanging neatly on a hook by the door. It was very much a single man's kitchen. She opened the cupboard by the sink and reached up for a couple of glasses.

'Food will be here soon. Good guess with the glasses.'

'Same place I keep mine,' said Megan, unscrewing the wine and pouring. 'Or rather, kept them.' She handed him a glass. 'Cheers.' They clinked their goblets together.

'Cheers,' said Sam. 'Shall we sit at the table?'

Megan sank down into a chair, glugging back the wine. 'This is a nice place you have, Sam.'

'Aye,' he said. 'It's not bad. Better than that place I stayed in Aberdeen.'

'Yes,' agreed Megan, 'this is definitely an improvement.' She looked at the sanded floors and the white walls with black and white pictures of Barcelona. 'Have you been there lately?'

'No. Not for a while. Was hoping to get out there sometime soon.'

'Do you still keep in touch with your friend there?'

Sam nodded. 'Aye. We hook up if I'm in town.'

He was a man of few words, and Megan knew that was all he was likely to say. She knew he had a sometime girlfriend who lived there. She was a graphic designer. And that was all he would tell her.

'How are you enjoying living with your sister?' he asked.

Megan knew he'd always had a bit of a soft spot for Joanna, which unfortunately wasn't reciprocated. 'She's okay, thanks. Doing a great job with George and juggling that with work in the women's refuge.'

He looked pensive for a moment. 'Does she ever hear from George's da?'

Megan shook her head. 'Not that I know of. Why do you ask?'

'I just wondered,' he said.

Megan decided not to probe any further. 'Thanks for letting me come over at such short notice.'

'No problem,' he said.

Megan looked around the room. 'This is a nice kitchen. Great view of over there.' She pointed at the window. 'Reminds me of that picture - what's it called?'

'*Windows of the West End*? I think that's the one you mean. Aye, it's not bad. You get a nosy into other people's worlds. See what they're up to . . . sometimes it's a good distraction, you know, if you can't sleep.'

'It's nice here, though. Quiet.'

'Aye, sometimes too quiet though.' He shrugged. 'That'll be the food. Two ticks.'

'Here — let me get it,' said Megan, grabbing her bag and pulling her purse out.

They sat with an assortment of foil trays between them, spooning chicken and sauces onto their plates.

'So how's work going? How's the Glasgow office?'

'It's fine. Quieter than Edinburgh, weirdly But I like it. Sam, I wanted to talk to you about a story. Can I run it past you?'

'Okay. Is this about the dead girls?'

Megan forked some rice onto her plate. 'Yes.'

'Have the police made any progress?'

'No, that's the thing. They've made an appeal, but they don't seem to have any positive leads. They seem to think they could maybe have been working as prostitutes.'

Sam sat back in his seat and considered this for a moment. 'Could've been. They're young girls, right? Both black?'

'Does that strike you as strange?'

'Not really. To be honest, there are so many refugees and asylum seekers in the city now, it's quite normal to see every colour of prostitute on the streets these days.'

'But that's the thing. I don't think these are street girls. Nobody seems to know them or recognise them. Surely someone would have recognised them from their patch?'

Sam sat chewing for a moment and then nodded his head. 'Of course so much stuff is going on behind closed doors these days.'

'Exactly. Which is why I think they were trafficked.' Megan rested her fork on her plate.

'How do you prove it though?'

'Well, for a start, the charity here helping trafficked women says Nigerian women are their highest nationality group. And it also reminds me of a story a friend covered in London,' said Megan. 'A girl from Moldova. She was kept prisoner in a flat and forced to have sex with scores of men.'

'And what happened to her?'

Megan laughed drily. 'She was one of the lucky ones. She escaped.'

'Why would they be bumped off?'

'What do you mean?'

'Well, from what I know about trafficking, these girls make their bosses *a lot* of money. I mean, a lot of money.'

Megan tore at the naan bread. 'So why would their pimps get rid of them if they were such a valuable commodity?'

'That's what you have to ask yourself,' said Sam. 'Maybe they're being made an example of, perhaps? But to who?'

'I don't know. That's where I'm drawing blanks.' Megan picked up the bottle of wine and refilled their glasses.

THE GIRL WAS *groggy but managed to sit up. It was dark outside, and she couldn't see any lights or buildings. Where were the toilets? You go there, said the man, pointing at the side of the road. The girl stumbled, shivering in the night air. She desperately needed to empty her bladder. She wondered if the man would look away and give her some privacy. He didn't. She had no choice but to squat down beside him, feeling the sense of relief as her pee flowed across the dry dirt on the ground. He stared at her the whole time. She stood up, her cheeks red with embarrassment and anger. Get in car, he said, pushing her into the back seat. Eat this, he said, and thrust a small bag towards her. The girl clutched it in her hands. She didn't want to eat anything. Her stomach still ached and she wasn't remotely hungry. But he stood there, waiting and watching. She prised it open and pulled out some bread, which felt stale, and a piece of yellow cheese. He handed her a bottle of orange juice. Drink this. Drink it all. The girl took small bites of the food and a few sips of the juice which was sweet but not refreshing. She tried to swallow down the food but gagged with every bite and sip. The man eventually moved away and shut her door. He sat in the driver's seat, staring at her in the rear-view mirror. Where you taking me to, she whispered. Am I going home? Yes, he said. I'm going home, she asked. I'm going home? He gave a harsh laugh. Yes. You go to new home.*

15

‘The boss has been marching around the place looking for you,’ said Katherine as Megan arrived at work.

‘Has he? Didn’t he try my mobile?’

‘Apparently it’s switched off.’

She reached into her pocket and pulled it out. ‘Oops, so it is. What’s wrong? What’s the drama?’

‘Well, you didn’t hear it from me, but he’s not very happy that you didn’t make it to the meeting yesterday.’

‘I know, but something came up. I did let him know.’

Katherine shrugged. ‘Just thought you should know, Megan. It’s just that he takes the editorial meeting on a Tuesday *very* seriously.’

‘Right, fair enough. Guess I’d better go and do some grovelling then.’

‘He’s upstairs just now, working in the conference room.’

Megan headed upstairs to Richard’s office on the fourth floor. As the lift door pinged open, a gaggle of women from marketing stumbled out. ‘Good morning,’ said Megan as they walked past, sniggering.

The door of the conference room was ajar. ‘No problem. I’ll get back to you on that, and maybe we can line up a few holes of golf one of these days?' Richard laughed as he hung up. 'Come in and sit down, why don't you?'

'Thanks. So. I hear I'm in trouble.'

He burst out laughing. 'Who's been stirring?'

'I've just been told you were stalking the corridors looking for me because I didn't go to the meeting yesterday.'

'Well, to be honest, it wasn't your smartest move, Megan. The thing is, we take the editorial meeting seriously through here, you know. We're a good team. It's important that we all gel. You're new here, so you need to make an effort to bond with the team. You can't just waltz off when you get the sniff of a story.'

'Even if it could be the scoop of the year?'

Richard leant back in his seat and clasped his hands behind his head. 'Go on, then. Tell me what this amazing scoop is.'

'Look. We're needing to sell copies of the paper. Which means we need hard-hitting and exclusive content. None of the rewritten wires rubbish which the others are full of. I mean, did you see the state of that new freesheet this morning?'

He rolled his eyes. 'Okay, I get that. I like the way you think. But, still, you need to come to the meetings and cover the other stories too.'

'I know that. And I'm really sorry. But I need to be out there investigating and asking questions, especially if you don't want to be buying in so much copy.'

'Look . . . I know where you're coming from, Megan. But we need to work out some kind of compromise, otherwise the board will freak. Especially when this is supposed to be a trial . . .'.

'A trial? What do you mean, a trial?'

He spoke quietly. 'They just want to keep an eye on expenditure before they commit fully to a permanent operation in Glasgow.'

'And why am I only hearing this just now?' said Megan, trying to keep the edge from her voice. 'I thought you said you were permanent. You've all been here for a year already. Why wouldn't they keep the office here?'

'Because I was hoping to smooth it all out without worrying you.

Look it'll all be fine, just as long as you don't ruffle any feathers.' Richard looked sheepsih.

Megan leaned forward. 'Regardless of budgets and all that, I have a job to do. I can't be worrying about the future of the Glasgow office when I'm on the verge of something exclusive with these two dead women. I really think it could be trafficking. Maybe even something worse.'

'Eh? What could be worse?'

'Well, I hope I'm proved wrong. But I just need some time to investigate an angle. The point is, we're all fighting for circulation. We need to sell copies and we need people to want to buy us. We're the best out there.'

'Well, let's face it - there's not exactly much competition.'

'Not at the moment. But that could all change, and so we need to build our readership now so we have brand loyalty.' She winked. 'See – I can the marketing lingo too!'

Richard sat back and tugged at his tie. 'Okay. Take a few weeks to try and pull this together. But I need you to be visible too, otherwise people will talk. And you need to attend some of the meetings.'

'Fine. Richard, I need you to trust me to do this.'

'Funnily enough, that's why I gave you the job.'

She gulped. She really wanted this to work. She didn't want to end up back through in Edinburgh. Megan pushed her chair back and stood up. 'Oh, and before I forget, Natasha Campbell has invited me to Sweden the week after next. An exclusive. It's an international conference on trafficking and she's unveiling new legislation there.'

'Mmm.' Richard's eyes were now focused on his tablet.

'So you're fine to take that from the budget then?'

'I don't believe it!'

'What?'

'Och, Hearts have bloody well gone and lost to Celtic.'

'So, Stockholm then. You're fine with that? Should be away two days max.'

'Mmm, yes,' he said. 'That's fine. Bloody wankers. That's so typical.'

Megan knew he had no idea what he'd just agreed to. 'Perfect. And thank you.' She walked out of the room, thinking to herself that she'd better get the flights booked now, before he changed his mind.

THE GIRL'S eyes were stuck together. She felt cold water being splashed across her face and heard a man's voice telling her to wake up. She didn't know who he was or where she was. Maybe she was at the airport? A sharp pinch to her arm made her sit up abruptly. It was dark. She was in the car, still in the same car. She noticed the green tree hanging from the mirror at the front. She looked to see where the cold air was coming from and saw the man standing there. She was hauled out of the car and bundled along a gravel path, then led through a door. She couldn't see where she was being taken. Then the light was suddenly bright and harsh, and the man shoved her into a room. The girl could see other girls - all standing there, trembling, with their eyes fixed to the ground. A different man, with a shaved head and a beard, started to brush her hair. He tugged it and she yelped when the bristles hit the tender part of her head. He thrust a cloth at her and told her to wipe her face. Then he shouted at all the girls to remove their clothes quickly. The girl looked to see what everyone else was doing. What was happening? The man shouted at them to take their clothes off otherwise he would kill them. The girl tried to cry silently as she removed her top, kicked off her shoes and socks, then peeled off her trousers and finally her underwear. The girl next to her was shaking violently she could hardly stand upright.

The man ordered them to follow him, and the girls all followed behind in a line. He took them down a dingy corridor. The brickwork was exposed and she shuddered as something furry brushed past her ankle. It felt like a long walk. Then the corridor opened out and the girl heard loud music thumping. The man told them to keep their heads up and walk slowly up and down the stage. They were each given a sheet of paper to hold with a number. Following the girl with the curly blonde hair in front of her, the girl gasped when she saw the audience. They were all men and all dressed in suits. They looked like the businessmen she'd seen at the airport that day with Auntie. She tried not to stare at them but wondered if they were there to help. She kept walking up and down the stage. The music was deafening, the lights bright, and she noticed one man taking notes. Her arms shook as she held the paper in front of her as she'd been told. Then all the girls were led off the stage and back down the corridor. The man took them to the room where their clothes were. He told them not to put them on yet as some of the men might want to try their new purchases out.

16

Paul, whose office was on the first floor, had developed a habit of appearing at Megan's shoulder. She'd even resorted to moving her desk, so her back was against the wall.

'Can I help you with something, Paul?' she snapped.

'No, not really,' he said, scratching his precisely trimmed goatee. 'I liked the piece you did last week, by the way.'

'Which one was that?' said Megan.

'Charity-shop chic. Important stuff.'

She didn't respond.

'Just wondered what you've got this week. I wondered if we could help you out with anything?'

'We're doing a spread on the best cleansers, lipstick and a guide on how to pull a bloke.' Megan didn't move her eyes away from her screen. She had spent all morning trying to rewrite freelance copy and was not feeling charitable. The wind was howling through the gaps in the windows and the raindrops were battering off the glass.

Paul stood there pouting. 'There's no need to be like that.'

Megan looked at the *No* badge pinned to his dishevelled shirt. It was the only reminder she'd seen of the Independence referendum in 2014. She wasn't quite sure what point he was trying to make.

'Look, Paul. You do this every week. I wouldn't dream of wandering into your office uninvited and asking you what your splash is for tomorrow.'

'Well, we do all work for the same company. We should be helping each other out.'

Megan was suddenly overcome by weariness. 'Look, Paul, we're not friends, we're not here to share copy, and we may work for the same company but we are different publications. Separate entities. Can you please go away and leave me to it.' She glanced at the clock.

He flared his nostrils, then sucked his stomach in. Megan knew he was trying his hardest to think of a smart reply. But couldn't.

'And make an appointment next time you want to see me.' She glanced up as he wandered off, muttering.

'What did you just say?' she said.

He stopped and turned. 'You heard me. I said it must be your time of the month.'

Megan burst out laughing. 'Really? Is that the best you can come up with? Might just have to report you to HR for that one, Paul. I think that could be interpreted as a sexist comment, don't you?'

He glared and turned away.

'By the way,' she said, turning back to her screen and beginning to type, 'I really like your trousers. I wish I could fit into my wee sister's clothes too.'

He stormed out the door, slamming it behind him.

Katherine burst out laughing. 'That shut him up.'

Megan smiled. 'Yes, well, he is quite the knob, isn't he? Why's he always sniffing around here? Did he always do that? Before I arrived?'

'Not so much, actually,' said Katherine, looking confused. Then she laughed. 'Maybe he's got the hots for you.'

Megan grimaced. 'Oh God, I hope not. He just seems quite obsessed with what I'm working on.' Sighing, she returned her attention to the screen. She was checking the press cuttings in preparation for the trip to Sweden. She wanted to know what the trafficking situation was in Sweden. Several articles came up and she hit 'print' for them all. In the corner of her eye, she saw an email drop and clicked it open before she realised who it was from.

Megan,

I know you're avoiding me but we need to talk. You know how good we are together. You know how much better things are when you're with me. I don't want it to end like this. What about your things at the flat? Should I just leave them out with the rubbish? Phone me, please.

Johnny

Damn. She'd forgotten to block him. Megan deleted the email straight away. She didn't care for the pleading tone or the underlying threat that he was going to bin her belongings. He could toss them out if he wanted to. She'd taken all the things that she wanted and needed. If she went back there she knew that would be it. Somehow he would convince her to stay.

She sat for a moment, tapping her fingers against the worktop, then quickly Googled 'Scotland domestic abuse'. The cuttings from Rachel Thompson's recent press conference appeared: the 'two strikes and you're out' policy. Megan scrolled down further until she found a cutting which revealed statistics. Maybe she should talk to someone at Women's Aid. Another mental note for tomorrow.

In her bag, her phone began to ring. The number was withheld. 'Hello,' she said cautiously.

'Megan. It's Jamie.'

'Oh, hi there,' she said, relieved.

'You got a minute?'

'Sure,' she said.

'Can you meet me?'

'When?'

'Whenever you can get away. I'm in Glasgow.'

'You're making a habit of this,' she said.

'So when can you get away?'

She glanced at the clock. 'I can leave in ten minutes. Where are you?'

'Queen Street station. See you there in half an hour?'

'Okay,' she said.

When Megan walked out of the underground, she saw Jamie by the taxi rank. Once again, and much to her annoyance, she felt excited to see him. He gestured to her to follow him down the small lane which ran into Buchanan Street. She tripped and stumbled, but Jamie caught her from behind and steered her towards a doorway. Her heart started to thump. This was unexpected. Where was he taking her? She braced herself as they went through the door. Relief rushed through her as she was greeted by light, heat and music. They'd gone in the back entrance of Waxy O'Connors. No wonder he'd brought her here. She'd been told it was one of the most discreet bars in town. It was a labyrinth of drinking corners spread over three levels - the sort of place you could get lost in.

They settled at a table in a dark corner and Jamie got them drinks.

'Are you driving back to Edinburgh?' she said, nodding at his glass of Coke.

'Yup.'

'So what's new then?' asked Megan, taking a sip of her gin and tonic and feeling herself relax.

'Well, I heard a couple of things that may be of interest to you.'

She leaned in closer. 'Me too.'

'Right - well, I'll show you mine if you show me yours.'

Laughing, she nodded. 'You first.'

'Okay. Well, forensics are now making a link between the women: some hair fibres found on both and similar markings. We know they were both Nigerian, but so far the databases are drawing blanks.'

'Right. I knew all that. What else?'

'There's also signs of prolonged sexual abuse.'

'And what else?' Megan was getting impatient.

'Well, I thought that was quite a lot to go with. Definite link and a near-firmed-up place of origin.'

'But no motive or suspects?'

He shook his head. 'Still too early. But we now definitely think they've been trafficked here.'

'What makes you think that?'

'The fact that we can't trace them and nobody claimed them. They must have been brought in from abroad.'

'Anything else though?'

He paused long enough for Megan to know there was. She narrowed her eyes. 'Is there anything you want to share?'

'We're keeping our eye on one or two people of interest.'

'Who?'

'Can't say at the moment,' he said, his eyes darting over towards the bar.

Megan decided she would have to launch the charm offensive. She needed him to trust her. 'So how long have you lived in Edinburgh then?'

'Four years or so.'

'Whereabouts are you?'

A ghost of a smile passed his lips. 'Tynecastle.'

'Ah, so you're a Jambo then?'

He laughed. 'Well, yes and no. I grew up in Glasgow, so when I'm through here it's Partick Thistle. In Edinburgh, I'm a Hearts fan.'

'My nephew supports the Jags.'

'He must be a good lad then,' said Jamie. 'How old is he?'

'Ten.'

'And how about you? How long have you been in Glasgow?'

'Oh,' said Megan, 'I've only been here a couple of weeks. I used to live in Edinburgh . . . but I live with my sister now and George. . . that's the nephew.' Megan noticed the way Jamie kept twisting his wedding band. 'How long have you been married?'

Jamie looked away for a moment then hesitated before replying. 'I was married for two years.' Then he waved a hand dismissively. 'Anyway, what about you?'

Megan didn't want to push or pry but she wondered why he still wore his ring. For a moment she thought he looked vulnerable sitting there, nursing his glass of Coke. Not at all like the confident cop who had met her in the pub the first time. 'I'm not married,' she said. 'Obviously . . . if I live with my sister. I was engaged. . . well, the wedding was called off.'

'Was that the guy who followed you from the pub that night?'

Megan hadn't expected him to say that. 'How did you know?'

'I wanted to make sure you were okay, so I hung about,' he said, shrugging. 'I watched him follow us from the pub and then I heard him shouting at you. Bit aggressive, isn't he?'

Megan's took a swig of her gin. 'Eh,' she said in a whisper. 'He can be.'

'Who broke it off?'

'Me,' said Megan. 'It was me.' She started rubbing the side of her temples.

'Well, I think you're well shot of him,' he said. 'Looks like a right wee shite.'

Megan laughed, her tension relieved now she'd told him.

'Let me get you another drink,' he said, standing up. His phone rang and he answered as he walked away.

Megan watched him talking animatedly into the phone. He must have felt her eyes on him because he turned and locked his gaze onto her. Megan looked away. What was wrong with her? She'd only just broken up with Johnny and she was going weak at the knees if another man so much as glanced at her. Johnny would be furious if he could see her right now. Just then, she remembered Craig's invitation to take her for a drink. Though, if she was honest, she really wasn't interested in him. When Jamie returned to the table, Megan looked up at him. 'Did they have any markings on them apart from the cuts?'

'What do you mean?' he said as he sat down. 'And anyway, how did you know about the cuts?'

Megan ignored his last comment. 'Did they have any branding marks? That's apparently quite common. Logos or signs tattooed onto them.'

Jamie sat back. 'No. But you're becoming quite the expert. Are you after my job?'

'Ha ha.' She paused as someone walked past their booth. 'I agree with you though. I'm convinced they're trafficked. I think someone is using witchcraft back in Nigeria to force these girls to come here.'

'But you're not going to say any of that in the piece? Jesus, I can already see the headlines: Black Magic. Voodoo on the Streets of Glasgow.'

'Do you know about this?'

He didn't answer.

'Well, I have a contact who does. She told me about the cases and the marks on their bodies. She's an expert on African religions and rituals. Her first impressions are that the women have been forced to come here. What I don't get, though, is why they're being murdered and dumped.'

Jamie nodded. 'I know. Normally they're sold on. They're worth a fortune to their pimps.'

'Unless they were, you know, damaged goods?'

'What do you mean?'

'Were they pregnant?'

Her words hung there for a moment and, eventually, Jamie shook his head. 'No.'

'Are you sure?'

'Not that I've been told, Megan. And I'd like to think I would have been.'

'Is it worth double-checking?'

'I would have been told,' he said, his voice tense.

'Okay. I just think there must have been something wrong with them. Something that we're missing . . . or something that you're not telling me?'

THE GIRL WAS EXHAUSTED. *She couldn't lift her head off the pillow. She just needed to close her eyes for a while. Everything that came after was hazy. She remembered the gentle soothing rhythm of a car engine. She thought she heard Auntie's voice, could smell her perfume, but couldn't remember actually seeing her face or touching her. It must have all been a dream. She just wanted to sleep for ever. It was cold and dark when the girl was bundled out of the car and up stairs. There was a smell of stale urine on the*

dirty concrete steps. Her head flopped over the shoulder of a man. He was muttering under his breath, and she couldn't understand what he was saying. She went limp, pretending to be asleep. There was no point in struggling; she didn't have the strength. She was dumped on a bed in a small cold room. A bottle of water was left by the bed. The girl gulped it down, curled up and fell asleep again.

That night she saw the priest from her village in her dreams. She could see his face looming large above her, his yellowing eyes staring at her, piercing all the way through her. His voice hissed at her, and he was shaking a bloody, squawking chicken. Its beak was pecking at her face and she screamed trying to hit it off her. She woke up trembling, curled in a ball, on a lumpy mattress with some grubby blankets wrapped around her. Flicking her eyes up at the ceiling, she stared at the brown stains and the fancy cornicing. Something was battering the windows outside. It sounded like a million stones being thrown at the windows at once. The girl didn't dare move. It could have been the priest coming to get her, or the spirits or anyone. Had she been bad? Disobeyed? She had tried so hard to do as she was told, even though she hated every second. Her mind was foggy and she couldn't remember anything clearly. Glancing down she could see she was wearing jeans and a T-shirt. They didn't belong to her. Where was she? How did she get here? There were noises outside the door and she scrambled further into the corner as she watched the handle turn.

17

Megan couldn't push away the feelings of guilt which seemed to plague her. She hadn't seen much of Joanna or George and knew she needed to talk to her sister about what George had said to her the other morning about his dad. And she was aware she had to fulfil her promise to take him surfing. Megan was also becoming increasingly anxious that she owed her sister an explanation about what happened with Johnny. Instead, she was burying her head in the sand and had come to work early while Joanna and George were still asleep. She logged on to the computer and waited for it to fire up. She leaned back in her chair and took a sip of the hot, strong coffee she'd picked up on the way in. The shrill sound of her phone interrupted her thoughts.

'I've got something I need to talk to you about.' It was Joanna.

'Is it urgent?' Megan's stomach twisted.

'No, nothing to worry about. There's just someone I'd like you to meet. When will you be home tonight? I can tell you more then.'

'Don't know if I can wait that long.'

'Well, you'll have to. I need to take George to school now.'

'Okay, fair enough. About seven?'

'And Megan?' said Joanna softly.

'Yes?'

'Johnny called me.'

'Called you?' *Fuck*. Megan's voice dropped. 'Eh, why?'

'He said he misses you and wants you back. I told him it was none of my business. But he asked if I would talk to you. Make you see some sense.'

Megan dropped her mouse with a clatter on the desk. 'What did he say exactly?'

'Not very much. But, Megan, I hope you don't mind me saying. He's a bit of an arse.'

Megan nodded. She never thought she would hear her sister say that. 'I thought you adored him.'

'Em, no. I just said I did because you obviously did. I've always thought he was a bit of a dick.'

Megan could scarcely believe what she was hearing: Joanna had never let on what she thought of Johnny.

'He's clearly got a bit of a bruised ego.'

'Just a bit,' said Megan. 'I'll explain later. But thanks for letting me know.'

'I'll catch up with you later. I need to get George now.'

Megan hung up and sat thinking for a moment. Maybe the trip to Stockholm would give her some head space, allow her to process what had happened and what to do. At the moment her mind was so chaotic she didn't know if she was coming or going.

The next few hours passed in a blur. Her stomach started grumbling just as Katherine placed a chicken sandwich in front of her.

'I'll get you a tea too. You've not moved from that seat all morning.'

'Thanks. You're an angel.' Megan wanted to drop her head onto the keyboard and weep. *Bloody Johnny*. She sank her teeth into the soft bread and chewed a piece of chicken coated in spicy mayonnaise. 'Katherine, your husband's a lawyer, right?'

'Yes,' said Katherine. 'Oil and gas.'

'Of course, I forgot. That's a shame.'

'What do you mean?'

Megan flicked her eyes back to the news wire. 'I could do with talking to someone.'

'What for?' Katherine waited for her to elaborate.

'I just think I could do with some advice.' Megan put down the rest of her sandwich. She'd lost her appetite.

A MAN STOOD in the doorway. The girl recognised him from the night before. He'd prodded her and touched her intimately while she and the others had been waiting. But then she'd been given something to drink. She couldn't remember much else. He was a white man with blond hair cropped close to his head. He wore jeans and a black T-shirt. His arms were covered in tattoos and he stood watching her for a moment. The girl didn't dare move. She held her breath. Then he walked away, leaving the door open. The girl wondered if she was supposed to follow him. But she was too frightened to move. A few moments later, he returned with some sandwiches and another bottle of water. He told the girl he was her new boss and she needn't be afraid. He said he would only hurt her if she didn't do as she was told. He smiled at her, but there was nothing nice about him. He offered her a sandwich, and when she didn't take it straight away, he gripped her arm tightly and squeezed it. He told her she had to eat to keep her strength up. He said he got annoyed when his girls didn't eat. It made him angry. She reached out and took one, biting into what felt like a damp towel. She had no idea what was in it. It looked like pink meat, but it was tasteless. She chewed each piece several times before forcing herself to swallow. When she finished it, he told her to eat another one and another. Then he told her she would have to be careful not to be greedy. He said he didn't like his girls to be fat and the customers didn't either. The girl was told that she wouldn't have to work that night. She could have the day to rest and then tomorrow business would begin. The girl knew what kind of work he was talking about. She wasn't stupid. All her hopes and dreams of babysit-

ting or housework had vanished. I own you now. I paid a good price for you too, he said, licking his lips. He ate the last sandwich in two bites, then wiped his hand over his mouth. He pushed the tray aside and walked back over to the door. He locked it, turned back to the girl and began to unbuckle his belt.

18

Joanna had company. A girl with blonde hair, dark at the roots. Chunky gold bracelets hung from her wrists and several delicate silver necklaces were swathed around her neck. She was wearing black jeans and a bright red sweater. Her thick black eyebrows dominated her face.

As Joanna shooed her sister into the lounge, she felt as though she had stumbled into a private party for two. Half-full mugs of tea sat on the coffee table, with demolished slabs of chocolate cake on plates.

'Sorry, I didn't mean to intrude,' said Megan as the girl stood up to leave.

'It's okay. This is Rhona. She works at the refuge. This is my sister, Megan.'

Rhona gave Megan a tight smile and then folded her arms.

'Nice to meet you, Rhona.'

'I'd better be going, Jo. Thanks for the chat and that. Maybe see you later on.'

'No problem at all. Any time. Come on and I'll see you out.'

'Bye,' called Megan, but Rhona didn't look at her.

Joanna returned, shrugging apologetically.

Megan pulled a face. 'I thought she wanted to talk to me.'

'She did. But she's a bit wary of the press. The *Record* turned her brother over. I tried to encourage her to stay and talk to you, but she's clearly not having a good day. I think she panicked.'

'Okay . . . so, what did her brother do?'

Joanna waved the question away. 'I'll fill you in another day. It was drugs. Do you fancy a cup of tea?'

Megan picked up the pot of lukewarm tea. This looks fine to me.' Megan poured some tea into the third, unused cup on the table and took a slurp of the tea, then stuck her pinky into the icing on the plate. 'Where's George?'

'He's at judo. Should be back in twenty minutes or so. His pal's mum is dropping him off.'

'Do you ever hear from George's dad these days?'

Joanna looked surprised. 'Eh, no, why?'

'Just wondered. Sorry, I know you don't like talking about it.'

'It's okay,' she said. 'No. I'm happy just with me and George, but why are you asking?'

'It's just that George mentioned him the other day.'

Joanna sat upright. 'What did he say?'

'Just that he wished he knew more about him . . .'

Joanna dropped her eyes and stared at the cup in her hands.

'Don't worry. I told him he was lucky to have you as his mum, and me as his aunt, of course.'

Joanna took a deep breath and shifted in her seat.

'Sorry, Jo. I didn't mean to upset you.'

'It's okay. Normally it's fine. Really. It just gets to me sometimes, you know.' She stared at the floor.

'Anything I can do?' said Megan, scooping up more icing.

Joanna looked up and half smiled. 'Yes, have a proper piece and stop playing with the icing.'

Megan smiled. 'Do you ever hear from him?'

Joanna shook her head. 'Nope. The last I heard was just after George was born. I managed to track him down to tell him he had a son, but I never heard back.' She shrugged. 'George is better off without him . . . Anyway, do you want to know what Rhona said?'

Megan nodded, letting Joanna change the topic of conversation.

'Rhona knows everyone and everything. But she's anxious, a bit jumpy, and she can get details a wee bit mixed-up. She's been a bit of a drug user in the past. Anyway, she says she knows one of the bouncers in a club in the town. He's told her that the girls in there pass through like cattle in a market.'

'Has she seen any of them?'

'Aye, well, that's the thing. Sometimes she's asked in to do some treatments for them. A bit of waxing, some nails and fake tans and that. Cash in hand, no questions asked.'

'And what does she think?'

'Just that she said she never needs to do any travelling. The women of the world are all in the centre of Glasgow. You name the country and she guarantees there'll be a girl from there. It sounds like the UN.'

Megan looked surprised. 'What's the club called?'

'The Tinkle Club . . . I know, classy, eh? And if my experience is anything to go by, then the police will know. They're just not doing anything about it.'

'Did Rhona say anything else?'

'No. She started freaking out about what she'd said. That's why she left.'

'What is it that Rhona does at the shelter?'

'She comes in and does treatments for the women there. Same kind of stuff. But all above board.'

'Does she paint their toes?'

'Yes,' said Joanna. 'If they fancy it.'

'What colour?'

'Eh? What's that got to do with it?'

Megan drained the rest of the tea and stood up. 'What colour does she paint their toe nails?'

'Why you asking that? How would I know?'

'Is there a chance she knows more than she's letting on?'

'What do you mean?'

'Well, I think she might know more than she's letting on.' Megan was getting impatient now.

'Look, leave it with me. The last thing I need is you running after her and frightening her. She's jumpy enough as it is, and she'll totally clam up under pressure.'

'The sooner the better. Time is kind of the essence here. Seriously.'

'That'll be George,' said Joanna, going to open the door. Then she turned and hugged Megan. 'Look, thanks for letting me know what he said. I'll have a chat with him, try to put his mind at rest.'

Joanna opened her mouth to say something else, but the buzzer rang again.

~

The girl was always moved when it was dark. The car weaved its way from the city, the harsh yellow lights disappearing until all she could see was the starry sky. None of the girls talked. They just shared brief, tense looks. There were three of them. The blonde, with her curly hair piled on top of her head, and another girl with short, cropped hair and delicate feature who looked like a little boy. The girl had to stop herself from staring. Maybe she was *a little boy.*

The car crunched up a gravel drive. The bossman and his helper, another face she hadn't seen before, told the girls to get out and pointed to the house. The bossman led the way. The door opened and they stood in the hallway waiting to follow orders. The girl noticed candles twinkling on the mantelpiece and heard music quietly playing in the background. Her stomach grumbled at the smells wafting from the kitchen. It was almost homely and welcoming. Then the bossman pointed at a door and told them to go through. They were taken into a large room, with several dining tables and lots of men. They were all smartly dressed, wearing suits. They looked like respectable men. Tidy, with nice hair and good teeth. The girl started to relax. Maybe this was going to be okay. Perhaps they were just there to help serve food. They were all handed a glass of something to drink.

The girl took a sip and didn't like the taste, but when the bossman glared at her she knew she had to swallow it all.

The girls were asked to walk around the room serving drinks to the men. There were perhaps a dozen. Then she noticed other girls in the corner of the room. They were perched on the edge of seats, clutching glasses which they too kept sipping from. They were all smiling, but the girl knew they were not having fun. When she realised none of the men would make proper eye contact with her she began to worry. Then when they started to clap and jeer she began to worry. Yet her head felt woozy and she couldn't think fast or work out what to do. She set the tray down on a table, then she felt someone clutch her from behind. His hands circled her waist and he pushed into her. I won, he kept saying. I won. I won. He grabbed a glass from the tray and swallowed it in a gulp. Cheers, darling, he said, handing her another glass. The girl didn't want to drink anything else. She felt spaced out and frantically tried to look for the blonde woman or the bossman. All she could see were blurred faces smiling and jeering at her. The man pulled her towards him and she stumbled, trying to grab onto something, anything. Come on now, he said. You're mine now for the night. I won. You're mine. She saw the bossman staring at her. She heard the village priest's voice telling her she had to do as she was told. The man dragged her out the room.

19

Megan started to clear up the plates. She heard George running up the stairs.

'Hiya, George,' she said as he came bouncing in. She reached out to ruffle his hair.

'Hi, Auntie Megan. Can I have some cake, please?'

Joanna smiled. She knew he was enjoying having Megan there and was happy to take a back seat.

'So tell me what you learned tonight. Show me some of your moves,' said Megan.

'Shall I show you the Ouchi Gari?' he asked.

'Just be careful with her now. No knocking her to the ground,' warned Joanna as she carried the mugs and plates through to the kitchen.

'What on earth is that?' said Megan.

George smiled. 'Don't worry, Mum. I won't hurt her. Auntie Megan, what you have to do is you have to remember your centre of gravity and keep your core tight. That's your tummy by the way.'

Megan tensed her stomach. 'Okay, I've pulled it in.'

'Okay, now keep it pulled in and watch.'

Megan watched as he talked her through the move and let him

gently hook his foot through her leg. 'You're a strong wee thing, George,' she said.

He beamed. 'I'll soon be taller than you,' he said as he managed to catch her off-guard and she tumbled slowly to the ground.

'Okay, okay, you win,' she said, hauling herself back up. 'Actually, do you know what, George? That's what you do when you surf.'

'What, the Ouchi Gari?'

'No. The holding your tummy muscles tight.'

'Okay,' he said, looking at her in disbelief. 'But we're not surfing. We're doing judo. Here, watch this.' He took her through the move again and Megan protested laughing, as she ended up on the floor.

Joanna stuck her head round the door. 'Okay, George, that's enough for now. Shower time.'

'But Mum . . .'

'But nothing,' she said. 'You've got school in the morning and Auntie Megan is catching an early flight.'

'Where are you going?' he said, looking at her.

'Stockholm,' she replied.

'That's in Sweden?'

'That's right, well done.'

'Will you bring me something back please?' he said, sticking out his bottom lip.

Megan laughed. 'Only if you go and have your shower right now, young man.'

He stuck his hand in the air to high-five her. 'Deal.'

When Joanna was sure she could hear the shower running, she turned to Megan. 'Why did you leave Johnny, Megan?'

Megan looked away and stared out of the window. Her voice was tight. 'Do you really want to know?'

'Of course I do. I've just been waiting for you to tell me the truth.'

Megan half smiled. 'I didn't want to disappoint you. I thought you liked him. Remember you said he was the perfect man?'

Joanna snorted. 'I never said that.'

'Yes, you did,' said Megan. 'You said I was on to a good thing and he was worth hanging on to.'

Joanna shrugged. 'Was that back in the early days? Are you sure I wasn't just being polite? I would never have said hang on to him if I thought he was making you miserable, Megan. No guy is ever worth that . . . So are you going to tell me?'

'Okay. Don't say I didn't warn you.' Megan walked over to the sofa, sat down and hugged her knees to her chest. 'Johnny was charming to everyone. He's handsome and charismatic . . . as you know. But when we got engaged, things changed. He started to challenge everything I said. Then when we started to talk about the wedding, he went in a sulk if I didn't agree with what he wanted . . .' Megan's voice trailed away. 'It was like dealing with a wee boy. In fact, no it wasn't. That's insulting to George.'

'Do you think he was stressed about the wedding?' said Joanna.

Megan sagged back into the seat. 'I don't know. But he started to criticise everything I did or said. Then he told me that I should be using my inheritance to pay for the wedding.'

Joanna's eyes widened in shock.

'It wasn't so much that that was a problem in itself. It was just the way he said it. He said that's what our parents would have wanted and if I was too stupid to see it then I would be letting them down.'

'Oh, Megan. Why didn't you say anything?'

'Because I thought he was right. And I didn't really know what to say. I was embarrassed. I mean, when you think about it, really it's just a lot of small things. And he's been stressed about work for a while. I just thought I should suck it up and deal with it.'

'Stress at work is no excuse for acting like a prick,' said Joanna.

'I know,' said Megan, her voice quiet. She clasped her hands together. 'I just kept thinking that I should be able to handle it and it wasn't that big a deal. He used to tell me how lucky I was to have him. That not every guy would put up with me and my strange habits. And that I was lucky that he didn't mind the long hours I worked. Apparently not every guy would put up with that either.'

'I take it he thinks it's the 1950s? He sounds like a dinosaur.' A flicker of disgust crossed Joanna's face. 'You're well shot of him, Megan. You've done the right thing.'

Megan sighed. 'I know. I just feel guilty. I did love him, you know. It wasn't *all* bad.'

'No,' said Joanna, her voice fierce, 'but you deserve so much better than that.'

'You know it's only since I moved in with you and have had some time to reflect on it all that it's started to sink in. He was controlling me, Joanna. And I feel like such an idiot.'

'You're not an idiot. Not at all.' Joanna reached out to hold Megan's hands in hers. 'You are strong and amazing and you got away. Imagine what it would have been like if you'd gone through with the wedding.'

Megan shuddered. 'I know. And he keeps calling me to tell me to reconsider. I wish he would just piss off and leave me alone.'

Just then George walked into the room, wearing his *Star Wars* pyjamas. 'Shall we have our game, Auntie Megan?'

'Oh, George, shall I do it tonight?' said Joanna. 'Megan needs to get ready for her trip.'

Megan watched his face fall and his shoulders slump. She wiped away the tear that had trickled down her cheek. 'Come on, wee man, let's play your game. Just the one, all right? Then it's definitely time for my bed too.'

She turned and hugged Joanna. 'Thank you for being there,' she whispered in her ear. 'Come on, George. Let's go.'

She woke up, her eyelashes sticky and clogged together. She looked around the room, confused. It wasn't where she normally woke up. It was a proper bedroom with a high ceiling and fancy bedcovers. There was even a window. She peered under the covers. She was naked and sore, extremely sore. The girl had no idea where she was or what had happened. The last thing she could remember was serving drinks. She lay there, willing herself to remember what had happened. Then she spotted her clothes slung across a chair by the window. That dress and those shoes. The fancy house and the well-dressed men. She heard the door

swing open and the bossman loomed. Hurry. We're leaving soon. Get dressed.

The girl desperately needed some water, her mouth was so sore and dry. She crept out of bed, pulling a sheet around her. A door was slightly ajar on the opposite side of the room – a bathroom. Wincing, she sat down on the toilet and felt a burning sensation between her legs. She watched as blood and urine trickled from her. She wiped herself gently and then washed her face and hands. Looking up at the mirror, she gasped. Bruises, like blooming flowers, circled her neck. There were purple welts on her breasts and more bruises on her thighs. She saw scratches on her legs, and when she turned to look at her back, red welts across her shoulders. She dressed as quickly as she could, pulling the dress over her head and pushing her feet back into those shoes. She wished she had a long coat to cover up with. Come on, said the bossman. Noticing her bruises, he slipped his coat off and handed it to her. Put that on. Cover that up. It's no good for business, he said.

For the first time, the girl felt grateful towards him. She followed him out and saw the blonde girl waiting, an unlit cigarette in her mouth. There was no sign of the girl who looked like a boy. The blonde's eyes met the girl's briefly and she detected a glimmer of pity in her eyes. The girl wondered if she knew what had happened to her last night. There were still ripples of conversation and laughter coming from across the hallway and the girl wondered if the men were still there - still dressed in their best clothes and still having a good time.

20

The conference was being held at the Waterfront Congress Centre in Stockholm, next to the harbour and close to the Central Station. Megan was desperate to get outside for some fresh air and to stretch her legs before it started. She'd visited Stockholm before, though the waterfront had been completely redeveloped since then. She was keen to explore and she had an hour or so until the next session began. She started walking towards City Hall, admiring its spire with the three golden crowns. She greedily breathed in the fresh, cool air and rolled her neck gently from side to side as she walked. It felt good to be away from work and home. She'd promised to catch up with Natasha later on. Other than that, all she had to think about was this investigation and the best angle to take for the trafficking feature. She thought about the conversations she'd had with Jamie over the past couple of weeks and how much she'd actually enjoyed his company. He was easy to talk to and funny. He actually made her laugh. She mentally sifted through the information she had on the two dead women. It was like trying to arrange the pieces of a jigsaw and there were still some significant pieces missing. Something was niggling at the back of her mind, but she just couldn't quite work out *what*.

'Picture if you can the following room,' said the Dutch psychologist standing on stage. She gripped the sides of the lectern, fixing her cool gaze on the back row of the audience. 'It's grey, with a dim, flickering light. In it are six beds with thin mattresses and cheap, dirty sheets and blankets. There is no carpet, just rough wooden floorboards. The room is sparsely furnished. No lamps or cushions.' She paused. The conference room was silent. 'Just the beds and six girls. Two from Romania, two from Nigeria and two from Moldova. So how do we know if people are being trafficked? Well, we need to be vigilant to what is going on in and around our neighbourhoods.'

Later, Megan scribbled in her notepad as a Swedish expert in gender violence and trafficking, talked. 'Men arrive at all hours of the day. The buyers. The girls are dragged from their beds and forced to strip. The men prod them like cattle, touch them and examine them. Often, they are taken out of the room and the men try them to find out how they perform sexually. They are degraded and dehumanised. They are made to feel worthless. They are treated like animals.'

Megan was sitting in a row near the front of the lecture hall. It was packed with delegates from around the world. There were a couple of other journalists, a woman from Reuters and a guy she recognised from the *Telegraph*; she was the only Scottish journalist.

'We've been told of girls forced to parade on stage as though they were in a fashion show, except that they're naked. The lights are dimmed. The audience is full of men in business suits. Professionals. Who look like many of the men here in this room today . . .'

Megan squirmed in the uncomfortable silence.

'These men and, believe it or not, sometimes women buy and try the goods. After being broken in, the women are auctioned off to the highest bidder.'

Megan looked up, catching Natasha's eye. The pair exchanged a brief nod.

'It's important to distinguish the difference between trafficking and smuggling,' said the academic. 'Does anyone know?' Without allowing anyone the chance to answer, she continued. 'Smugglers are paid by people to bring them across borders. Traffickers *force* people to cross borders.' She paused. 'What we need to do is raise awareness.

Where there are men, there will always be a demand for supply of these women.' She took a sip of water.

Megan continued to make notes as the lecture turned to the 1999 Kvinnofrid law, which made buying sex illegal in Sweden. 'In this country, protecting the sanctity of human life is more important than protecting the sexual desires of men. There needs to be a serious penalty for men buying sex. Let us pause for a moment as we think about this,' she continued, fixing her eyes on someone at the back of the room. 'And I'll end on the fact that Sweden now has the lowest rate of trafficking.in the EU.' She strode from the stage and took her place in the front row. The delegates applauded.

*T*HE SUN WAS RISING *when they walked outside. It was cold. The girl pulled the coat closer around her. She had done as she had been told but she didn't feel okay. She felt disgusting and ashamed. She tried to focus her gaze on the world outside. She wanted to record any details at all which might help her. Forest, gravel tracks and an ocean which looked as though diamonds had been scattered across it. Everything about the setting should be beautiful. The girl stood stared at the pale blue sky. She couldn't remember when she'd last seen the sky in daylight. She was surrounded by trees. There was nowhere to run. The bossman told them to get into the car. The blonde sat next to the girl and passed her a bottle of water. The girl took small sips from it then closed her eyes, her head falling against the window. When she woke later she was back in her room, groggy and with a thumping headache. It was dark, and she had no idea how long she had been sleeping or what time it was. She heard the key in her door turn and someone entering. It is me. Sssh. It's okay, said a voice. It was the blonde woman. She sat on the girl's bed and helped her sit up. She had a banana and some crackers on a plate. You eat. You hungry, she said. The girl gnawed on a cracker. You sore, yes? The girl nodded. You be okay. You did good. She sighed. You there two days. The girl frowned. I cannot remember, she said. The boss, he happy. You good girl. You have special drink to help you forget. Is better that way.*

When the blonde left, the girl gently edged her way back down onto the bed. It didn't matter that she had no memory of what had actually happened. She knew bad things had happened to her. She could tell from the marks on her body. She knew from the pain she felt inside. She didn't feel like a good girl. She felt dirty and sore and bad. She wondered if all those men were bad. Or was it just the one who had claimed her. She wondered about the priest from her village and if he knew this was how her life would be. Did Auntie know about all this too? How could any gods let this happen to her? Then she thought about her mother and brothers. If she kept obeying then perhaps one day she would get to go home, to her real home and be with them.

21

Later that night, Megan lay in the bath until the water cooled and her skin shrivelled. She stepped out, wrapped a large white towel around her and went through to the bedroom. She reached over to check her phone. Three missed calls, fifteen texts and twenty-two emails. It was seven o'clock, and she was due to meet Natasha in the hotel restaurant in half an hour. She quickly scrolled through her messages, looking for anything that needed to be dealt with urgently. It could all wait. Megan curled up on the bed, wrapped in her damp towel. Her eyes felt heavy and before long she was fast asleep.

'Glad you could make it,' said Natasha as Megan walked towards the table.

'Sorry, I'm late.' Megan sat down. 'I fell asleep.'

'So what did you think?'

'I thought it was pretty impressive. Good range of speakers. Packed audience.'

Natasha raised an eyebrow. 'Yes, well, Angelina Jolie was

rumoured to be one of the keynote speakers, which probably had something to do with it.'

Megan laughed. 'Good PR strategy if you can get away with it.'

'This will need to be a quick bite,' said Natasha as the waiter approached. 'There's a drinks reception at the embassy, which I need to go to. I've ordered you a glass of wine. Red okay?'

'You're a star. Thank you.' Megan reached for the glass and took a swig. 'So, are you all ready for your big announcement tomorrow then?'

'Yes. Absolutely.' Natasha reached into her bag and pulled out a bundle of papers. 'Here you go. A wee sneak preview just for you.'

'Thanks.' She flicked through the documents. 'Is there anything classified here? Anything that I could be arrested for having?'

Natasha laughed. 'No. Just a few of my wee doodles on it. I know the dailies will mop up tomorrow's news so I've made a few notes which may be useful to you for your piece. If you can't understand my writing then just give me a shout.'

Megan quickly glanced through the briefing papers and saw a section which had been underlined. 'The forty-five-day rule. What's that?'

'Good question. The National Referral Mechanism grants a forty-five-day period for recovery and reflection, which basically gives the teams a chance to work out whether their asylum process can be processed.'

'And if not?'

'Well, to simplify it, it's more than likely they face deportation.'

Megan frowned. 'But that's not a very long time, is it?'

Natasha shook her head, picking at her food. 'No, it's not. Not if you've been beaten and raped and are terrified for your family back home. But at the moment it's a bit out of our hands. It's not a devolved issue.'

'Even though you're bringing in this new legislation.'

'Yes.' Natasha took a sip of water. 'Our hands are tied.'

'Right,' said Megan. 'Okay, so what you're saying is, if this *was* a devolved matter then you would have more flexibility?'

'Yes, but as you can imagine, it's a tricky one. Everything mired up with Westminster legislation is tricky.'

Megan snorted. 'Yes. Somehow I imagine this might not be such a priority down there - especially when plenty of them are probably cavorting with victims in the clubs they go to.'

Natasha sucked her cheeks in. 'Don't get me started.'

'I know, I know. You couldn't make it up.'

A man came to the table and put his hand on Natasha's shoulder. 'Excuse me, Natasha, we need to head to the reception. The car is due in five minutes.'

'Okay, thanks, Peter. I'll be with you in two minutes.'

'I'll fix the bill,' said Megan, 'Off you go. Are you okay? You're actually looking a bit peelly-wally.'

'I'm fine, just a bit tired. I need a holiday,' she said. 'In fact that's not a bad idea. Do you fancy it?'

Megan didn't know what to say. She couldn't remember the last time she'd had the freedom to decide on a holiday. 'Yeah, maybe.'

'We could have a surfing holiday?'

'Maybe,' said Megan, liking the sound of that. 'Somewhere warm?'

'That sounds like a brilliant idea. Let's have a chat later.'

'Well, thanks for this,' said Megan, stashing the papers safely in her bag.

'Oh, no problem. Megan,' she leaned down to whisper in her ear, 'strictly between you and me for the moment, I spoke to some of my Swedish colleagues earlier. I'm going to push again for bringing in the Nordic model when we get back.'

Megan knew that if anyone could push through new legislation it would be Natasha. 'Good for you. Okay, see you in the morning?'

She sat for a moment, sipping her wine, processing everything that Natasha had just told her and wondering which angle to take.

Better Deal for Trafficking Victims in an Independent Scotland?

Government's Plans to Undermine Westminster's Trafficking Laws?

Minister Makes Justice Pledge for Victims of Trafficking in Scotland?

Her mind was whirring now. She pushed her plate to the side.

She didn't feel like heading back to her room. So, after settling the bill she went to the hotel and ordered a Mackmyra Brukswhisky.

'Would you like ice with that? Or water?' asked the barman.

She looked up. 'Neat, please. Thank you.' She took a small sip of the whisky and enjoyed the sensation of the warm liquid slipping down her throat.

'Well, hello there,' said a voice.

Megan bristled when she felt a hand on her back. Turning round, she smiled when she realised who it was. 'Oh, hello there.'

'Mind if I join you?' Craig the photographer sat down, not waiting for her to reply. 'That looks good. The same for me, please,' he said to the barman.

'Cheers,' said Megan when his drink arrived. They clinked glasses. 'Katherine said you would be here. When did you arrive?'

'Got here last night. Thought it would be a good chance to get some shots of the city. I've never been here before.'

'Isn't it lovely?' said Megan.

'Well, yes, the city is. Not so much the conference.'

Megan took a sip of whisky. 'Did you get some pictures of the Justice Minister?'

'Aye. She's quite formidable,' he said.

Megan snorted. ''What, because she has an opinion on things?'

'No, no. Sorry, that's not what I meant.' Craig smiled. 'No, I just think she's pretty impressive. Very good in her role and seems to actually get things done rather than just talk about them. Unusual for a politician.'

Megan relaxed slightly. 'So are you just here for the paper? Or have you managed to blag any other jobs while you're here?'

'Nope. Just the paper. Flying home tomorrow.'

Megan couldn't take her eyes off him. He really was very good-looking. 'When are you heading back home?'

'Tomorrow,' he said and laughed. 'That's what I just said.'

Megan could have kicked herself. God, she was *so* out of practice. She glanced at her watch. 'I should be heading off soon. I've got quite a lot of preparation to do for tomorrow.'

'Time for another quick one?'

'Well, okay. Just a quick one.'

He smiled. 'I can't get you to go for a drink with me in Glasgow but I can in Stockholm, eh? Same again?'

'Perfect,' she said. 'I didn't realise Swedish whisky was so nice. Excuse me a moment while I use the Ladies'.'

Some days the girl was raped by eight or nine men. Sometimes more. One after the other. One day, there was a knock at the door and a youngish, overweight man skulked in. He had a paunch, a hairy chest and larger breasts than the girl. Then came the man with the pale, sweaty face covered in eruptions of pus-filled acne. The third man blew ragged, rancid breaths in her face. He had long greasy hair, lips twisted into a sneer and a purple face. Then there was the man with the hate-filled eyes whose hands gripped her neck while he panted and gasped.

Some nights, the same two men came into the room together and took it in turns to watch. Sometimes she was allowed a break between customers. She might be left for half an hour or so to be allowed to make herself presentable or use the toilet. It hurt all the time when she peed. She bit back her tears. There was no point in crying. She knew she must do as she was told. But as she waited for the seventh man to come into the room, she felt a twist in her stomach. When three men were shown into the room by the boss, she started to panic and her mouth filled with saliva. The boss gave her a hard stare then turned and left, locking the door behind him.

22

Megan opened her eyes slowly, unsure of where she was. She couldn't lift her head off the pillow. Reaching out, she clicked on the bedside lamp. She looked around. She was in a hotel room. It took her a moment or two to remember which city the hotel was in. Stockholm, she was in Stockholm. Her head was pounding, her mind foggy, as she tried to grapple with just exactly what had happened last night. She must have forgotten to set her alarm. What time was it? Shit. She couldn't get up. Couldn't move. Drifting in and out of sleep, she managed to haul herself up, grabbing the edge of the bed. What *had* happened last night? How much had she drunk? And where was her phone?

Easing herself off the bed, she stumbled into the bathroom and just reached the toilet in time to vomit. Grabbing the sides of the bowl, she felt waves of nausea sweep over her. There was a blinding pain behind her eyes too. Her bare knees felt cold against the floor and she reached out to grab a towel. She was still wearing her clothes from last night, but she had no idea how she had got to bed. Megan was used to holding her drink and the Swedish whisky had seemed okay at the time. Famous last words. Pulling herself up to the sink, she splashed her face with cold water, then flinched as she saw her reflection staring back at her. What had *happened* to her? Her face was smeared with last night's make-up and her hair stuck up like a bird's nest. Tottering back into the darkness of the bedroom, she glanced around quickly, checking everything was there. Her laptop sat on the desk where she'd left it. Her handbag was slung over a chair. Reaching into it she pulled out her phone. The screen was dead so she plugged it into the charger and switched it on. Fifteen missed calls, thirty texts and forty-two emails. Oh God. She dialled voicemail.

'Megan, it's Natasha. Just to let you know you can have a chat with the Justice Minster at eleven.'

She checked the time. It was ten-thirty. She groaned and held her head in her hands to stop it spinning. Feeling nauseous again, she collapsed onto the bed and let her head sink into the soft pillows. She let herself doze for two minutes then opened her eyes. A vague memory of a hand on her back steering her towards the bed flitted through her mind. Craig must have walked her back to her room. But she couldn't grasp anything else; the rest of the picture was fuzzy. A quick shower would help clear her head. She quickly washed and dressed and swallowed some paracetamol.

Downstairs in the lobby, she looked for the signs to the conference room and prayed there was coffee.

'There you are,' called Natasha from behind her. 'Just in time. I thought you'd gone AWOL.'

'No, just slept in.'

'Oh, aye,' said Natasha, with a wink. 'That kind of night, was it?'

'You have a one-track mind, Natasha. No, it wasn't that kind of night. Just a quiet drink with a colleague. That Swedish whisky is stronger than you think! I need a quick coffee and then I'll be fine.'

'Well, come this way. There's coffee and pastries in the conference room.'

'Thank God,' said Megan. She parked the thought of Craig to the side for the moment.

~

The girl was given some cream to put on her bruises, and when they had healed, normal business resumed. Occasionally she and the blonde women were taken to house parties. Sometimes other girls would be brought along. The girl had stopped caring. She never again saw the girl who looked like a little boy.

Mostly the girl was kept in her room and men were shown in, though sometimes she was allowed to sit in the living room with the others. Every morning, she woke feeling sick and sore. Her hips jutted through her skin and her stomach was concave. She was given white bread to eat which tasted of nothing, bright red soups and sometimes a bruised banana or a bashed apple. One day she was given a sickly, fizzy orange drink from a can. She looked at the writing on the can. Irn-Bru. She'd never heard of it.

Sometimes she was let out of the room, under the bossman's supervision, and into the kitchen where he chain-smoked and checked his phone. The girl preferred to stay in her room. The only laughter she ever heard was when the blonde was talking to the bossman. The girl began to wonder if she was in fact a friend of his, rather than someone like her. But she had noticed bruises on her, the lines on her arms, and wondered what had happened to her. She wondered if she had been tricked into coming here too.

The blonde knocked on her door, before business started, and came into the room with some new underwear for the girl. It was red and lacy. The girl knew it would be scratchy. You put this on, said the blonde. Taking it from her, the girl asked, where are you from? Moldova, she said. Why you here? The blonde shrugged. Same as you. For your family? asked the girl.

Yes. I have daughter. She safe only if I work here. Have debt to pay. Debt, the girl said. Debt? Yes. Same as you. We owe money.

I have no debts, said the girl, confused. The blonde looked at her and sighed. Yes. We all have debts. More work we do, make bossman happy and then maybe we get home. The girl shook her head. I do not understand. The boss. He is our owner. We belong to him. He decides when we get home. Best do as you are told. Best be a good girl. She pointed at the underwear on the bed. The girl knew there was no point in arguing. She would put it on. Maybe if she did as the blonde woman said, and worked harder and harder, then perhaps she would get home. It felt itchy against her skin. But she had to focus on doing her best. If she could focus on doing well for the bossman maybe he would let her go home soon. She grimaced as she adjusted the bra strap. She knew there was no point in complaining. There was a knock at the door and the bossman showed in her first customer of the night.

23

Megan grabbed her clothes from the floor and threw them in her bag. If she hurried she could be on the next Arlanda Express train to the airport. The interview with the Justice Minster had gone well: she had spoken to Megan in great detail about the new anti-trafficking legislation. Megan wasn't quite sure if there were any exclusive lines; she would have to wait and see how the dailies covered it. She longed to crawl back under the covers and sleep. Or have another quick shower to wake herself up, but there wasn't time. She *had* to be on the flight. She bent down to pick up her handbag - and that was when she remembered the papers that Natasha had given her the previous evening. Of course. Natasha had said something about notes she'd made on them that would give her the extra line she was looking for. She peered in her bag. They weren't there. Megan began to feel panicky. Surely she couldn't have lost them? She scanned the room to make sure she hadn't left anything lying around. There was nothing there. She grabbed her bags and headed to the station.

Megan sat in a corner of the departure lounge, eyes down, fixed on her phone. She couldn't believe she had allowed herself to get into such a state. She felt utterly wretched and ashamed of herself for losing the papers. She'd never, ever been so stupid before. Her phone rang. It was Natasha.

'Megan, do you want to tell me why the *Daily News* are running an exclusive line that I gave to you?'

Megan's stomach lurched. 'What do you mean?'

'I mean,' snapped Natasha, 'that the information on those papers I gave you last night were for your eyes only. And now it's splashed across the *Daily News* site. Not only that, but *someone* appears to have got hold of my memory stick too. The details are all over the paper too. I didn't realise you and Paul were so close.'

Megan closed her eyes. 'Natasha, I swear I didn't tell Paul anything. I didn't tell *anyone* anything.'

'Then how the hell does he know what the Justice Minister is planning to do with the Nordic Model?'

'I don't know. But I swear to God I did not tell that man anything. He's a wee scrote.'

Natasha didn't reply.

'I'm sorry, Natasha, I'm telling you the truth. You're not saying I would steal your memory stick, surely?'

'I don't know what to think,' said Natasha. 'I need to go and deal with this. The shit has hit the fan here. It wasn't ready to be released to the press yet.' She hung up.

Megan wanted to close her eyes and erase the past twenty-four hours. A voice came over the tannoy announcing that her flight was boarding. She couldn't think rationally about what had happened. And she couldn't face telling Natasha that she'd lost the papers. She'd have to deal with that disaster later.

When Megan finally stepped through the terminal door at Glasgow Airport she braced herself against the cool wind. Head down, she focused on walking as fast as she could to the taxi rank. There seemed to be people everywhere. She sighed in irritation as she tried to get past a crowd of older American golfers who had spread themselves and their clubs across the pavement. One backed into her as he tried to get a group selfie with his friends.

'Sorry, ma'am.'

Megan wanted to scream.

'Fancy seeing you here.' Megan flinched. It was him, Craig. She felt a mixture of embarrassment and guilt as she turned to look at him. 'I didn't realise you were on that flight. Wow, you're not looking too great. Are you okay?'

'I'm fine,' she stuttered. 'Think I must be coming down with something.'

His face was earnest and she started to wonder if she was going mad. 'Do you need a ride?'

'Sorry, what?'

'A lift. Can I give you a lift?"

'No.' She shook her head. 'I'm fine, thanks. Just heading to the taxi rank.'

'Well, I'll chum you along. I'm going that way, anyway . . . Look, I just wanted to say thanks for last night.'

Megan's face drained of any remaining colour. 'What do you mean?'

'You were great company. It was good to finally have a drink and a chat with you.'

Megan was unable to say anything for a moment. 'No problem.' She kept walking then gave him a sideways glance. 'How many drinks did we have?'

'Just a couple,' he said, walking alongside her. 'Why? Are you feeling rough?'

'A bit,' she said. 'It's all a bit hazy . . . Craig, did you walk me to my room?'

He looked sheepish. 'Yes. But that's all, I swear. I just wanted to make sure you were okay. Megan, is anything wrong?' His expression looked genuinely full of concern. 'You seem a bit jumpy.'

'Em, I'm okay. Honestly. Probably just too much whisky.' Was she becoming paranoid? Maybe she was just run down and coming down with something. She seemed to have lost a grip on what was making sense.

'Okay, well, I'd better let you go.'

'Bye then.'

He caught her arm, pulling her back. 'One thing,' he said quietly. 'Maybe don't say anything to Sunita about last night.'

'Sunita?'

'Yes, Sunita in the office.'

Megan was baffled. What on earth was he going on about?

'It's just that I'm taking her out on a date at the weekend. I don't want her to think I'm that type of guy. Best keep schtum.'

Megan nodded, tired of the confusing exchange. Then she hurried towards the taxi rank. Glancing back, she saw him watching her. But all she could see on his face was a friendly smile.

The girl woke up drenched in sweat, gagging on the stale taste in her mouth. She tried to sit up but her arms were pinned above her head. She couldn't feel her feet. It took a few moments to realise she was tied to a bed. Her heart started to race in panic, and she tried to control her breathing by counting slowly inside her head. breathe slowly and count inside her head. It wasn't the first time this had happened. Flashes of the previous night sparked in her mind and she shuddered. She hated that man. Maybe he was gone now. Then she heard the sound of the toilet flush and knew he was coming back for more. He flicked on the light as he walked back into the bedroom. His paunch hid his private parts. His chest was hairy and his head bald. The girl's mouth was dry and she tried to lick her cracked lips. Taking it as an invitation for more, he came to the foot of the bed and untied her. Then his phone rang. He tutted. I'm a bit tied up at the moment, he said. Can this wait for later? Yes, I'll be at the meeting. Two? Righto.

Afterwards, he collapsed on his back and groaned. The girl managed to roll onto her side, curling herself into a tight ball. She stared at the wall ahead of her, wrinkling her nose at the smell. There was a picture on the wall, an ocean on a stormy day. The waves were inky blue and foaming; the sky was dark. There was nothing soothing about the scene; it looked eerie hanging there on the orange wall. But the girl wished she could fall into it and sink beneath the waves. She tried to imagine what it would feel like to have the icy water rush into her lungs, and to gasp for breath. Maybe there would be sharks in the sea too. Their sharp teeth ripping at her flesh, devouring her in a few bites. Death by drowning, being eaten by sharks, surely that had to be better than this. At least her life would be over for good.

24

The next day Megan called in sick to work. She was knackered and still felt mortified that she had allowed herself to get so drunk that she'd lost the documents Natasha had given her. The only person she felt she could talk to was her sister.

When Megan eventually got out of bed, Joanna was hovering in the doorway with a furrowed brow. 'Are you okay?'

'No. I think I'm going mad,' she said, pulling her dressing gown cord tightly around her waist. She followed her sister through to the kitchen and took a seat at the table.

'Are you going to tell me what's wrong, Megan? You look awful.'

'I don't know who else to talk to about this. It's a bit mad. I think I may be going crazy.'

'I've probably heard worse,' Joanna said gently. 'Try me.'

Megan gave her sister a brief outline of the trip to Sweden and her recollection of waking up with a terrible hangover.

Joanna's face remained composed throughout. 'And how did you know this guy?'

'Through work. He's a photographer.'

'Right. And what's his name?'

'Craig James.'

Joanna took a sharp intake of breath. 'I know him.'

Megan looked up.

'Yes. He's been to the refuge before to take pictures for one of the papers. I remember him. He's a handsome bloke.'

Megan ignored the comment.

'So you had a few drinks too many. Don't beat yourself up about it. Do you think he took you to your room?'

Megan clutched at her forehead. 'Joanna, that's the thing. I don't really remember. It's all a blank. He said he did. *And* I lost important stuff that Natasha gave me - stuff that was exclusive to me and which has now appeared on the *Daily News* website. And she's accused me of stealing her memory stick. Apparently there were more details on that too which appeared. She's furious.'

'Surely she doesn't think you would have stolen her memory stick though? She knows you're not that kind of journalist. Anyway,' said Joanna, 'it's not the end of the world. It was an accident.'

'These things don't happen to me, Joanna. I'm really conscientious.'

Joanna blew through her cheeks. 'Okay . . . tell me what you can remember.'

'I remember having dinner with Natasha. I had one glass of wine and she headed off. Then I sat at the bar and ordered a whisky. Craig joined me and I nipped to the loo while he ordered another drink . . .'

Joanna's face betrayed nothing as she asked, 'Could he have gone into your bag while you were at the loo?'

Megan's voice was quiet. 'Well, yes, but surely not. And why would he?'

'Well, doesn't he do some work for the daily paper as well? Would it be a way of earning some more cash?'

Megan nodded. 'Yes, but how shitty would that be? And how would he have stolen Natasha's memory stick? I didn't have it.' She groaned. 'Why do I keep attracting all the shits?'

'Seriously, Megan, I'm worried about you. Maybe you're working too hard.' Joanna paused for a moment to look at Megan. 'You know, maybe having some time off work wouldn't be such a bad thing.'

'No.'

'It's okay to accept help, you know. It's not a sign of weakness.'

'I know, but I need to work. It's the only thing that's keeping me going right now.'

'Okay. At least let me make you a cuppa.'

Sinking back into the seat, she started to cry. 'I just wish I hadn't got so drunk.'

'Maybe you didn't . . .'

'What do you mean?'

'Maybe your drink was spiked . . .'

The possibility of Rohypnol had seeded in Megan's mind earlier, but she had dismissed it. She couldn't bear to contemplate that Craig would do such a thing. 'I don't think so . . .'

'Look, a couple of days' rest will do you good. Sleep and lots of water and good food.'

'Okay, but at least let me go out and get the papers,' she said, turning to go and get dressed.

'Right, but straight back and into bed,' ordered Joanna.

Megan's mind was whirring as she left the flat and headed towards the newsagent on Clarence Drive. A man across the street crossed over. By the time she was close to the newsagent, she realised he was following her.

The girl crept into the kitchen. The blonde was sitting staring at the wall and smoking a cigarette which smelt of flowers. She glanced up at the girl and offered her a smoke. The girl shook her head. You should try it. Might make things easier for you. It helps me a bit. The girl went to the sink and rinsed out a dirty mug. She filled it with water then gulped. Sit down, said the blonde, pulling out another chair. Neither of them spoke for a few moments. The girl focused on the puffs of smoke coming from the blonde's mouth. She asked if she had ever tried to escape. She nodded and flicked her eyes around the room. Yes. I did. One time, not from here. She took another long suck from her cigarette. I am very stupid. I was okay. I escape in

London. But they found me again, she said. How? They always watching. I thought I was safe. The police said I was safe. It was okay for a while. But then they found me. Said I had to pay off debt, then they would let me go, she said. I ended up here. Bloody cold. Did you ever try to go here? Yes. One time, she said.

The girl's eyes widened. The door was unlocked, she said pointing at the main door at the end of the hallway. Someone forgot to lock it. It was now or never. I got out. To bottom of stairs. Then he came. The bossman. That was it. No point trying to run.

What happened? whispered the girl. They beat me . . . other things too. I could not walk for a week.

Neither the girl nor the blonde spoke for a moment. Nobody cares. Nobody would help. We be put in jail, she said. We are bad. Not doing as told. We not supposed to be here. They own us. Take our passports, documents, everything. The blonde shook her head slowly. There is nothing left. Best do as told. She fell silent, and the girl turned round to see that the bossman had come into the room. We are off out tonight to a party, girls. Both of you. Get a shower and make yourselves look respectable will you? The girl and the blonde shared a tense look. Look pretty, Big night tonight. It's a party night, he said.

25

Megan had been on edge since the incident the previous day. Convinced the man was following her, she had flagged down a passing taxi and asked the driver to take her round a few blocks until she was sure it was safe to go back. He'd vanished, of course. But she still felt jumpy. She was back at work. Her phone buzzed.

Hope you're okay. Sorry we fell out. I was stressed. Any progress on the trafficking report? You and Karen are being tweeted about! #jacketgate

Megan wondered if Natasha had found the missing memory stick. She clicked on the picture. A TV journalist had copied a picture of the Justice Minister and Megan wearing matching jackets while in Sweden and captioned it with: *They're all at it. Copying each other's style.*

Megan swore under her breath. She knew the journalist in question. He was a patronising prick. She opened Twitter and saw it had been retweeted 500 times. Smiling wryly to herself, she typed Natasha a reply.

Wow. Two women wear blue jacket. Ground-breaking stuff! Sorry we fell out too.

Natasha replied immediately.

Yip. Amazing. Don't worry I'm about to sort it. Watch out!

Megan watched her screen. A picture of the journalist alongside David Cameron, carrying leather satchels, popped up. Natasha had added the caption: *Breaking news! Male journo and Prime Minister carry bags! Check out those shoes too! #manbaggate #jacketgate*

Megan burst out laughing. Then she noticed Katherine was watching her. 'Just having a bit of fun. Or my friend is, on Twitter.'

Katherine was about to say something when her phone rang. 'It's Richard. You're wanted upstairs.'

'Thanks.'

She made her way up stairs to the conference room, which had become Richard's room of choice. She knocked on the door and went straight in. Richard was standing in the corner lining up a putt and jumped when he heard her voice.

'Oh, come *on*. You made me miss that one.' He frowned.

'Really, Richard? Putting in the office?'

'Yes, why do you think I spend so much time up here? It's so much bigger than my shoe-box downstairs. And I just wasted that shot. Haven't you heard of knocking?'

'I did.'

He scratched his head and gently placed his shiny club against the table. 'I'm just having a wee screen-break, you know. It's not good to be glued to a computer all day. Anyway, thanks for coming up so quickly. I wasn't expecting you to move that fast.'

Megan sat down. 'Tell me, when you're not golfing, Richard, how do you spend your time?'

'There's no need to be sarcastic.'

'I'm not. It just seems to me that most of your journalistic work is done on the golf course. Even a carpeted one.'

'It's all about networking, Megan, you know that. Look, this investigation you're working on, I just want to make sure we have it locked down. Rock-solid. The lawyers have been on to me. Their budget's been slashed and they're worried about us taking risks.'

Megan shook her head in disbelief. 'Risks? Bloody hell. I'm a professional, Richard. I'm not just having a wee play-around with this to keep me occupied while my husband is out doing a real job!'

'Easy, Megan' he said in a soothing tone. 'I know that perfectly well. They're just worried about money. We can't afford to defame anyone right now.'

'But who would I be defaming, and anyway, how would they know what I'm working on?' Megan's voice grew louder. 'I mean, have they been talking to the trafficked girls or the folk behind it? Because unless they've been reading my copy then they don't know a thing about this. Unless they're trawling through my files, which would be highly unethical, don't you think?' She glared at Richard.

'They're just jittery at the moment, you know, with the fall out from the Leveson stuff.'

'Really?' Megan paused. 'Who's been putting the pressure on you, Richard?'

'What do you mean?' he blurted.

'I mean that last week you were all gung-ho about cracking ahead with the trafficking investigation and now you're stalling. Are you trying to save it for the *Daily News*?'

'That's just insulting, Megan. I'm as furious as you are about that story being gifted to that wee dick of a crime reporter.'

'So why are you stalling?' she persisted.

'You're so suspicious. You should be working for MI5. Actually, maybe not . . . '

'I've every right to be suspicious. I know how these things go. What's happened to change your mind?'

'Look, my hands are, er, slightly tied here for the moment . . . we just need to tread very carefully in the current climate.'

'Really? Do you think someone is trying to cover something up?'

'No, not exactly. We just need to make sure we have enough evidence to run the story. And I mean solid evidence.'

She stood up. 'Maybe the lawyers are involved. Maybe they're key clients in this trafficking ring. It's like bloody Jimmy Savile - all these old farts covering up for each other.'

Shock stopped him in his tracks and Megan wondered for a fleeting moment if she'd gone too far.

'Megan, we can hardly compare this to Savile.' His voice was terse. 'And, please, never say anything like that outside these four walls.'

Megan couldn't stop herself. 'Why not? A cover-up is a cover-up.'

'Look, it's not a bloody cover-up. We just need to sure before we go ahead to print. I don't think anything is being covered up. It's just a case of making sure we're totally watertight.'

Megan tutted. There was no point in this fruitless exchange. "I *will* make sure this is watertight, Richard. And I *will* go to print with it. Regardless of what they say.' Now she *really* was treading on thin ice. How could she go to print with it? She made to leave and then paused. 'You're supposed to be my mentor. Now I'd like to give you some advice.'

'What's that?' he said wearily, rubbing his eyes.

'Man up and grow a set.' Megan couldn't quite believe the words she had just uttered. What on earth was wrong with her? She felt a lurch in her stomach. This time she'd gone too far. So much for her great plans to settle here. She hadn't lasted five minutes. Jesus. Her heart was beating faster and her palms were sweating. She tried to control her breathe.

Richard smiled in spite of himself. 'Megan Ross, you are one tough woman.' There was admiration in his voice. 'You are a great addition to this team. You'll go far.'

Megan nodded, then walked away. She was just grateful she still had a job.

The girl could hear screaming. She stood trembling by the door, hands heavy and clammy, hanging uselessly by her sides. She knew she should try to help. She wanted to. But she just couldn't bring herself to reach out and touch the handle of the door. It was always locked anyway. But she couldn't just stand there listening and waiting. There was a piercing wail which reminded her of the goats being slaughtered in her village. She felt sick. She had to do something. The girl grasped the handle and turned it. She felt it open easily. She stumbled into the hallway, squinting her eyes to

adjust to the light. Then the screaming turned to pleadings of no, please no, please no. Then silence. The girl saw another door off the hallway start to open. As quickly as she could, she backed into her room, leaving the door ajar. She pressed herself up against it, holding her breath as she watched the bossman walk out of the room with the blonde hanging over his shoulder like a dead dog. The girl's legs were quivering as he walked past the door.

The girl couldn't move, though she knew she needed to get away from the door. She padded as quietly as she could back to the corner, but she couldn't stop shaking. Then the bossman suddenly kicked the door open and stood there, staring at her. The girl felt her insides liquify and she tried her hardest to hold everything in. But in a flash he had a knife at her throat. She could hear his heavy breathing, smell the metallic scent of blood. Then someone else came into the room.

You didn't lock up properly, you daft fuck, said the boss. Silly, silly girl, he said in a low voice. His skin felt clammy against hers and she could smell his aftershave, feel the stubble from his chin. You really shouldn't have done that. You need to do as you are told. You know we can't look after you properly unless you are doing as you are told. You don't want to end up like your wee pal across the hall.

26

It was pissing with rain, blowing a gale and already pitch-black. Megan sighed as she looked at her watch and realised it was only just after four o'clock. So much for spring. This weekend's investigation feature was on Italian crime bosses in Aberdeen. An old freelance friend had offered it to her exclusively and she had managed to get Richard to agree to it. She stretched and had a swig of water from the bottle which was a permanent fixture on her desk. Her phone buzzed in her bag.

'Hello,' she said.

'It's me,' said Jamie.

'Oh,' she said in surprise and smiled. 'How are you?'

'Well,' said Jamie, 'you've been ignoring all my calls. But apart from that I'm fine.'

'Sorry, just been busy,' she said. 'I was actually about to call you.'

He laughed. 'Of course you were. Look, I just wanted to check in with you.'

'Has something happened?' said Megan, reaching for a pen.

'This and that, you know,' said Jamie. 'What about you though? Are you going to tell me what's going on?'

Megan took a sip from her bottle. 'What do you mean, me tell you? Have you got any more leads on the lap-dancing bar?'

'Yes,' said Jamie briskly. 'We're keeping our eyes on that situation.'

'And what about the women there?'

'We can't do anything unless we have evidence, you know that.'

'What if I get you the evidence? I mean . . . I may as well go into the club and check it out myself, seeing as you won't tell me anything.' She dug her nails into her palms.

'Megan, you steaming straight in there and blowing everything up would be a *disaster*.' His voice had a warning tone to it.

'You're right.' She sighed.

'Megan, are you okay? You sound a bit pissed off.'

She sniffed. 'Ignore me, I'm just tired.'

His voice softened. 'You sure it's just that?'

'Yes, honestly, I'll be fine,' she said. She could hear the concern in his voice and she wanted to tell him everything. She wanted to tell him about work and Johnny and the thing that happened in Stockholm. But the last thing she needed to do right now was get close to anyone else.

'Well, if you're sure,' he said. 'But, please, give me a call if you want to chat. Maybe I can help.'

Megan glanced up as she saw Craig walking into the office and heading straight to Sunita's desk. Tosser, she thought, remembering how he'd told her not to mention their evening together in Stockholm. Clearly he'd been hedging his bets.

'You still there?' said Jamie.

'Yes. I'd better go though.' She hesitated for a moment, wondered if she should suggest meeting up, but then she caught sight of Craig. He was very obviously ignoring her. No. What was the point? Men were more trouble than they were worth. 'Keep in touch,' she said and hung up.

~

Was she dreaming? She could hear Auntie talking to her mother, who was at their kitchen table at home, sobbing and rubbing her hands over and over. She is a good girl, said Auntie. She will be okay and make you proud. But she is only a child, said Mother. Why did I send her away? Because you needed the money, said Auntie harshly.

The piercing sound of her mother's wailing woke her up. The girl sat up abruptly. The pain in her arms was burning. She felt as though she'd been split in two. The screaming was still there. She could still hear it. Auntie's voice too. This is too risky, she said. I'm not coming here again. Next time you meet me somewhere. The girl swung her legs from the bed and tiptoed across to the door. She bent down and put her ear as close to the frame as she could. The wailing had subsided to snivelling.

Oh, be quiet, said the woman impatiently. Go home, want to go home, whispered a voice. A new addition to the family, thought the girl. Shut up, said the woman and then the girl heard a loud slap. Then a gasp. A door slammed and a key turned. I'll deal with her later, said the bossman.

The girl was certain she could smell Auntie. That cloying perfume she wore. The smell of cherries. Feeling a surge of anger, she threw herself against the door. What the hell is going on in here? said the voice. Sounds like a zoo. The priest won't be happy when he hears about this. He won't like it at all.

The girl froze, her breath tight and rasping. She tried to calm herself down. She must not anger the spirits. She must not. She had to do this for her family. If she didn't then they would be in danger. The girl rocked back and forth in the corner of the room, trying to soothe herself as much as she could. But all she could think about was Auntie behind that door. And the streaks of blood she'd seen on the hall carpet. That girl had been her only friend and now she had vanished.

27

Richard appeared by Megan's side. 'I'm going to get a coffee, a proper one instead of the shite you get here. Can I bring you one back?'

'Yes, please,' said Megan. 'I don't think I've ever seen you doing the coffee run before.'

'Well, you may never again.'

Megan looked at him in surprise, and was about to probe further, when Katherine appeared.

'Hello,' she said brightly. 'Everyone okay?'

'Mmm,' said Richard. 'Well, the golf was terrible this morning. Think I may need to take up something else.'

'Like gardening?' suggested Megan.

'I was thinking more of squash.'

'Oh no, not at your age. Too dangerous.'

'Anyway,' said Richard, ignoring her comments, 'I'm off to get some coffee. Katherine, can I get you something? A latte, maybe?'

'Oh, that would be lovely, thank you.'

'Course not,' he said. 'Better not interrupt the love birds,' he said, eyeing Sunita and Craig in the corner. 'Back soon.' He strode out of the office, wafting aftershave behind him.

Megan watched Katherine watching him and smiled. She knew

Richard used to have a way with the ladies when he was younger. Obviously, for some, he still oozed charm.

'Two coffees for two lovely ladies,' said Richard, placing the cardboard cups onto Katherine's desk.

Megan blew through her mouth. 'That was quick.'

'I don't hang about, Megan. You know that.'

'Thanks,' she said.

'Better dash,' said Richard. 'Catch you later. Hello, Ronnie. You just missed out on a free coffee. What a shame. Maybe next time?'

Ronnie muttered 'hello' to Richard and then scowled when he was sure Richard couldn't see him.

'How are you?' Megan said, picking up her cup and taking a sip of the strong black coffee.

'So- so,' he said.

Megan stood up and walked over to Ronnie's desk. 'What's up?'

'Nothing,' said Ronnie, frowning. 'Just man trouble.'

'Tell me about it,' said Megan. 'They're not worth the bother.'

'You're not wrong,' he groaned.

Katherine waved a piece of paper at Megan. 'Hey, Megan. Just in case you need it.'

Megan took the paper and unfolded it to see the name and number of a top Glasgow lawyer.

'She's one of Tony's colleagues,' said Katherine. 'She's the best.'

'Thanks a lot,' said Megan. 'That's great.' But she knew the reality was that she wouldn't do anything. It would just make things worse if she took legal action. Johnny *was* a lawyer and would know how to make it worse.

She emailed Sam.

Fancy a freelance job?

Need a background check done.

Call me.

She pressed send. A second later, her phone buzzed.

'Megan. Sam here.'

'That was quick. Just wondered if you fancied a job?'

'Aye, well, we need to chat. When you free to meet?'

'That sounds ominous,' she said. But when Sam didn't make a sarcastic comment back, she felt curious. 'Okay. Tinderbox?'

'Aye, that's fine. I'll be there in ten minutes.'

'See you then,' said Megan and put down the phone. She pulled on her coat and ran down the steps onto Byres Road. A homeless man, sitting cross-legged in a doorway, wolf-whistled at her.

'Hello to you too,' said Megan, smiling.

He rewarded her with a grin that revealed his three front teeth.

When Megan reached the coffee house she ordered a green tea and sat facing the door so she could see Sam come in. There was a constant clatter of cups and the whirring of the coffee grinder. Then, when the door opened, the noise of a bus trundling past.

'All right, Sam?'

'Aye,' he said, looking more flustered than usual. His face was bright red and he looked like he'd lost weight since she last saw him. There was a line of sweat where his moustache used to be.

'Going for a different look?' said Megan, raising an eyebrow.

'Aye, something like that.' He wiped away the sweat with the back of his hand. 'Look, let's not beat round the bush, Megan.' He glanced around as he sat down. 'What is it you're wanting?'

'Bit of background on Warren McGregor.'

He eyed her warily.

'The nightclub owner.'

'Aye, I know who he is.'

'You okay, Sam? You're not looking so good.'

'Thanks, Megan. Trust you to cheer me up.'

Megan studied his face, which had suddenly gone pale. 'Can I get you something?' she said, pointing over at the counter.

'No, it's okay. Just my back giving me gyp.'

'What's wrong?'

'I think I must have pulled something.'

Megan wagged a finger at him. 'You need to look after yourself, Sam.'

'I'll be fine. I've signed up to start Pilates. Just need to work on my core strength.'

Megan nearly spat out her tea. 'That's something I never thought I'd hear you say.'

He laughed. 'Look, I'll make a few calls and see what I can find out. He's a fuckin' shady bastard.' The smile slipped from his face and he frowned. 'What are you wanting with him, Megan?'

'Proof that he's trafficking girls into the country.'

He sat back and sighed. 'Jesus. Not a tall order then.'

'Can you?'

'I'll see what I can do,' he said. 'But, Megan, there are a lot of folk not happy with the sniffing about you're doing on this trafficking article.'

Megan's eyes widened. 'But how do they know?'

'You know how these things work.' He shrugged. 'Word spreads. Look, my sources have told me that there's some new police project about to be launched.'

'To do what?' Megan leaned. *Why hasn't Jamie told me any of this?*

'To keep an eye on the West Coast in case folk are being brought in that way.'

'And do you think they are?'

'Aye, probably. I mean there's shitloads of coke being brought in on tug boats. No reason why women and kids can't be brought in that way too. Supply and demand.'

Megan processed the implications of what he was saying. 'When is it being launched?'

'Very soon. Any day now. Surprised there's not been a release about it yet.' He stood up and winced. Megan moved to stand up too. 'It's okay. You finish your tea. And Megan, you watch yourself . . . Watch your back. There are some vicious bastards out there. And not just in the police.'

Megan raised an eyebrow. 'That's a bit cryptic even for you, Sam.'

He patted her on the shoulder. 'Just watch yourself and those around you.'

'Thanks, Sam. I will, I mean it. I appreciate you looking out for me.'

He shrugged. 'I'll be in touch.' He waved at her over his shoulder as he sauntered out the door.

Megan sat for a moment. She'd never seen Sam looking so jittery. She decided to text Jamie. She needed to find out what was going on.

Fancy a drink later? Have an update for you.

Megan ran her fingers through her hair and sighed. She didn't really have an update for him, she just hoped he would take the bait so she could probe him further in light of what Sam had said. It could help the story and, well, she actually did want to see him. Her phone buzzed.

Okay. Quick drink after work. 7 @Cottiers?

So he was in Glasgow again, she thought, as she watched three young mums and their toddlers come into the café and sit down next to her. She smiled as one of the little boys reached out to hold the hand of the girl in the buggy next to him. The women were all slim with glossy hair and, she noticed, wearing sparkling engagement rings and wedding bands. A large splash of water landed on her cheek and she looked over to see the cute little boy not looking quite so adorable. His mother, whose face was flushed, mouthed 'sorry' and then quickly lowered her eyes as the boy started to wail.

Megan stood up. It was time to leave.

Being slapped, kicked and punched was normal now. She'd had clumps of her hair ripped out, and whenever she caught her reflection in the mirror she shuddered. She'd been told plenty of times she was past her best, she was an ugly bitch. It didn't stop the bossman using her himself though. When he was forcing himself on her she wondered why he didn't just do it to a hole in the wall. He'd started to wear condoms. Called her a dirty cow. Some of the men paid more to go without. She didn't like that. She didn't

like the way, when they'd finished, that it would all slide back out of her and down her legs. It didn't matter how many wipes she used in between the men, she never felt clean.

She knew the bossman was up to something. She'd heard him about a delivery being made in exchange for that black one. For her. She didn't know why he'd lowered his voice when he was talking about her. It didn't make any difference. He'd talked about a ship and cargo. Then she couldn't make out what he said as he started talking so quickly. Then he mentioned cargo again. Value added cargo, going to its final destination.

She stared at the swirls on the curtains when she heard him say that. Maybe she would be taken back home? Maybe she'd paid off her debts and she could go home now. She was struggling to remember what it was like. Would her mother still be there? And her brothers? When she heard footsteps, she moved away from the door. A cold gust swept through the room when the bossman flung it open. He stood in the doorway for a moment, his face hard.

A woman walked in, straight towards the girl, high heels catching in the ragged carpet. The girl couldn't help staring at her. Had she come to rescue the girl? Had she come to help? The girl's knees wobbled and she collapsed to the ground, her eyes pleading with the woman. The woman looked so out of place standing there, in a smart black dress and a cloud of flowery perfume. She shot the girl a look of disgust. The bossman shouted at the girl to her to get on her feet. There was no emotion in the woman's eyes. No sympathy or concern. The woman circled her, looking up and down the girl's body. She grabbed the girl's face in both hands and turned it left and then right, scrutinising her for something. Then she lifted the girl's top up and sneered. The woman made no eye contact with the girl as she stuck her finger inside her mouth and felt her teeth. Then she left without a word. The bossman locked the door and the woman said she would do.

28

Jamie stood up and smiled at Megan as she entered the bar. After they got their drinks, they sat beside each other in a booth.

'So, you said you had an update?' said Megan.

Jamie eyed her warily. 'Eh, you said you had an update. You said you wanted to meet.'

That was just a ruse. I believe you may have something to tell me.'

He sighed. 'Right. Still, off the record though, okay?'

Megan hadn't expected him to cave so quickly. 'Of course.'

'A woman walked into a police station in the South Side a couple of days ago. A Thai woman. A punter apparently dropped her off there.'

'Why would he do that?' said Megan, her eyes widening in surprise.

'More common than you think. Probably wants to be her knight in shining armour. My guess is he took pity on her and gave her the chance to escape.'

'And how is she?'

Jamie scratched his head. 'Hard to tell. She's a bit disorientated, thought she was in New York.'

'How come?'

'That's what she'd been told. And why wouldn't she believe it? She's probably never been out of her village before. She would have anything.'

'Is she saying much?'

'Not right now. We've got a translator sorted, but it'll take time. At least it's a start.'

'Where is she?'

'In a safe house. There's an agency working with her to make sure she's okay. It'll take them time to reassure her that she's safe.' Jamie took a sip from his pint.

Megan leaned in towards Jamie.

He shook his head. 'No.'

'No what?'

'I know what you're going to ask. Would she talk to you?'

Megan sighed.

'No, not just yet,' said Jamie. 'It's not straight forward, you know. We can barely get these women to talk to the police. They're terrified.'

'But she must know she's safe now.

Jamie shook his head again. 'No, that's the whole point, especially with the Nigerian girls. They're scared to death that evil spirits will come and get them.'

'What do you have to do to reassure them they're safe?'

Jamie gave a bitter laugh. 'It's not a quick-fix solution, Megan. It's a long, long process. These girls have been to hell and back, and everyone's fucked them over. They trust nobody.'

'Okay, I understand that, but how do you get the Nigerian ones, say, to trust you, to get round the Juju thing then?'

'It just take time and the right support,' he said.

'They don't have time though, do they? Not with that forty-five day limit. Megan took another sip of her drink. 'God, it's awful.'

'I know from previous cases that if the woman is Nigerian, the agency workers will tell her that they have colleagues in her village who can go to the shrine and remove the things that are hers. They tell her she's not broken the oath. It's the traffickers.' Jamie drained the rest of his pint. 'They've been promised jobs in shops or as nannies. All bullshit. The traffickers lie to them. We need to reassure the girls that it was the traffickers who broke the oath.' He rubbed his chin. 'The main thing is, this Thai woman has come forward and asked for help. It's a start. She should be able to tell us where she was being held and who else was there with her. We need to solve this before . . .'

'Before what?'

'Nothing. Doesn't matter.'

Megan glared at him. 'What are you not telling me, Jamie? Apart from the new project being launched to keep an eye on what's coming in on the West Coast?'

'How the hell do you know about that?'

'Doesn't matter. Just shows you're not telling me everything.'

'Look, I have to remember who I'm talking to. I can't tell you everything . . . And that's not definite, by the way. As far as I know it's still in the early stages. But it's the same with you, Megan - you don't tell *me* everything.'

Megan wondered, for a moment, if she should tell him about Johnny. Maybe he could actually help. 'Fancy another?' she said, pointing at his empty glass.

'Pint of Best, please. But don't think you're going to get me drunk so you can get some information from me.'

'Just watch me,' she said, and winked.

Megan went to the bar. She just wasn't sure if she could trust Jamie or not. She glanced over at him. But then again she didn't want him to know *everything* about her. Not quite yet. He was supposed to be a contact, nothing more. Yet she could definitely feel a connection between them. Surely she wasn't imagining it? He looked up from his phone and clocked her looking at him. Flustered, she turned away.

'Is there any news on the Tinkle Club?' she asked when she returned to the table.

'There's not a lot we can do just now, other than keep a close eye on them. The guys running these places are smart. We're watching them, but unless the women in there talk to us then it's our word against theirs. Their passports have been taken, they don't trust anyone, so why would they risk talking to us?'

Megan tapped her foot slowly against his chair. One, two, pause. One, two, pause.

'Are you trying to annoy me?'

'No,' she said quietly. 'I was just wondering why you're always in Glasgow these days.'

Jamie rolled his eyes. 'Megan, you ask too many questions.'

'It's my job,' she said, stopping herself from reaching out to touch his hand.

He stared at her in a way that made her break eye contact with him. Then she looked back at him. 'What happens now?' She realised, too late, how loaded her question was.

Jamie frowned. 'That's a very good question,' he said, unsure of whether to continue.

'Yes,' she said, her head cocked to the side. 'It is?'

'Do you remember when that businessman went missing last year? Murray McVey?'

'The guy that invented that fitness app? What's it called ... Heartbeat?' she said. 'Yeah, I remember him, though I was never quite sure what the app did. He never did turn up, did he?'

'No. He was depressed, had some debt issues. He vanished without trace.'

'Why do you ask? Do you think he's involved somehow?'

'It's just a hunch I have.'

Megan guessed it was more than a hunch, but she knew he would only say so much.

'Did you ever hear anything about McVey through the grapevine?' Jamie asked, sitting back in his chair.

Megan shook her head. 'No. I was working in Edinburgh, remember, and it wasn't a big deal through there. I think people just thought he'd fled to the Cayman Islands or South America. He's probably living the life of Riley on a yacht with a completely different face. Wouldn't surprise me if he's never heard of again.'

Jamie took a sip of his beer and didn't say a word.

~

THIS MAN WAS different to the others. He looked at her properly. He wore tatty jeans, a grey sweatshirt and dirty white trainers. His hair was dark and thinning, and he had tattoos on his hands. When he was shown into her room and said thanks to the bossman over his shoulder, she slowly stood up and started to undress. Her head hung so she didn't see him shaking his head. She glanced up only when he began to talk. No, he said, shaking his head. Stop.

The girl wondered if this was a trick. Was the bossman testing her? She watched as he walked towards her, his hands now shoved in his pockets. She felt her heart race. It wasn't the first time a customer had pulled something out of a pocket. But she was surprised when he sat down on the bed. She flicked her eyes to the door.

It's okay, he said quietly. I don't want anything from you. I just want to talk. She remained standing, unsure of what to do. The room was strangely quiet for a moment, and then he spoke. Where are you from? he said. She didn't reply. It's okay, he said looking at her. You can just nod. You are from Africa? She nodded her head. Can you tell me where? Nigeria, said the girl. Where in Nigeria? She bit her lip. It's okay, he said. His tone reassured her. Where is your home? A village in Edo, she said. He smiled. I have been to Lagos. This focused the girl's attention and she looked properly at the man. Why are you here? he asked. I work, she said. There must have been a better job? She started to shake. She felt nervous again and didn't know what to do or say. This hadn't happened before. She looked at the door. Working, she said. He stood up and walked towards her. It's okay, he said. I want to help you. You want sex, she said. No, he said. I want to help. Can I help you? The girl bit her lip and felt tears trickling down her cheek. She could hear soft cries coming from the room next door, a thumping and then a howl. She saw the man's distressed expression as he listened. He looked at his watch and sighed. I need to go now. But I will come back. I promise. I am here to help. Can I take your picture, please? It may help, he said.

The girl's heart sank. He wasn't here to help. He was the same as all the others. Maybe worse. She nodded as he took out a phone from his jean pocket. He held it up and she began to unhook her bra. No, no, he said. I just want a picture of you. What is your name? Itohan, she whispered. They call me Mercy.

I promise you, Mercy, I will come back and help, he said, tucking the phone away again. He took some money from his pocket and counted out several notes. For the boss, he said, gesturing at the door. He smiled at the girl, then turned to walk away. He slipped through the door and didn't look back.

29

Megan's heels skidded on a wet cobble and she grabbed at Joanna's arm.

'Anyone would think you'd be drinking,' Joanna said.

They passed a teenage boy who had just stumbled into a doorway to throw up. His friend was pissing against a lamp-post as he watched.

'Lovely,' said Megan. 'The youth of today, eh?'

'Thank God we're sober,' muttered Joanna as they quickened their pace, walking along Gordon Street and then onto Buchanan Street. 'To think that could be George one day . . .'

Megan tightened her grip on her sister's arm. 'Never! He'll be a judo champion.'

'Hopefully. Or a chess champion. Anything that keeps him off the streets.'

They walked in silence for a while. 'Look, thanks for agreeing to come with me tonight, Joanna. I don't think I could do this without you.'

'Mmm,' said Joanna. 'I was hardly going to let you do this on your own, was I? Plus it's not often I get the chance of a night out on the town. And George is over the moon to be having a sleepover at Ben's.

They can practise their judo moves without me worrying about the neighbours.' She paused. 'Does anyone else know you're doing this?'

Megan gave her a sideways glance. 'No.'

'Not even Richard?'

'No. It's better that we don't complicate things. Come on.' She gestured ahead. 'We can cut through this way.'

Joanna ran a hand through her hair, patting it at the back. 'Actually, I could do with a cigarette. It's been a while since I felt like this.'

Just then a woman walked past sucking from her e-cigarette. She blew out a cloud of tangerine-scented vapour.

'I know what you mean. But I'd like the proper stuff. You know, actual nicotine.' Megan's eyes narrowed as they walked past the Gallery of Modern Art. 'I just hope this thing doesn't fall off.' She smoothed her hands over her wig. She giggled at the traffic cone on the statue of the Duke of Wellington, pointing it out to Joanna.

'So jaunty!' She laughed. 'During the Referendum there was a Saltire draped over it too.'

Megan glanced back at the illuminated building with its grand pillars. 'Strange to think that happened, eh?'

'Aye, well, no doubt there'll be another one before too long.'

'True,' said Megan. 'Look, here we are.'

'Do we have to stay long?'

'No way. Just a drink or two. A wee recce and then we're out of there.'

'Do you think we'll even get in?'

'Just leave it to me,' said Megan with a grin.

The entrance to the Tinkle Bar was down a cobbled alley. It was flanked by two burly bouncers with shaved heads and black puffer jackets. 'Evening, ladies. How are youse?' said one, his pale blue eyes fixing on Megan.

'Aye, all right, thanks,' said Megan, flashing her best smile.

'Dying for a drink,' said Joanna.

'In youse go.' He stood aside to let them pass.

Megan knew his eyes were lingering on her backside for a moment more than was necessary. She almost turned to say something but checked herself and kept walking. The women passed the cloakroom and the ATM. An unsmiling security man opened the door into the club. Megan exchanged a brief look with Joanna. It was pitch-black, and it took a few moments for Megan's eyes to adjust. She walked confidently towards the bar.

'Didn't realise you got cash machines in clubs these days,' said Joanna.

'Yip,' said Megan.

'This place actually looks okay.'

Megan looked around casually while catching the eye of one of the seated at the bar. It wasn't at all the dive she had been expecting. She had had visions of it being dark and sweaty with too many bodies pressing into hers. In fact, it actually looked as if its owners had invested quite a lot of money in making it look like a quality establishment. Chandeliers were strung across the lowered ceiling, the floor looked like it was made of granite slabs, and the seats at the bar were covered in dark-brown leather. Even the bar staff looked like they should be working in a fancy hair salon with their black jeans and T-shirts and heavily made-up faces.

'Well, this isn't what I was expecting,' Megan said. 'What do you fancy? Prosecco? Gin?'

'A vodka and tonic, please.'

A blonde woman leaned over the bar to Megan. 'What can I get you?'

'Two vodka tonics please.' Then she frowned. 'Don't I know you?'

The blonde woman threw her a blank look and shrugged.

'You look like someone... you look like Anastasia.'

The blonde shook her head. 'I get you drinks.'

'What is it?' Joanna asked.

'She looks like a girl in a story a friend of mine wrote.' She laughed. 'But that would be too much of a coincidence. And a tragedy.' When the blonde handed Megan the drinks she realised the woman was older than Anastasia. Her eyes were dull and flat. Megan wondered if she'd seen the same things as Anastasia.

'Where are you from?' Megan asked her.

'Poland.' The blonde flicked her eyes at someone behind Megan.

'It's okay,' said Megan. 'You just remind me of someone I know. Thanks. Keep the change.' She picked up the glasses and pointed to a table in the corner. 'Come on, let's sit over there.'

The music, a Calvin Harris track, was deafening, so Megan and Joanna struggled to hear each other speak.

'So now what?' shouted Joanna. 'What happens next?'

'Well, firstly, cheers.' Megan clinked her glass against Joanna's. 'Thanks for coming along.' Her eyes flicked around the room. 'The dim lighting is handy, eh?'

'Do you really think we're going to find out anything by being here?'

Megan was suddenly aware of someone watching her from the bar. 'I just don't know.'

'Hang on. Is that Rhona over there? Rhona from the refuge. Collecting glasses.' Joanna stood up.

'The nail girl?' said Megan. 'Jo, Jo, don't try and talk to her,' Megan tried to pull back her sister, but Joanna had already walked away. Megan watched as she made her way towards the bar, which was now busier, sliding past several men to make her way towards Rhona. Megan tried to appear relaxed as she checked out the club, taking in as much detail as she could: the colour of the walls and the floor, the number of bouncers flanking each door, how many girls were serving at the bar, the punters by the bar. They were a smart bunch. Businessmen in navy suits, with open-necked shirts, older men in jeans and blazers. The place wasn't exactly a dive.

'Bloody hell,' said Joanna, sliding back into the booth. 'That was an expensive round. Twenty quid for two drinks.'

'London prices.' Megan shrugged. 'Did you get a chance to talk to her?'

'No,' said Joanna. 'She looked at me like she'd seen a ghost and then disappeared through that door. Not sure what that's all about.'

'Maybe she didn't recognise you?'

'Nope. I don't think it's that.'

'She's maybe just a bit thrown seeing you here out of the blue.'

'Maybe. I thought I should at least buy a round while I was up at the bar, try not to make it look too obvious . . . what are we going to do now then?'

'Well, not dance,' said Megan, nodding in the direction of the poles just to the side of their booth, which two women were sliding up and down.

'Jesus Christ. Where did *they* come from?'

'Well, they're not local by the looks of it,' Megan said.

'Jeez, I feel about ninety.' Joanna watched as one of the women thrust her leg around the shiny pole. 'Clubs weren't like this in my day.'

'That's because you didn't *go* to clubs, Jo.' Megan laughed, feeling the vodka starting to relax her.

'Aye, that's true. See what being a young mum did for me. Saved me from these places. Did you do much clubbing in Edinburgh?'

'A bit,' said Megan. 'But it was nothing like this. The clubs in George Street were full of posh students. Girls in pearl stud earrings, hoping to snare a royal. The pubs full of rugby types. Not my cup of tea.' She wrinkled her nose.

'What *is* your type going to be then, Megan? I mean, apart from the wanker lawyer type?'

Megan took a swig from her tumbler. 'Let's just see what happens. Who knows? Look - do you think those girls over there look okay?'

'The ones on the poles?'

'Yes.'

'Hard to tell,' said Joanna. 'The girl who served me at the bar was definitely not a local though. Neither was her friend.'

Megan glanced over at the bar. It was the same girl who had served her when they arrived. 'Where do you think she's from?'

'Pretty sure, Moldova.'

'But she said she was from Poland. What makes you say Moldova?'

'Just from some of the words I've picked up in the refuge. They sounded familiar. I've become quite the linguist, you know.'

Megan looked over at the women dancing. They were pale and

far too skinny, and Megan noticed that they were avoiding all contact with the punters 'You look good, sis. Your hair suits you like that.'

Joanna was wearing her hair loose over her shoulders with a black shirt and trousers. 'I've always fancied being blonde. Anyway, stop trying to change the subject.'

'So, listen, don't freak out but I think we're being watched.'

'Who by?' said Joanna, keeping her voice neutral and her eyes fixed on Megan.

'A couple of guys at the booth across the way. They're wearing suits, expensive ones, and I have a feeling that one of them may be the owner. Just keep calm, and if they come over then just be yourself.' Megan's cheeks flushed as she tried to work out what to do next. There was no point in leaving abruptly. That draw even more attention. Instead, she concentrated on chatting to Joanna, until she suddenly felt a hand on her shoulder.

The girl hadn't seen the blonde woman since the night of the party. She knew the blonde must have upset the bossman. He'd screamed at her, his eyes wide and bulging, and the veins throbbing in his neck. Then slammed his fist into her nose then spat on her as soon as they arrived back at the flat. He pushed her into her room, followed her in and slammed the door shut. The girl knew what he was doing. She could hear screams of agony. The girl had been kept locked in her room since. She didn't dare ask questions.

She kept thinking about her brothers: Osato and Dmiklo. They would never be safe. Not if she disobeyed. She wondered if she would ever see them again.

30

'Hello, ladies,' said the taller man. He smiled, his white teeth luminous in the dark club, and sat down. 'Mind if we join you?'

'Eh, I think you already have,' said Joanna.

Megan kicked her under the table. 'Of course, be our guest.' Megan tried to remain composed as the man blatantly checked out her chest.

'What brings you here?' he asked.

'Just fancied checking it out and seeing what all the fuss is about,' said Megan.

'And?'

'And it's okay. It's quite nice.'

'Thanks, Tom,' said the tall man to his companion, who had arrived back from the bar with a bottle of Cava on ice.

Megan could see Joanna trying not to snigger.

'That's very kind of you,' said Megan. 'But we're actually just about to leave.'

'No,' he said. 'I insist.' He gestured to Tom to sit down on Joanna's other side, trapping them both in their seats.

'Stay and have a drink with us. Then we'll let you go,' said the man.

‘Okay. Well, only if you introduce yourself,’ said Megan.

‘Of course. I’m Warren McGregor,’ he said, reaching out a hand and grasping hers. ‘And you are?’

‘Sophie. This is my friend Ros . . .’

Joanna smiled and reached out her hand. ‘Pleased to meet you.’

‘What about your wee pal there,’ said Megan, pointing at Tom. ‘He doesn’t have a lot to say for himself. Is he okay?’

Warren smirked and nodded his head. ‘Aye. He’s not the brightest. I’m sorry, ladies, let me introduce you to Tom. This is Tom.’

‘Hi, Tom,’ said Megan, extending her hand and fixing her eyes on him. She couldn’t believe this was happening. What on earth was Jamie playing at? Why was he pretending to be called Tom and acting like he and McGregor were best friends? ’It’s lovely to meet you.’

‘Sophie,’ he said. ‘It’s a pleasure to meet you too.’

Megan watched as Warren opened the bottle and poured everyone a glass. When she looked across at Tom she gave him a hard glare.

‘What do you do, Warren?’ asked Megan, pretending to take a sip from her glass.

He laughed. ‘Oh, this and that.’

Tom interrupted. ‘He’s the manager here.’

Megan had already checked out the exits, which were all guarded by security guys, and she knew there was no way of getting out of there until Warren said they could go.

‘What about you, Sophie? What do you do?’

‘I’m a teacher.’

‘What do you teach?’

‘Modern studies.’

‘And you’re out on a school night?’ said Warren, reaching for the glass and swallowing the rest of his Cava. Topping his glass up, he said, ’A bit of a naughty girl, are you?’

‘I can be.’ Megan forced herself to giggle.

‘And you?’ He turned to Joanna.

‘I’m a counsellor,’ she said. ‘People tell me all their problems.’

‘That’s good to know,’ said Warren.

'You've got some nice-looking staff in here,' said Megan. 'Are they all Polish?'

'A few of them. But we like to mix it up,' said Warren. 'Get them from all over. Why, you fancy any of them? Choose whoever you want and I'll sort it out, sunshine . . . as long as I can watch.'

Megan resisted the urge to smack him across his greasy forehead. 'Ha ha. Maybe next time,' she said. 'I'm not really in the mood tonight.'

'Excuse me for a minute,' said Warren, who was staring towards the bar. His eyes narrowed and a flash of fury crossed his face. Megan jumped as he abruptly stood up, then marched towards the bar where another man was standing. Two bouncers seemed to appear out of the shadows to flank him.

'What's happening?' said Megan, glancing at Jamie. His eyes were locked on Warren too. He spoke urgently. 'You two need to get out of here *now*.'

Megan watched as Warren slapped his hand across the man's back. He spun him round and pressed his face right up to the man's. Then suddenly he backed away and grinned, snapping his fingers at the girl cowering behind the bar. She handed him a glass. The other man began to edge away from Warren but the bouncers closed in at his side. Warren took his time drinking his whisky and then signalled for another. Megan gulped; her throat dry and raw. She felt stiffen next to her.

'What's going on over there?' Joanna's voice had dropped to a whisper.

Megan looked over at Jamie. His eyes were flicking between Warren and Megan. Her heart was racing now, and she knew that she and Joanna needed to leave, but at that moment, there was a scream from behind the bar as Warren smashed his glass on the bar. Shards went flying, and one of the girls brushed pieces from her arm. Nobody moved. Then Warren held the jagged glass at the man's throat. The bouncers grabbed the stranger and bundled him towards a fire exit. Jamie didn't utter a word. He sat, motionless, and observed.

'Right, girls,' he said, when he could see Warren was out of sight. 'It's time you were on your way.'

'Yes, we're going.' Megan stood up shakily.

'Your friend Ros isn't looking too great,' said Jamie.

'I'm fine,' said Joanna, her face tense.

'You're not. Come on,' said Megan, digging her nails into her sister's arm and pulling her to her feet.

'Please thank Mr McGregor for the drink, Tom,' she said, turning to Jamie.

'I'll be sure to,' he said, ushering the women to the exit. His arm was holding Megan's a little more firmly than was necessary, urging her to get away. 'Get a taxi and go straight home,' he said in her ear. Then more loudly to both of them, 'Lovely to meet you.'

'Bye,' said Megan.

'You sure I don't know you? We've not met?' said Joanna.

'I'm sure,' he said, turning away.

'What do you think was going on there?' said Joanna as they walked towards the main road.

Megan looked around desperately for a cab with an orange light on. 'Something very dodgy.'

'The Cava was a bit naff, wasn't it?' Joanna shivered.

'Yes, it was. Oh, thank God for that, a cab,' she said, flagging it down.

Neither of the women spoke until the taxi pulled up at Joanna's door.

'I can't wait to get this off me. It's really itching,' said Joanna as they walked up the stairs.

'I know,' said Megan, tugging at her wig. As soon as she was inside, Megan pulled her phone from her bag and quickly sent a text.

WTF Tom?

I can explain. Sophie? Are you home yet

Megan bashed out her reply.

Yes.

What the hell had he been playing at? Was he undercover or something? And what else wasn't he telling her? Wild thoughts were whirling around her head as she tugged off the wig and wiped the make-up from her face. She shivered when she thought about the man who'd been hauled out the back. What had happened to him? Sam Martin was right. Warren McGregor had a vicious streak and didn't care who witnessed it. She really needed to talk to Jamie.

THE GIRL FOLLOWED the blonde into the dark stairwell. She'd been told to keep her eyes down, follow her and not to speak or look at anyone. The girl clung to the banister as she tottered down the stairs. The wood felt smooth under her palms. Her eyes were fixed on each stair and she tried hard not to stumble in the cheap platform shoes.

As they got to the bottom of the close the man pushed her and the blonde through the door. It banged hard behind them making the girl jump. She had to step round a puddle of vomit and piles of rubbish bags on the street. There was a smell of urine at the door, as if someone had been standing there peeing into it for hours. It was night-time and the street was empty. The girl noticed a car with a flashing blue light passing by. The bossman linked his arms tightly through hers and the blonde's, and told them to keep smiling and walking. The girl watched the flashing blue light fade. The bossman jerked at her, shouting at her to keep her eyes down, and she cried out in pain. The blonde gave her a stare and the girl knew to say no more. The car was waiting for them a few metres away. Parked on a double-yellow line, its engine throbbed.

Get in, he said, opening a door and pushing her in the back. The blonde got in after her and the door slammed shut. It was warm inside the car at least. Warm and dry. The girl was always cold. Whit you parking there for, you daft cunt? he said. Polis just passed by. The driver laughed harshly. Like they give a fuck. They'll be on their way home for their tea. They don't have time to piss about wasting their time with yellow-liners. The bossman clicked his teeth. Next time, don't fuck around, he said. Park further down.

The girl tried to concentrate on what they were saying. Sometimes she could make out random words. Mostly she couldn't. The bossman turned up the radio and lit a cigarette. It smelt of flowers. He inhaled deeply and turned and passed it to the blonde. The girl saw her close her eyes and suck on it. Her eyes flicked open and she offered it to the girl. She hesitated for a moment then shook her head. The blonde shrugged then took another draw and let her head fall back.

The girl watched. Perhaps she should take the blonde's advice and just take what they offered her. Maybe it would help to dull the pain. At least it smelt nice. Maybe she would just take it, after all.

31

Megan woke to hammering at the front door. She sat up abruptly, rubbing her eyes with her knuckles. The room was in total darkness. For a moment she had no idea where she was. Her heart was thudding as the banging on the door grew more urgent. Glancing at the clock, she saw it was just after four o'clock.

'What the hell is going on?' she muttered and sprang out of bed, pulling a fleecy sweatshirt over her pyjamas. She crept to the door of the room, her teeth chattering.

The pounding had stopped but her phone started to ring. She ran to the bedside table and picked it up. Eight missed calls. *Oh God.*

'Hello.'

'Megan. It's me. Jamie. I'm at your door. Let me in.'

She ran to the hallway. Joanna was standing in the doorway of her room, rubbing her eyes. 'What's happening, Megan?'

'It's okay. Ssh. Go back to bed. Sorry Joanna. It's for me. It's all okay.'

'You sure?' she said, sounding unconvinced. 'Is it him? Is it Johnny?'

'No,' said Megan. 'It's a cop friend. It's fine. I'll explain in the morning. I promise everything is okay.'

She waited for Joanna to turn and close her door, then she unlocked the snib and opened the door. Jamie practically fell in.

'What are you doing, you idiot?' she said.

'Trying to make sure nobody spots me.' Jamie shut the door behind him.

'Unlikely at this time in the morning.' Megan scowled at him. 'Anyway, you're the one making all the noise with that banging.'

'I tried calling you. Several times. But you were obviously dead to the world.'

'Can you keep your voice down? My sister is trying to sleep.' Megan turned and walked towards the kitchen. 'Cuppa? Or something stronger?'

'Aye, a cup of tea would be good.' Jamie yawned and raked his hands through his hair. 'Are you going to tell me what the hell you were playing at tonight?'

Megan spun back to look at him. She narrowed her eyes, gesturing for him to go into the kitchen. She closed the door behind them. 'Are you having a laugh, Jamie? Or — sorry — should it be Tom? What am *I* playing at?' She slammed the kettle down on the worktop and forcefully flicked it on. 'I think I'd like to know what exactly *you* are playing at. And just who you are.'

He sighed. 'Megan. This isn't a game, you know. It's not just about you dipping in and out of these places and playing games.'

Megan resisted the urge to throw something at him. 'I was out with my sister for a drink. That is it.'

Jamie raised an eyebrow. 'Is the Tinkle Club one of your regular haunts?'

Megan shrugged, the muscles in her jaw tense.

'Why did you give false names?'

'You think I should give dodgy strangers my real name? And *you* can't exactly talk.' She reached to get two mugs out of the cupboard. 'Coffee or tea?'

'Tea please.' He perched against a stool and crossed his arms.

'Well, are you going to tell me what's going on?'

Jamie sighed. 'You're playing a dicey game Megan . . . I can't tell you everything.',

'Well, tell me what you can then.'

'We've been watching the Tinkle Club for a while now. And the owner. Warren.'

'I see,' said Megan dropping the teabags in the mugs and pouring on the boiling water.

'Megan, I'm not sure you do, actually. Which is why you need to tread carefully. You're lucky he didn't recognise you.'

'What do you mean?'

'Because he seems to know that the press, and you in particular, are sniffing around him.'

Megan's face paled. 'And how would he know that?'

'Because he has contacts everywhere, Megan.' He paused for a moment. '*Everywhere.*'

She gave a wry smile. 'It's lucky I wore a wig then, isn't it?'

'Aye. Probably the most sensible decision you have made in a while. And those clothes too. Even took *me* a while to work it out.'

'So how did you, then?' she said, handing the mug to him. 'How did you know it was me?'

'I just know the way you move. You walk in a certain way.'

'Is that right?'

Neither of them spoke for a moment and Megan blushed, suddenly aware that she was wearing just her pyjamas in front of a man she didn't know all that well. 'And what about you, Jamie? Why are you in there cosying up with him and calling yourself Tom?'

'Police stuff.'

'Really?'

'Aye.'

'So why the fake name?'

'I'm hardly going to tell him my real name, am I?'

'I don't understand.'

Jamie chewed at his bottom lip. 'Look. I'm not supposed to tell you any of this.'

Megan swallowed some tea. 'Is that the real reason you're always in Glasgow then?'

He nodded. 'Yes. For this job. It's undercover. They need someone who's from Glasgow and can fit in. I've been away for long enough that nobody recognises me. And I've got the accent.'

'But how do you know he won't work out you're a cop?'

'Just have to keep my fingers crossed.'

'You sure?' said Megan, dubiously.

'Look, I'm not in there very often. I've another guy who goes in a lot. Has his ear to the ground more than me. I just wanted to do a wee check. I said to Warren I've been away for a while.'

'You look different, too, with the glasses. And that suit?' she said pointing at it. 'Did you get yourself down *Slaters* or something for that?'

He frowned. 'Anyway the point is, Megan, that I don't want to hear that you've been in there again.'

'Why would you? Nobody knows it was me.'

'Promise me you won't go back there. There is some nasty stuff going on.'

'So why can't you arrest him?'

'There's stuff you don't know about.' Jamie put down his mug on the worktop and folded his arms. 'There are things that I can't tell you about. Operational details that I can't go into.'

'Why not?'

'Because you're a journalist, Megan, and I would be breaking the law.'

She glared at him and gulped down a mouthful of lukewarm tea to stop herself from speaking.

'It's not as easy as just arresting him. It's not just him. It's like a bloody spider's web. You would not believe. The girls won't speak. Believe me, we have tried to get them to. But they are terrified. They don't have their passports. They don't trust anyone. Best we can do for just now is get him where it hurts — and that means getting his assets.'

'What is the point in all of this? It's just going to keep on happening over and over again. What's the point in the bloody legislation if it can't be used?'

Jamie didn't reply.

'Sometimes I wish I hadn't bothered with all of this, you know.'

'What do you mean?'

'I just think Richard's getting cold feet about the trafficking feature. Says he's getting pressure from the lawyers.'

'Yes, well, most of the press are fairly paranoid these days.'

Megan gave a brittle chuckle.

'Anything else I should know?'

Megan shook her head. She wasn't going to tell Jamie anything else about the feature. Not after tonight.

Jamie yawned and belatedly covered his mouth.

'You must be knackered. You should go.'

'Aye,' he said. 'You're probably right.'

She hesitated for a moment, then walked towards him as he pulled on his coat. He leant down and hesitated before kissing her on the cheek. 'Take care of yourself, Megan. I'll see you soon,' he said.

She closed the door behind him and bolted it shut. Her face was flushed and, despite her best attempts not to, she was smiling.

The girl listened to the rain hitting the windows which rattled in the wind. She longed for the sound of the rain battering off the corrugated iron roof at home. Her nose constantly streamed a clear river of mucus. Not that it put any of the men off. They probably didn't notice anyway. The girl had forgotten what it felt like to be warm. She longed for dry, dusty heat. For the earthy scent of her mother's kitchen. Here, the smell of cooking oil seemed to always linger in the air, mingled with the cheap perfume the girls were told to spray on. The girl missed the blonde. She had been kind to her. The girl didn't want to talk to any of the others. They were still being kept locked in their rooms anyway. When they were taken out in the car to the parties, they were the first to be won and taken away.

She heard the key turn in the door. The bossman walked in and came right up to the bed. His cheeks were red and had a map of broken veins stretched across them.

You've got a customer, he said. Get dressed. He grinned at her, his tongue lolling from his mouth. The girl hastily brushed her hair, which had started to thin, applied some lipstick and pulled the nightie over her head. The bossman watched. She stood waiting. In you go, said the bossman when he walked into the hall. She's all yours.

When the man entered the room she felt a faint flicker in her stomach. Not fear, something else. He was older, well-groomed and wore a suit and tie. He looked vaguely familiar. He was the first black man she had seen in a long time. She could smell his aftershave as soon as he stepped over the threshold and walked his polished shoes towards her. The bossman shut the door, leaving them alone.

She stood still as he slowly circled her, his lips pursed, his arms folded and with a finger to his mouth. He was behind her and out of sight but she daren't turn to look. Instead she braced herself waiting for a thwack or the sound of a zip and a prod from behind. She stood there waiting and waiting, her eyes fixed on the door. What was he doing? Her legs started to feel stiff and her neck began to ache. She was cold too in the flimsy nightdress. Then she heard something click and the man started to slowly move again. Click. Click. He held up his mobile phone and took her picture. Was he like the other man? Was he going to help? But then he told her to undress and took more pictures. The other man had told her not to undress. She was confused and tense, ready for the man to pounce. But he didn't touch her at all. Just kept clicking his phone. Then he put it in his pocket, walked towards the door and left the room.

32

A few hours later Megan was running towards Hyndland Road. It was light out but not bright. The sky was grey and oppressive and she shivered, focusing on her breathing as she forced her feet along until they found their own gentle rhythm. Then her breathing steadied. The streets were quiet apart from a few folk coming off night-shift or making early deliveries. A man, his head down, hands buried deep in his pockets, brushed against her and tutted. Megan gasped in fright, muttered an apology, and then mentally shook herself. He was in the wrong, not her. She turned to make sure he was still walking in the opposite direction. He was. Since the day she'd realised she was being followed, after leaving Joanna's flat, she had been more vigilant about which routes she took. She glanced over her shoulder again, then continued running. She was at Argyle Street now and almost at the Kelvingrove Museum. The sky was turning paler, highlighting the red sandstone of the museum. She kept running on, no idea of how far she had come or where she was going. Thoughts swirled inside her head. She found herself running in a loop up towards Charing Cross and back down Great Western Road. Her breath was starting to become laboured and she knew it was time to head home.

Megan stood at the kitchen sink gulping from a glass of water.

Then she refilled it and quickly drank it all down. She was trying to make up for the lack of liquid in her daily routine — there never seemed to be time at work. The radio provided some background chatter, a bit of company, which distracted her from her thoughts of work.

'Good morning. It's the nine o'clock news,' said the newsreader. 'A man has been killed by a train at Partick Subway Station in Glasgow. The incident, which British Transport Police said is not suspicious, happened at ten-thirty on Tuesday night. Emergency services were called but the man died at the scene. Subway services were suspended for four hours but normal service has since resumed. In the rest of the news....'

Megan flicked the radio off when Joanna came into the kitchen. 'Good morning,' she said.

'Morning,' said Joanna, stifling a yawn. 'Wondered if you had company?'

Megan blushed. 'As if,' she said. 'Don't be silly. I got rid of him.'

Joanna raised an eyebrow. 'Fancy heading out for some breakfast?' she suggested. 'I don't need to pick George up until eleven.'

'That sounds perfect,' said Megan. 'Give me five minutes to have a shower.'

Just as they were about to leave, Joanna picked up the mail from the mat and quickly flicked through it. Bills and pizza leaflets. Then she saw a small white envelope. 'It's for you,' she said, handing it to Megan.

Megan tore it open.

Megan,

I don't trust emails. Especially when I realised someone was following me when I left you in Byres Road that day. So I thought I would deliver this direct.

I've done some digging on WM. Fuck me. He's a sneaky bastard. I wouldn't go anywhere near him. But then when have you ever listened to me? Seriously though, watch yourself. Yes, there're women coming in from all over the place. Mainly Eastern Europe. And if anyone asks any questions then they disappear. The usual story.

This'll interest you most. One of his cronies is running an offshoot. An online business. Like a VIP online escort service with online auctions and all sorts. That's where the African girls seem to be. Nasty stuff. Be careful. There are some big names involved. Some people you know.

Megan, the truth is closer than you think. You're a clever girl. You'll work it out. I'll get in touch if I hear any more. I'll be laying low for a while, so wait to hear from me.

Sam

She automatically reached for her phone and called him. It went straight to voicemail. Why hadn't he been more specific? Who did she know that was involved? Did that mean she now had to suspect every man she was in contact with? Richard? Jamie? Her colleagues? Joanna had started to walk down the stairs ahead of her. Slipping the note in her handbag, she slammed the door behind her and caught up with her.

'Who was the mystery caller then?'

'A cop friend. And I'm sorry. He shouldn't have turned up like that. Not on your doorstep. I told him.'

'How did he know where you stay?' she said.

'I told him,' said Megan, though wondered how he knew exactly which flat they lived in. 'He just wanted to check everything was okay'

Joanna frowned. 'Why wouldn't it be?'

Megan hesitated. 'Because he spotted us in the club and was worried.'

Joanna pushed the door of the café open and glanced around for a free table. 'Look over there,' she said, pointing to a table in the corner. 'He sounds keen.'

Megan ignored her comment. 'I'm starving. Are you ready to order?'

'Yes,' she said to the waitress. 'A latte and a bacon roll please.'

'The same,' said Megan. 'Actually make that two bacon rolls. I'm starving.'

'What's giving you an appetite?' said Joanna.

'All the sex I'm having,' said Megan drily.

'Really?'

'No. I was being facetious.'

'Well at least you've still got your sense of humour. So tell me really — why did he come and see you last night?'

Megan gave Joanna an outline of what Jamie had told her and she listened quietly. The women didn't speak as the coffees and rolls were placed in front of them. Joanna opened hers to squirt ketchup on the bacon. 'I don't know,' she said, licking her greasy fingers. 'Sounds like you need to tread carefully.'

'Yes. I think you're right.' Megan's stomach began sinking as the reality of what her sister said started to make sense. 'And I am sorry. I shouldn't have involved you in this. Not when you're a mum and you've a wee boy. That was thoughtless of me.'

Joanna reached over the table and grabbed Megan's hand. 'Stop it. Stop being so hard on yourself Megan. We're fine. I wouldn't have come with you unless I wanted to.'

Megan looked back at her older sister. 'I know.' She forced herself to smile. 'I'm wondering if Jamie might help me with Johnny.'

'How do you mean?'

'I just mean I wonder if he would be able to advise me. I thought about taking legal advice. But I think he would crush me.'

'Why what has happened?'

'Well nothing major,' said Megan. 'It's just that he won't leave me alone. He keeps calling and texting and emailing.'

'Stalking?'

'Well, maybe that's a bit strong,' began Megan.

'No. It's not. If your cop friend can help then talk to him.'

Megan nodded. The cafe was busy and soon the tables around the women were packed. Megan could hardly hear what Joanna was saying. She was talking about work and budget cuts to women's services. 'I think they may need to let some of the workers go,' she said. 'Which is a shame. As we have such a great team.'

'Do you think the funding will come through?' said Megan.

'It just depends. On a number of factors. We've got some of our trustees to put in funding applications. But you know how these things work. Nothing is guaranteed any more. I feel bad for some of the younger girls. They're on contracts and they can't get mortgages. They've got no financial security and they end up moving on elsewhere to a place where their job is guaranteed.'

'But is any job guaranteed anymore?'

Joanna shrugged. 'I guess not.'

'How is Rhona, by the way?'

'I've not seen her for a while. But that's not unusual. She tends to come and go.'

'Did you find out why she ran off that night at the club?'

'No.'

Megan glanced around. She had a strange sense she was being watched. A fleeting frown crossed her face as she read the blackboard on the wall behind, using it as an excuse to quickly scan the café. Ooh — she could bring George here, she thought, spotting bagels with smoked salmon on the menu. A feeling of uneasiness settled in her stomach and she began to wish she hadn't eaten two bacon rolls. She looked around again, her voice tense, and said, 'Do you think anyone heard us?'

'No. You've been talking quietly. And the only people next to us were pensioners so they were probably hard of hearing anyway. Come on now. Don't get suspicious.'

'You're right. I just need to be careful.' Though Megan wasn't quite sure whether she was talking about work or Johnny. All of a sudden she wanted to get out of the café and get back to the flat.

'Just watch yourself,' said Joanna. 'Watch your back. You're working in a ruthless business. Be careful who you trust.'

THE GIRL GLANCED over the bossman's shoulder. They were in the kitchen and she felt the cold air whoosh through from the hall outside. He grabbed her wrist and caught her chin roughly in his other hand. I wonder how your wee brothers are getting on, he said, his face twisted in a sneer. He let go of her abruptly, then the door banged shut. He sat back and lit a roll-up. Sucking greedily at it, he blew a smoke ring in her face. It stung her eyes

and she wiped them with the back of her hand. Don't get any silly ideas love. Remember that wee pal of yours.

The girl wondered what they had done with the blonde. Where had they dumped her body? Not that anybody cared, she reminded herself. The bossman stood up and walked over to the cupboard. He pulled out a bottle, sloshed some clear liquid into it and passed it to her. The girl knew better now than to argue. She swallowed it quickly, feeling the burn at the back of her throat. When he passed the cigarette, she took it and inhaled. The edges of her mind became woozy again.

Let me tell you a wee story, he said. A wee story about one of our girls. Worked here for us. Had a huge debt to pay off before she could go home to her family and her wee baby. He paused to belch. Stupid cunt decided she'd had enough. Did a runner. He leaned forward suddenly and the girl shrank back. She got away, he said. But we knew where she was. We knew she was gonna testify against us in court. Stupid bitch. He took another drag from the cigarette. She was sent a wee present in the post from home. He smiled at her, baring his yellow teeth. Her wee man's foot.

The girl's eyes widened in shock and she hung her head, rubbing her fingers together quickly. Over and over.

Fancy another drink doll? You look like you could use one, he said, standing up and turning to fetch the bottle.

The girl wished she was stronger and braver. How she wanted to launch herself at him, scratch at his eyes and hit the bottle over his head. She watched him pour another glug of the liquid into the glass. This time when he handed it to her she swallowed the lot at once.

Want to know the ending to the story? he said, not waiting for her to respond. He sat down nearer her this time and the girl could smell his rancid breath. She missed us so much that she decided she'd come back and join us again, he said. She was a pretty wee thing, he said. Shame she didn't last much longer after that. She moved on to greater things. Know what I'm saying doll?

33

Megan was apprehensive as she sat down at Richard's desk. Even though she'd known him for years, his dark eyes could bore into her in a way that made her feel queasy.

He leaned forward. 'I wanted you to do a brilliant job through here and transform the team, Megan. That's why I gave you the job.'

Shit, thought Megan, here we go. He's going to fire me. No job, no prospects and nowhere to go. Washed up before I've even hit thirty.

He smiled, showing his perfect white teeth. 'The thing is, Megan, you're doing something the others aren't.'

Megan sighed. She could no longer be bothered to suppress what she was thinking. 'It's okay, Richard. Shall I just make this easier for you?'

His smile wavered. 'What do you mean?'

'Do you want me to quit?'

The smile became a puzzled frown. 'Why would I want that?'

'Because all of a sudden it seems that I'm not doing such a great job.'

He sat down and clicked his fingers. 'No. That's not what I said. Or what I want. The fact is, I am really impressed.'

'Really?' Megan's voice was doubtful.

'Yes.'

'I don't understand. So why have you called me in here?'

Richard sat back and folded his arms. 'Look, Megan. You know how it works. It's all game-playing. You scratch my back and I'll scratch yours.'

'In other words play the game by our rules or don't play it all?'

'Yes. For the moment. Look, I'm sorry Megan but I need you to hang fire just now over the trafficking piece.'

'I just don't understand why there's such reluctance over this article? Unless certain board members have something to hide?'

Richard didn't reply.

'Well, do they?'

'Don't be silly.' Richard dismissed her question with a flick of his hand.

'Then why the intervention?'

'I can't say at the moment.'

Megan gave a harsh laugh. 'Right. They want me to stick to nice, safe little articles on how to apply lipstick properly or how to give the perfect blow-job? Even better: what about I run a fashion spread on what punters like their trafficked hookers to wear?'

'Well, I think you're being a bit dramatic.'

Megan stared back at him defiantly.

'Look. Have a think about it. We'll chat later.' He looked at his watch. 'I've a meeting to get to.'

'Okay.'

'Oh — and Megan. Go easy on Paul. I know he's a bit of a tosser. But I've just been told he's been diagnosed with cancer.'

'Oh,' said Megan. Right enough she hadn't see him for a few days. She felt a flicker of guilt as she thought about the most recent run in she'd had with him. She walked back to the office and slammed her bag down on the desk. She drummed her fingers impatiently. Grabbing a pen, she pulled her large desk-pad towards her and started to make some notes. She *had* to work out a way of joining up the dots.

Any further forward on the trafficking stuff? NC

It was the fifth text she'd received from Natasha since she'd returned from Sweden and she knew her friend was getting impatient. She'd tried to give Megan an exclusive, and had promised her an interview with the Lord Advocate. She must know Megan was stalling. She didn't want to piss her off any more than she had done already.

Getting there. Just waiting to tie up a few loose ends.

Megan glanced down at her watch. It was time she was at work. Her phone buzzed again.

Sure. Keep me posted. Have some update on NM. Do you want to surf at the weekend?

NM? What did that mean? Megan couldn't think who she was referring to and was about to text her back when her phone started to ring, interrupting her train of thought.

It was Sam. 'Paul at the *News* is dead.'

Megan was shocked and it was a moment before she could react. 'What do you mean?'

'He's dead.'

'What, already? What happened?'

Sam was confused. 'What do you mean already?'

'Well I thought it had just been diagnosed.'

'Eh?'

'The cancer,' said Megan. 'I've just been told it's only just been diagnosed.'

'Cancer. He was ill?'

'Well, yes. That's what I've just been told.'

Sam paused. 'I see. Well that maybe makes sense then.'

'What do you mean?'

'I mean that would all make sense. He got hit by a train at Partick. Must have thrown himself in front of it. Maybe it was all too much.'

'Paul? No,' said Megan. 'No way. There's no way Paul would have done that.'

'How do you know? I thought you didn't like him.'

'He wasn't my favourite person,' said Megan, 'no, but I do know he hated jumpers. His brother was a train driver and had been left traumatised by the number of jumpers he'd faced. It was something he always went on about when he was in the pub.' Megan scratched her head. 'There's something very dodgy about this, Sam.'

'I think you're right,' said Sam.

'Who told you?'

'My police mate. He thought I might know him. I mean *everyone* knew him. Are you sure about this — he might not have been thinking straight.'

Megan felt a flash of frustration surge through her. 'I am telling you that Paul did not jump in front of a train. Someone pushed him. Maybe he was being followed.'

'Who by?' said Sam, dubiously.

'The other day I came out my sister's flat. I was being watched. Maybe he was being watched too . . . ? But why?' She stood up, her legs trembling. What was going on?'

'Megan. You *have to* tell me what's going on. If you think there's more to this then you have to tell me. We need to talk to the police. This could be murder.'

Megan's heart was racing and her teeth started chattering. 'I think someone has been watching me.' A shadow crossed her face. 'I thought it might have been Johnny . . . but now this has happened to Paul. But the police are not going to believe me. I need to prove it.'

Sam's voice was low and tense. 'Watch your back, Megan. I'll sniff around and see what I come up with.'

She hung up. She needed to tell Richard. He wasn't in his office, so she ran upstairs to the conference room.

'Paul is dead,' she said.

Richard missed the shot. 'What?'

'Paul is dead. Fell in front of a train.'

Richard lined up his next putt. 'Are you having a laugh?'

'No. I'm not. A mate has just rung to tell me. But I think there's more to it.'

Richard looked up. 'Good God. When did this happen?'

'The other day,' she said. 'Took them a couple of days to identify him.'

Richard's face paled and he let his putter clatter to the ground.

'But Richard, I think there's more to it.'

'What do you mean?'

Megan suddenly felt exhausted. 'I think someone pushed him in front of the train.'

THE GIRL DREAMT the man came back for her. He'd crept into her room, roused her from her sleep and beckoned her to follow him. The door of her room was ajar. When she hesitated he held out his hand. The girl grasped it. He clutched her tightly and gently tugged her alongside him. She tried to warn him about the bossman but the words wouldn't come out of her mouth. He looked at her and jerked his head towards the front door. Everything was quiet and still. She did as he said and followed, feeling the grit from the floorboards stick to her bare feet. She had nothing to take with her anyway apart from the memories. They would be etched inside her mind forever. A sense of calm fell over her as the man opened the front door. This was it, she thought to herself, she was really leaving. She was going home. Then a hand yanked her shoulder back and she woke abruptly. She was still there. In her bed, in her prison. The bossman stood sneering over her.

Having sweet dreams were you? He yawned. You look awful happy when you're sleeping. He laughed and dug his hand deeply into his pocket, pulling out a small foil packet. He threw it at her. Your tablets, doll. Make sure you take them. We dinnae want any accidents do we? He walked away, whistling, then suddenly stopped and turned. Mind you that might do it for some. He rubbed his hands together. I'll do a wee bit research and get back to you on that. Take them the now. He turned, slammed the door behind him and turned the key. The memory of the dream was so vivid the girl couldn't believe she was still there. She reached out for the foil and clutched it in her palm. Pushing out a tablet for day one, she swallowed it.

She'd always dreamed one day of having her own family. But not like this. Panic gripped hold of her chest and her breathing became shallow. Could they really do that to her? Force her to get pregnant? She needed to think about what to do if they took the pills away. She needed the man to come back for her. It was her only option right now. Yet he would surely turn out to be a liar. Just like everyone else.

34

After work that night, Richard insisted on taking them to the pub. 'I think we could all do with a stiff drink,' he said.

News of Paul's death was now widely known throughout the building and everyone was in shock. There was general disbelief that their colleague had committed suicide.

'You never can tell with people,' said Ronnie knowingly as they walked to the pub. 'It's a growing crisis, and the biggest killer of men under forty-five.'

Sunita shrugged. 'But he didn't seem all that depressed.'

Ronnie looked at her and raised his eyebrows. 'Well he would never have said anything would he? I mean how often do you ask people how they are and they say they're fine?'

Sunita chewed her lip. 'True,' she admitted. 'It's just that he didn't seem down or depressed . . . I mean I know he could be a miserable bastard. But I didn't think life was that bad.'

'Did you know he'd been diagnosed with cancer?' said Megan.

Sunita and Ronnie both looked puzzled. 'Really?'

Megan nodded.

'That kind of makes more sense now,' said Sunita, as if the penny had finally dropped. 'Poor guy.'

Megan decided to keep her suspicions to herself for the moment. She didn't see the point in clouding things any further, especially when everyone was still in shock.

'Come on troops,' said Richard who had walked on ahead. He stood holding the door of the pub open. 'It's not often drinks are on me.'

'That's for sure,' muttered Ronnie.

'What was that?' Richard said, raising an eyebrow.

'I said that would be very nice,' he said.

Katherine had already left, so it was just Megan, with Ronnie and Sunita and a couple of the subs. Their local bar was in Ashton Lane and was packed. Even Richard groaned as he fought his way to the bar.

Megan wasn't really in the mood for this. She was shocked about Paul, worried that she was being watched and wanted to go home. Joanna had taken George away to Crieff Hydro for the night. She had been looking forward to having a lazy and indulgent night on the sofa followed by a lie-in, without seeing or speaking to anyone.

'Over there,' said Megan, pointing to a group who were pulling on their coats. 'Grab their table.'

Ronnie managed to grab the bar and a couple of stools and guarded them, a fierce look on his face.

'Goodness me,' said Richard when he spotted him. 'If only he would apply such passion to his job.'

Megan sniggered.

'The usual,' he said.

'Yes please,' said Megan.

Richard signalled to the woman behind the bar, ordered the round and then turned to Megan who was waiting to give him a hand. 'How you doing Megan? Is everything okay?'

Megan looked at him, curious. 'What do you mean?'

'Em, it's just that you look a bit tired and . . . well you're working hard. I don't want you overdoing it. And today's news has been a bit of a shocker.'

Megan shrugged. 'I'm fine. Though thanks for asking. It's just been a bit of a week,' she said, not knowing what more to say.

'Aye it has been a bit of a week.'

'I just can't believe it about Paul.'

Richard leaned closer. 'I think you might be right, Megan. I think there may be more to this. Something funny's going on just now and I can't quite put my finger on it.' He leaned back and took a sip of his drink.

Megan stood for a moment in silence. Richard was never normally so open about things with her. She wasn't sure whether to laugh or cry. 'Cheers,' she said when he handed her glass. 'To Paul. Shall we go and join the others?'

It was noisy and crowded and she had to shout to make herself heard. After about an hour, she tried to fight her way to the ladies' toilet and glanced over to see Craig deep in conversation with Sunita. He'd not bothered to even say hello to Megan since he arrived and when she saw him ensconced with someone else she decided that she would rather be at home. She was shattered. 'I'm off now, Richard,' she said, pulling on her jacket. 'See you later.'

'You make sure and get a taxi back,' he said. 'Do you want me to see you into one?'

Megan laughed weakly. 'No. But thanks. I'll be fine. The rank is only out there.' She shuddered as she remembered Sam's warning. As she walked out of the pub and down the lane, once again she had the feeling that she was being watched.

The corners of the man's mouth turned up into a wry smile as he walked towards her. She sat watching from her chair in the corner as his hand reached up. Then his palm smacked against her cheek. A bubble of sick crept into the back of her mouth but she managed to swallow it back. Look at me will yay, he said, looping his hand through her hair and yanking her head hard. It was the fifth time he had done this since he'd arrived. Sometimes the men smelt of aftershave or cigarette smoke. But this man stank of

piss. The girl's head hurt but he wasn't the type to care. He flipped her over on her stomach, her cheek pressed against the damp floor.

As she lay there, she caught a glimpse of the small patch of grey sky, which hadn't quite been covered up by the plywood on the window. There were thick curtains too, old and dirty and splattered with blood. She thought maybe the blood belonged to the girl who lived in the room before her. The girl wondered briefly what had happened to her. She could hear the wind whipping around the window and thought maybe her own blood might join the pattern of swirls. She closed her eyes again and lay there like a rag doll, while the man finished grunting. He heaved himself off her and she listened as he zipped up his trousers and cleared his throat. Then he spat on her as he left the room. She lay there for a few minutes no longer able to sob. All she wanted was her mum. But she realised that she would probably never see her again. Slowly, she picked herself up off the floor, brushed herself down and brushed her hair, like she'd been told.

35

A few days later, as Megan sat at her desk chewing on a pen, her landline began to ring. 'Hello.'

'Megan, it's me. Joanna. I've just had a call from the school. It's George. He's not there. He's missing.'

'What? Since when?' Megan was gripping her phone hard.

'Since lunchtime. He was in the playground and didn't come back into the classroom. None of his classmates seem to know what happened.' Joanna's voice was on the verge of becoming hysterical.

'Okay, Joanna. Listen to me,' said Megan in what she hoped was a calm, practical tone. 'Where are you?'

'At work,' she said, her voice a whisper.

'You go home and check in case he's there. Go right now and phone me when you get there. I will walk round to the school right now, okay, and phone you when I get there.' Megan hung up and ran out the office, grabbing her jacket. She started to retrace the steps she took on the mornings after she had dropped him his school. Then she called Jamie.

'Hi it's Megan. Sorry to bother you,' she said.

'That's okay.' His tone was curt.

'Look. I need your help. It's my nephew. George. He's gone missing from school.'

'What? Where are you just now?' he said.

'I've just left the office and I'm on my way to the school. It's on Hyndland Road.'

'I know it. I'll meet you there,' he said.

As Megan walked briskly, scanning the street ahead, she felt growingly uneasy. What if something had happened to him? Was he being watched too? Had she put his life in danger? She willed Joanna to call her. Maybe he'd just got fed up at school. Perhaps he was at home watching TV. Megan knew he had a key for emergencies. The school was less than five minutes away from Byres Road but there was no sign of George or any kids as she approached the locked gates. Pressing the buzzer, she willed someone to answer quickly.

'Hello,' said a voice.

'Hi. This is Megan Ross — George Ross's aunt.'

'Oh. Please come in.'

There was a hiss and Megan swung the gate open and walked through the empty playground. She frantically cast her eyes around wondering if there was anywhere that George could possibly be hiding. Joanna's number flashed up on the screen. 'Is he there?' she said.

'No,' said Joanna, her voice trembling.

'Right, think Joanna. Is there anywhere else he might have gone to?'

Joanna had started to sob. 'No. He's never done anything like this before.'

'I'm at the school,' said Megan softly. 'You stay where you are and I'll phone you back.'

The head teacher was standing waiting for Megan at the door. 'I'm Megan Ross. George's aunt,' she said, trying to sound bright though she felt anything but. 'I've just spoken with my sister. She went home to check whether George had gone there.'

'I'm Mrs Bradley,' said the woman sticking out her hand to

Megan. 'I just don't know how this could have happened. We have playground monitors. The gates are locked.' Her face was strained.

Megan looked around again. 'Is there any way he could have climbed over?'

The head's cheeks flushed. 'Well — they know not to. I mean, there is a small hole in the fence that we've been waiting to have fixed. But . . . well, it doesn't matter. The children know they shouldn't go near it. The janitor had tried to patch it up.'

Megan studied her for a moment. The poor woman was in a state of shock. 'Okay. I think you should call the police,' said Megan.

She nodded. 'Yes,' she said. 'I have done that. They're on their way.'

'Okay. Well in the meantime I'm going to start looking for him.'

'But the police?'

Megan shrugged. 'Who knows when they'll get here. I can't just stand around waiting . . .'

'I'm so sorry this has happened.'

Megan could see the worry in her eyes. 'Let's just focus on finding him. Here's my card with my number,' she said, taking her card out of her pocket. 'Keep in touch and let me know what the police say.'

The woman's face paled when she read Megan's job title on the card. 'Oh God. You're a journalist.'

Megan smiled reassuringly at her. 'Don't worry – just now I'm only George's auntie and at the moment he is all I care about.' She turned and walked away then dialled Joanna's number. 'Joanna. The head teacher has called the police. I've told her you are at home in case George appears there. I'm going to look for him.'

Joanna's voice was strained. 'Megan . . . what if something has happened to him? My baby.'

Megan forced herself to remain calm. 'Come on. Don't think like that. We'll find him. I promise.' Why did she just say that? She couldn't promise anything. She forced herself to take a few deep breaths. 'I'll phone you as soon as there's any news. Keep in touch.' Megan walked out of the school and stood for a moment wondering which way George could have gone if he had decided he'd had enough of school. She glanced down the street and saw a black car slowing down. It pulled up and stopped beside her. She staggered back slightly as the driver leapt out and ran towards her. What the hell was going on?

The girl pressed her clammy forehead against the car's tinted window. She stared at the sky heavy with dark clouds, rubbish blowing across the pavements and a man who had stumbled into a doorway to vomit. A blur of glowing colours flashed in front on her eyes and she turned to take a long, deep drag of her cigarette. The boss sat in the passenger seat talking quietly to the driver. The girl shifted uncomfortably in her seat, her bare legs sticking to the cool leather. Earlier, when she'd been to the toilet, she'd wiped away thick, dark clots. She was sore everywhere. Constantly aching and dirty. Her mind was woolly, she wasn't sure how long they had been at that party. A few hours maybe? Or even days? She picked at the scab on her knee. How much had she had to drink? Where were the others? Suddenly the driver jerked the car around, ignoring the blaring horns, and sped back the way they had come. The girl shrugged and flicked her gaze back to the street and its dirty tenement buildings looming against the slate grey sky. A few buses wheezed past and a police car, its siren blaring, raced past.

What you playing at, shouted the boss. I'm going back, said the driver. The boss didn't speak for a moment. The girl's breath quickened and she looked down, tracing her thumb over the bracelet of bruises around her wrist. Pull over, said the boss in a sour tone. The driver glanced over but didn't stop. The girl's eyes widened as she stared at the driver. I said pull over, repeated the boss, now jabbing a gun into the driver's neck. The car skidded to a stop. The girl held her breath. She knew the boss wouldn't hesitate to shoot him. Alright, said the driver. No need for any of that business, he said, jerking his head towards the gun.

36

'Come on. Get in,' said Jamie, his voice calm and even.

Megan was surprised at how relieved she was to see him. She had to stay calm for her sister's sake but inside she was in turmoil. She was petrified that something awful had happened to George.

'Thanks,' she said, pulling open the door. She slid in next to him and took a deep breathe, willing herself to remain strong.

'Okay. Let's think rationally about this,' said Jamie staring ahead. 'The police will ask your sister all the usual questions about his friends and what his routine normally is. But you're his aunt. You've got a bit of perspective.'

Megan sat back in the passenger seat, exhaling. 'Okay,' she said, waiting for him to continue.

'Has he had any problems? Or mentioned anything unusual?'

'Yes,' she said. 'Yes! He asked about his dad. He wanted to know why he wasn't around.'

'Okay. Where is his dad?' said Jamie, starting the ignition.

'He's not around and never has been. George doesn't even know his name.'

'Are you absolutely certain of that?'

Megan nodded. 'As certain as I can be,' she said, rubbing her thumb against the palm of her hand.

'But this is something that has been on his mind?'

'Well, yes,' said Megan. 'He mentioned it to me the other week.

'Okay. So tell me what does he like to do?'

Megan fumbled around desperately for answers. 'He does Judo. And he wants to go surfing. I promised him I would take him. And he likes going to the park. . .'

'Which park?' said Jamie.

'The one by the school. And the one at the Botanics.'

He glanced in the rear-view mirror and then pulled out. 'Let's head there and you keep an eye out.'

Megan felt as though the short journey to the Botanics was a long-haul flight. She drummed her fingers on her lap, constantly checked her phone whilst scanning the street and pavements around her.

'When did the school notice he was missing?' asked Jamie as they waited at the traffic lights to turn onto Byres Road.

She glanced at her watch. 'I think at the end of lunchtime. The kids must go out in the playground about twelve thirty. The alarm wasn't raised until after one. And it's now almost two.'

'Okay,' said Jamie, softly. He reached over and patted her hand, then grasped it tightly for a minute. He let go when the lights turned to green.

'What if someone's taken him?' she said in a low voice.

'Taken him?' asked Jamie glancing across at her. The traffic was slow moving and the car was at a standstill.

Megan nodded.

'Who would have taken him?'

'I think someone has been following me,' she said.

'What! Why didn't you say anything?' said Jamie.

'Because I couldn't be sure. I don't know if I was being paranoid.'

'Oh bloody hell, Megan. You should have said something to me.'

'I didn't want to make a big deal out of it,' she croaked.

'Well, you should have said something. Honestly.' Jamie's mouth was set in a tight-line and he pulled into a space close to the gate.

'I just don't think he would have come here,' said Megan doubtfully. 'What if something terrible has happened?' Her voice was panicked now and at that moment she hated herself. She would never forgive herself if someone had taken George.

'Football,' interrupted Jamie. 'You said he was a Partick Thistle fan.'

'Yes,' said Megan, confused.

'Does he know how to get there? To the stadium?'

'I don't know.' Megan's voice was growing desperate. 'I mean I think he's been to a match before with Joanna. But he's only ten. I don't know if he would know.'

Jamie raised an eyebrow. 'You'd be surprised at how much a smart ten-year-old can do.'

'Well plenty of time for him to catch a bus.'

'But it's still a long way.'

'I reckon it would take him half an hour on the bus at the most. And then a short walk.' Jamie tightened his grip on the steering wheel as he pulled out of the space and back onto Queen Margaret Drive.

'What makes you so certain this is what's happened?'

'Because,' said Jamie, 'it's very unusual for children to disappear from their school playground, especially when the gates are locked. It sounds like he's managed to find a wee gap and escape. He's seen it as an opportunity.'

Megan's breath started to steady. His certainty was reassuring and she hoped he was right.

'I ran away when I was a kid,' he said, glancing over at her.

'You did?'

He nodded. 'My parents were getting divorced and the house was always noisy.'

'Where did you go?'

'The very same place I'm hoping we find your nephew.' He hesitated for a moment. 'Mind you — we did stay a bit closer. Not too far from here,' he said, pointing at the row of tenements in Fergus Drive.

Neither of them spoke for a while. Megan kept checking her phone for updates from Joanna. But there was no news from her end. Megan just hoped Jamie's hunch was right. She pressed her face against the window as he pulled off and drove down Northpark Street.

Megan saw the block of student flats ahead just as they came to a T-junction. 'Look,' she said, pointing to the right. 'There's a bus.'

Jamie took a right and drove slowly, waiting for the bus to pull in at its stop. The street was quiet, apart from a student carrying a packed bag of groceries. The bus hissed and drove away.

'Look,' she said, unclipping her seatbelt and opening the door. She ran ahead to the small figure she saw huddled in the bus-stop.

'Is it him?' said Jamie appearing beside her.

'Yes. He wears a blue jacket. That's him. George,' she yelled. 'George.'

He looked up, his face white and streaked with tears.

Megan threw her arms around him. 'George. There you are. We were so worried.'

He clung to her and started to cry again. 'I'm sorry Auntie Megan. I'm sorry.'

'You're okay. You're okay. Oh George. What a fright you gave us.'

'I'm sorry Auntie Megan. I just wanted to see the stadium. I didn't think it would take that long.'

'It's okay,' she said, rubbing his back. 'It's okay. But I need to phone mum, okay? She is *so* worried about you.' Megan pulled out her phone and dialled Joanna's number.

'Megan?' she said.

'I've got him,' she said. 'I've got him and he's fine.'

'Where are you?' Joanna stifled a sob.

'Bloody Firhill. We'll be back soon.' Megan looked over at Jamie who was watching from a distance. 'Thank you,' she mouthed.

Jamie gave her a small smile and a shrug.

THE GIRL WATCHED the driver's shoulders tremble beneath his leather jacket. The boss clicked the gun and the smell of piss filled the air. Think you call the shots do you, said the boss. Naw . . . I just thought we should get the others, the driver said, his voice trembling. Did you now? Silence. The others? The boss gave a hard, brittle chuckle. 'There are no others you fuckwit. They're all gone. Gone, whispered the driver. Aye. Gone, said the boss with a click of fingers. Just like that. But that wasn't part of the deal, the driver said slowly. With a smile, the boss jabbed the driver again with the gun. Deal. What deal? You stupid fuck. There is no deal. The boss pointed ahead. Bet you wished you'd stuck in with the train driving, eh? Now you do as you're told otherwise we'll be making a detour past the Clyde. The driver turned the keys in the ignition and gripped the steering wheel. The girl stared at his white knuckles, then turned to watch the raindrops which were now sliding down the window. She knew the clock was ticking. She was damaged goods, with her cold sores and bruises and her straggly hair. I could just get rid of you now, the boss had told her earlier. But someone else can do that for me. And they'll pay me lots for the privilege. The girl shuddered. The blonde woman had talked about that. How men would pay to watch girls like her die. She thought about her friend, the blonde. She closed her eyes and thought about home. She had happy, sunny memories of being a child. Never could she have imagined that this is what would become of her. She wondered if her family would ever want her back after what had happened to her. She would bring shame on them if they knew what she had done. How could she even get back home?

37

Megan hadn't slept well. The wind had howled around the windows all night and she couldn't stop thinking about what had happened. To George and to Paul. Bloody Glasgow weather, she thought, as she opened the blinds in the lounge. Megan had never imagined that she would miss Edinburgh, but she was beginning to long for its drier climate. Mind you, at least the people here made her laugh. That did something to make up for the rain and gales.

She knew after yesterday's excitement that Joanna and George would still be fast asleep. The police had been, the head teacher had popped by and George had certainly learned his lesson. He would never try and skive off school again. Or take any solo trips to Firhill any time soon. Megan smiled when she thought of Jamie's promise to George, whose eyes had widened in excitement when he realised they supported the same team. 'How about I take you some time?' he had asked. George was beyond excited.

She padded through to the kitchen to make some coffee. Something had started to niggle at the back of her mind as she thought back to something Jamie had said to her when he'd brought her and George home. She had insisted he come in for a cup of tea and to meet Joanna. While she and George spoke to the police and the teacher, Megan had taken him into the kitchen.

'Did I tell you about my wee argument with the boss the other day?'

Megan shook her head.

'She's getting impatient about the two Nigerian girls. Wants to shut it down. Says we've had plenty of time to get to the bottom of it and having the deaths unsolved, as she put it, was not helping us reach our targets.' He gave a short, bitter laugh. 'She sat there tracing her finger over the pile of papers on her desk and said that some of the city councillors were starting to ask questions. That they were complaining that there was too much negative attention surrounding the force just now. That we needed some good news. Something positive to focus on.'

'What, so she wants you just to write them off?'

'Aye. Can you believe it?"

'I can, actually. Nothing surprises me.'

'I told her she was being short-sighted and that these investigations take time.'

'How did she take it?'

'Um, not so well. Said that there are no witnesses, no sightings, nothing. And if we have nothing to go on then we can't be seen to be wasting our budget. Everyone is having to watch their spending right now.'

'It always comes down to money, doesn't it? Even with the police.'

'Aye, well I haven't told you the latest development. That soon shut her up.'

'What's that?' Megan's interest was suddenly piqued.

'My contact in the lab called me last night. The blood tests are back.'

'And?'

Jamie drained the rest of his tea. 'Looks like both women were HIV positive.'

As Megan waited for the kettle to boil, she thought about what he had said. There was a missing link and she felt as though she was getting closer. She just couldn't work out what it was. Carefully spooning the coffee into the cafetiere, she added the water and stirred the granules. She waited for a moment and then plunged the lid down, inhaling the scent of the Colombian blend. Megan closed her eyes as she took her first sip of the scalding drink. Why would Paul throw himself in front of a train? He wouldn't. It made no sense. Her eyes snapped open. She was sure someone had pushed Paul. He obviously knew something that he shouldn't. But what? She tried to quickly mentally scan through all the brief, sarcastic exchanges they'd had lately. had said he'd been hanging about more than he usually did. Why was he so obsessed with what *I* was doing? What was it he had said about the girls at the police conference? Something about drugs? But then she'd just assumed he'd made that up to fool her. Helping her out on stories certainly wasn't his style. If only she could get in touch with Sam. But his phone seemed to be permanently switched off and he'd not opened her Facebook messages or replied to her emails.

She decided that a run would help clear her head before she went into the office. And besides, her Fitbit had been adding to her guilt by regularly buzzing to remind her that she hadn't reached her steps target for the current hour or day – or actually *any* day. She pulled on her leggings and a sweatshirt, and scraped her hair into a ponytail. Then slipped on her trainers by the door. Megan gulped in the fresh, damp air as she jogged down up Clarence Drive and then onto Hyndland Road. She wasn't sure what route she would take. She just let her breath finds its rhythm, focused her eyes ahead and ran.

*S**he opened* *her eyes and watched as the boss muttered to the driver. She couldn't make out what they were saying. The car turned down a side street that she didn't recognise. Where were they going? Why weren't they going back to the flat? The car slowed and stopped. The girl looked up at the boarded windows on the red sandstone block above the row of shops, with heavy grilles on the windows. A sunbed salon and a grocer's. Maybe the*

boss needed more cigarettes. Drop us here and wait for me. Moving closer to the driver, the boss's mouth was pressed against his ear. And don't ever fuckin' try anything like that again. The girl caught the driver's gaze in the rear-view mirror and she felt the familiar surge of nausea rise from the pit of her stomach. She trembled and clenched her fists together, trying to steel herself. Was this it then? She had to do something. But what? How could she get away? He had a gun. The bossman slid out of the car and she frantically looked back at the busy street they'd come from. Would anyone notice if she screamed? Would they care? The bossman turned, waiting for her to follow as usual. The girl sat there, her knees knocking together, her teeth chattering. This was it. She would never see her family again. She was going to die. She looked pleadingly at the driver. Then she glanced down at her spiky-heeled stilettoes. Could she make a dash for it when she got out of the car? Should she try and run? She watched as the bossman sneezed, then reached to open her door. Then his mobile rang. He paused and snatched his hand back, reaching into a pocket to pull out the phone. The girl stared as he started to laugh, his mouth wide open exposing the mercury fillings in his molars. The girl looked again at the driver and in that split second she knew this was her chance. I'm gonna talk to him, the driver said. I'm not going to lock the doors. The girl slipped off her shoes, moved as quickly as she could out of the other side of the car. Then the girl ran.

38

The rain was falling in steady sheets and Megan turned into Dumbarton Road where a bus, lurching in and out of a pothole, sprayed her with dirt. She ran harder and faster, slapping her feet beneath her. Wiping the beads of rainwater from her face, she looked up at the red sandstone flats above the rows of shops ahead. A sunbed shop, with a luminous yellow sign, a shabby-looking medical centre and a grubby-looking sandwich shop. She felt a quiver of panic when a drunken man banged into her. Then pity for him when he mumbled 'sorry' and stumbled on. She dodged an elderly lady pushing an empty supermarket trolley.

Her chest felt tight as Johnny popped into her mind. Then she realised she'd actually managed a day or two without thinking or worrying about him. Though she knew she would have to face him sooner or later. Megan saw a commotion ahead. Someone ran onto the road. Why weren't they stopping? It was a girl. And she wasn't stopping. Neither was the orange double-decker bus heading straight towards her. It bounced in a pothole, someone shouted, there was a scream, a squeal of brakes, then a thud and a thwack. A moment of silence. Then more screeching brakes and a bang. The sound of a car slamming into the one in front. Then another shout. 'Someone call the polis and an ambulance. A lassie's been hit.'

Megan twisted behind her to see a man frantically shouting in his phone. Shopkeepers were gathered in the doorways, watching.

'It's okay. They're coming. They're on the way,' shouted the man.

Rain dribbled down Megan's face. She made herself walk on, people were out of their cars now, there was nothing she could do. As she passed the spot where the girl had been hit she glanced over. All she could see was a crumpled heap on the road. A woman was beside her, cradling her head. Someone had covered her with a jacket. There was a dark shadow on the road. Megan wondered if it was oil, or rain. It seemed too dark to be blood. She needed to go home, wanted to get away. Horns were blaring, help would soon be here. An elderly woman ahead of her stood staring, then gave a gargling sob. Turning away, Megan retraced her steps and returned home.

'You're not too bad with a mop,' she said as she walked in the front door to find Joanna mopping the floors.

'One of my many talents.' She pointed at Megan's wet trainers. 'Watch your feet.'

'How's things? Is George still asleep?' Megan sat down at the door and pulled off her shoes.

'Yes,' she said. 'I'm going to let him have the day off. I think he's exhausted after all the excitement. It'll give us a chance to have a chat about things.' She bent down to wipe the floor with an old towel.

Megan looked at her sister fondly. Cleaning had always been her way of coping. She noticed Joanna's normally perfect nails were now ragged and chewed. Megan could barely imagine what she had gone through yesterday. She herself had been terrified that something awful had happened to George, and it must have been so much worse for Joanna.

'Have a good run?' she said, looking up.

'Not really.' She sat down at the door and pulled off her shoes. 'I saw a girl being knocked over on Dumbarton Road. Looked pretty bad.'

'Oh dear. That's not so good.'

Megan shrugged. 'No. It was horrid. Anyway — guess I'd better get ready for work.'

39

Half an hour later Megan was about to walk up the steps to the office when a teenager cut in front of her. She had her iPhone plugged into her ears and Megan could hear the thump of the bass. 'Watch where you're going,' she muttered.

'Megan Ross?'

Megan turned round to see the teenage girl looking at her warily.

'Who wants to know?'

'I've got something for you,' she said. 'Delivery from Sam.' She reached into the Morrisons shopping-bag she was carrying and held out a padded envelope.

Megan's pulse quickened. 'From Sam?'

'Aye.'

Where is he?'

'Dunno. I'm just doing as I'm told. Do you want it or not?'

Megan reached to take the package from her. 'Thank you.'

'No bother,' said the girl. 'See ya.'

The yellow envelope was thick. Her name was written on a white label in spidery handwriting that she recognised. She ran in through the doors, nodding at the security guard, dumped her bags on the floor by her desk and ripped the envelope open.

'You okay?' said Ronnie from across the office.

'Mmm.' Megan didn't look up as she shook the contents onto her desk. Her hands spread out several photographs, her fingers sticking to the glossy paper. It was a series of shots of people, men, going in and coming out of a building which looked as though it was somewhere in the West End. A tenement building with a close, which looked familiar. Megan frowned. Where was it? And a picture of a girl. A young black girl. Then she noticed the memory stick which had also fallen out of the envelope, and a note with a scribbled message on it.

Megan,

If you've got these then you know things have got a bit tricky and I'm laying low. I know I was taking a big chance going in there. But I had nothing to lose. Us freelancers have to earn a living, right? And I thought I could help you. The girl is one of several. She said her name was Idoto or Ito something. I couldn't make it out. Then she said she gets called Mercy. She said she was from Nigeria. I promised I would go back and help her. But they're onto me. And I don't want to end up like Paul. Megan, will you please help her. The others, well, you can work out who they are, can't you? Dirty pricks. Hope they get all that is coming to them. Good luck with it. I'll be in touch. And be careful.

Sam

Megan felt a prickle down her spine and she shivered. She had been right about Sam and Paul. She knew something wasn't right with Sam, and she had a hunch he'd maybe gone off to Barcelona. Not that she would be telling anyone that. She sat there for a moment, too stunned to speak. She rubbed her eyes, knowing they were bloodshot and swollen. Then she picked up the memory stick and was about to slot it into her computer when she decided it might be safer to use a device not linked to work. Just in case their systems were being monitored. She walked over to Ronnie's desk.

'What you doing?' he said huffily, shutting his Facebook page down. He always brought his own Mac into work. He said it gave him something to put in the manbag he liked to wear.

'I've got this memory stick. Can we see what's on it?'

'I hope you're not going to get me into trouble with dodgy pictures Megan. Is it porn?'

'No,' she said, pleading. 'I hope not. I don't trust mine and this is what we're waiting for, Ronnie. Stuff for the trafficking piece.'

He rolled his eyes, snatched the stick from Megan and slotted it in. Then he began clicking on the folder of the images. They were copies of the pictures on Megan's desk.

'Fuck me,' said Ronnie.

Megan stood in silence and watched as Ronnie clicked through the images of men including an MSP, a judge and a football club chairman. There were other faces, including one who looked strangely familiar but which she couldn't immediately place.

'What do you want me to do with them?'

'Can you make copies please? And not a word to anyone for now. I need to think.' She waited for Ronnie to save the copies, then he clicked on another folder. It was video footage. Ronnie opened it and allowed it to play. It was footage from inside the building. A dark, dank stairwell and boarded up doors. Then the footage cut to show the inside of a room. Megan sat down next to Ronnie, the pair of them silent as the camera moved slowly around the dimly-lit space.

'Jeez,' said Megan. 'What a shit-hole.'

The footage ended and Ronnie sat back, his face pale.

Megan stood up and walked back to her desk, shaking her head at what she'd just seen. She picked up the pictures again and slowly she sifted through them again. Then she gasped, catching her breath. Closing her eyes, she allowed herself a moment. 'I don't believe it.' Pushing her chair back, she stood up and started to pace.

'You okay, Megan?' said Ronnie, looking over.

She looked blankly at him and nodded. Snatching up her phone, she walked out of the office and called Jamie.

'We need to talk,' she said.

'Okay. What is it?'

'I've just been sent some pictures. Of a brothel.'

She heard Jamie take a sharp inward breath.

'McGregor *is* involved isn't he?'

Jamie lowered his voice. 'I'm not sure what you're talking about.'

A surge of anger flashed through Megan. 'Yes, you are.'

Jamie exhaled loudly through his mouth. A sigh of resignation.

'You may as well confirm it to me Jamie. I have a picture of him standing outside it with several well-known men.'

'Look,' he said, reluctantly. 'This can't come from me. I'll get the bloody sack if anyone finds out I've been telling you stuff.'

'So I am right then?' said Megan.

Jamie's silence spoke volumes.

40

Something about the body in the Botanics was niggling at the back of Megan's mind when she arrived home later that night. Joanna was working and George was still out at judo. She reached up into the kitchen cupboard and poured herself a large measure of Macallan. The pale liquid slid down her throat and she stood there for a moment enjoying the burning sensation trickling down her throat. Kicking off her shoes, she sat down at the table. It had been a long day. When she'd spoken to Richard he'd looked ashen-faced. He'd called her half an hour later to tell her not to mention the contents of Sam's envelope to anyone. She'd heard nothing from Jamie since and she couldn't help feeling disappointed. As she sat nursing her drink, she reached for her mobile and called her contact at the morgue.

'The nail-varnish,' said Megan. 'Was it the same colour on both feet?'

'I cannae remember. I'll check and call you back.'

It didn't take him long. 'Pink. It was bright pink.'

'Thanks,' said Megan. 'I owe you one.' She finished off her whisky, poured another, then called Joanna. 'It's me. What did you say Rhona did at the shelter?'

'She comes in and does wee treatments for the women there.'

'Does she paint their toenails?'

'Yes,' said Joanna. 'Why are you asking?'

'I'd just like to talk to her,' Megan said impatiently.

'She's here just now.'

'Don't let her leave,' said Megan, pulling her shoes back on. 'I'll be there soon.'

She called a taxi and, while she waited, looked longingly at the drink sitting on the kitchen worktop. It would have to wait.

Ten minutes later she was pacing the reception area at the refuge waiting for Joanna to come downstairs and sign her in.

'What's the matter?' Joanna tugged at her lanyard.

'I've got some pictures. I just want to show them to her.'

'Okay ... well, take it easy. I don't want you freaking her out. She's prone to anxiety attacks.'

Megan shook her head. 'I won't. This won't take long.'

'Come on. She's having a break in the kitchen.'

She followed Joanna back up the stairs into a stark white kitchen, made even harsher by the strip-lighting, where Rhona sat dipping a biscuit into her mug of tea. It crumbled into the mug as she looked up and saw Megan.

'Don't worry,' said Megan. 'I just want to show you some pictures. Just want to check if you recognise anyone.' She reached her hand into her bag, not taking her gaze off Rhona's pale face.

'Megan, come on,' said Joanna. 'Do we have to do this right now?'

'Yes. It's important.' She stared at Rhona. 'Can you tell me if you recognise this place, Rhona? Or any of the people?'

Rhona bit her lip and looked up at Megan. She reached out and took the pictures from her. Megan watched her reactions as she looked through all the shots. She handed them back and nodded.

'Do you know where that is?'

Rhona nodded.

'Have you been there?'

She nodded again. 'Yes. It's not that far from my house.'

'Why did you go there?' asked Megan, gently.

Rhona looked at Joanna. 'Am I going to get in trouble?'

'No.' Joanna frowned at her sister. 'Not if you tell the truth.'

'I went there. Just to do some nails and things. I needed the money.'

'Who asked you to go?'

'The man.'

'Which man?' Megan was trying desperately to keep her voice calm.

'At the club.'

'Do you remember his name?'

Rhona nodded.

'Can you tell me?'

Rhona glanced over at Joanna, blinking hard.

'It's okay, Rhona. You can tell her if you know.'

'Warren. Warren McGregor,' she whispered.

Megan's heart was thudding. 'Thank you.' She pointed at the other picture with the judge and the MSP. 'Do you recognise these men?'

Rhona nodded. 'I, I saw him on the telly the other night.' She pointed at the politician.

'Thank you. Thanks Rhona. That's all I need to know for now.'

'Are you going to tell the police?' she said, her voice cracking.

Megan didn't reply.

'Because I don't want to talk to them. I don't want any trouble.'

Megan pursed her lips together. 'I can't force you to, Rhona. But these are bad men. You might be the only witness.'

'I'm not saying anything.'

'It's okay,' said Joanna. Her voice was soothing. 'Megan, come on. That's enough. It's time you went.'

Megan couldn't argue, especially as Joanna now had her hand on her arm and was steering her towards the kitchen door. 'I'll trust you to see yourself out,' she said curtly. 'I'll see you at home. I'll be back soon.'

'Okay. Thanks, Joanna.'

But she gave Megan a tight smile. 'Please go.'

~

THE NEXT DAY Jamie called Megan to tell her the police were re-examining the circumstances of Paul's death.

'Finally,' she said. 'Let's hope your lot can work out what has been going on.'

'I'll keep you posted,' he said.

'Okay. Thanks.' She wanted to say more but didn't know where to begin. Instead she sighed. 'I need to go. I've a meeting with Richard in a minute.'

'Good luck. Bye.'

She put down the phone. She didn't have time to dwell on Jamie just now. Megan had to find a way to move this story along. Though she knew there was no way Richard would agree to printing the allegations or the pictures. Not when one or more of their own board was involved. It was far too messy, not to mention the potential links to the owners of the media group. No wonder there had been such resistance over the investigation. Megan glanced at her watch. It was time to talk to Richard. As she predicted, when she walked into his office he could barely meet her eye. He stood, leaning against his desk, attempting to look relaxed as he rolled a golf ball around in his hands.

'Playing with your balls again?' Megan strode in and took a seat, not waiting to be invited.

'Sit down, make yourself comfortable.' He placed the ball on his desk. He tried to smile, but was showing too many teeth — which was a tell-tale sign.

Megan frowned. 'This doesn't bode well.'

'Well,' he said, scratching his chin, 'It's a bit of a sensitive situation. I mean it doesn't look good does it? Plus, the lawyers are having none of it. It's all far too defamatory without actual proof.'

Megan snorted. 'But you have the proof. The pictures. What else do you need?' She wanted to tell him that she had found a witness who could confirm she had seen the men. But she knew there was no way Rhona would talk to the police.

'I know.' He shrugged his shoulders. 'It's just not tight enough for them to allow us to run with. I mean it's all a bit bloody embarrassing, isn't it?'

'Are you losing your nerve, then?'

'No. I just think we need more.'

'As I expected.' Her voice was steady but venomous as she spoke. 'Though I have to say, Richard, this is so unlike you. What happened to the old Richard? The one who loved the chase of a story and getting to the truth?'

Richard sighed. 'He got a bit broken.'

'Who is putting pressure on you though? I mean, surely you have the upper hand here now?' Megan's face paled as the pennies started to drop. 'Unless . . . Richard — is there something you're not telling me?'

'What do you mean?'

'I don't know. You tell me.'

A flash of anger crossed his face. 'Look, Megan. I am telling you that we can't run with this at the moment. Please leave it and trust my decision.'

'It's okay. I get it. You don't want to rock the corporate boat.'

'Look Megan, even if I did fight them it wouldn't make any difference. It's not up to me. It's the powers above. They have the final say.'

'And do they want to cover their sordid tracks or something? God it's like the Westminster old-boys' network.' Megan eyed him up and down. 'Nothing ever changes, does it?'

He had the grace to look embarrassed. 'It's not the old-boys' network, Megan. I think you'll find there is a very powerful woman at the head of it.'

Megan pulled a face. 'What do you mean?'

'I've said enough.'

'Of course you have. Whereas you have in fact said bugger all. You're talking in riddles, Richard. Who are you talking about?'

'I'm not saying anything else. Megan, listen to me. You need to leave it now. There's a lot going on behind the scenes that you don't know about. Trust me when I say leave it.'

'Fine. But I hope you do realise that you leave me with no option, Richard? I quit.' She stood up and turned to leave.

He coughed. 'Come on now. Stop being so bloody dramatic. I'm not saying you can't run the story. I'm just saying you can't run it *yet*. We just need more.'

'What?' Megan stopped in her tracks.

'You need to get more to back up the pictures. And I'm just not sure it's worth the risk . . . I mean, look what happened to Paul.'

Megan grabbed the golf ball from his desk, and grasped it in her hand. She watched Richard wince as he waited for her next move. She gently placed the ball back on the desk. 'Sometimes I wonder if your golf balls are the only ones you have, Richard. Surely our job is all about risk and uncovering the truth? I don't want to write about knitting competitions and chocolate cake recipes.'

Richard's face darkened. 'All I'm saying is be careful. Just watch yourself and don't do anything stupid.'

'Right,' she said determinedly. 'Leave it with me. I won't let you down.'

'But please be careful, Megan.

She threw him a withering look, turned and walked out.

41

The blue sky did nothing to disguise the bleakness of the tower blocks. The pavements were covered in chewing gum and cigarette ends. Teenagers wearing tracksuits and tacky-looking gold jewellery loitered on corners. They didn't look the types to ever engage in anything sporty. The roads were unkempt and the tarmac chipped. The few vibrant patches of green grass were soiled with cola cans, smashed glass and used condoms.

Megan shuddered as the taxi drove towards the flats in the pictures. This was where Rhona said she sometimes came. It wasn't far away from her sister's place but could have been in a different world. The taxi driver pulled up outside the high-rise blocks and stared at the rust-stained windows and dilapidated doorways. Outside, the forecourt was covered in ripped cardboard boxes soggy from last night's downpour. She looked up at the blocks before her, an assortment of boxed lives piled on top of one another stretching up to hell. If only she could just get inside and have a wee look around.

'You sure about this, hen?' said the driver. 'Do you want me to wait?'

Megan was tempted to ask him to come in with her. 'If you could hang on that would be great. I won't be long.'

Megan walked across to the door, her heart thudding. She pressed a few of the buzzers hoping someone, anyone, would let her in. There was a crackling sound and she pushed the door. The floor was cracked and the wallpaper peeling off the walls.

She pressed the button for the lift. The door slowly swung open and she stepped in. The lift was covered in graffiti. Broken glass crunched under Megan's foot. Megan studied the walls. Sectarianist slang. Something that looked like Urdu. Swastikas.

'Hold on,' shouted a voice.

Megan put her foot in the door as she saw a petite, elderly woman coming towards her.

'Thank you,' she said.

'Which floor?'

'The top one please . . . you get a great view.'

The lift groaned as it lumbered upwards. Megan smiled at her. 'Have you lived here long?'

'Aye,' she said. 'Most of my life.'

'Seems quiet.'

'Yes, it is mostly.' She shrugged. 'It can be noisy at night. That's when the lift is going up and down all night. Drives me demented. But what can I do?'

Megan was curious. 'Do you know who it is?'

'Aye. Those bloody foreigners on the floor below me.'

The doors opened and the women stepped out into a small dark lobby. The doors were boarded up, the floor covered in rubbish. Megan looked around to check for bullet marks on the walls. She felt as if she was reporting from Bosnia.

'Jesus,' said Megan.

'Not the prettiest. But as I said, the view is nice. And the rent is cheap.'

The air was thick with rank smells. Stale ash, urine, solvent and vomit at the very least thought Megan. 'Are you okay here?'

'It's home,' she said quite matter-of-factly. 'Where else would I go?' She looked at Megan suspiciously. 'Are you from the council?'

'No, no. I'm just . . . looking for someone.'

The woman nodded slowly, clutching at her shopping bags. 'Watch yourself, hen. A nice wee lassie like you shouldn't be hanging around a place like this.'

Megan wanted to agree but she felt awful for leaving the woman here alone. It didn't seem right that a pensioner should be living in such a shit-hole of a building. 'Will you be okay?'

'Aye,' she said. 'This is me here.' She unlocked the door, turned and closed it.

Megan glanced over at the door to the stairs. Maybe she would just have a quick look at the floor below and then go back to the taxi. At least she had plenty of description of the place for when she did eventually write the story. She felt her feet sticking to the stairs as she tried to tread quietly. It was dark outside and the light in the stairwell was flickering. She thought she could feel something rustling against her ankle and shuddered. Why had she thought this was a good idea? And why hadn't she told anyone other than the taxi driver what she was doing?

She could hear doors closing below and some men talking, their voices echoing. She paused, hesitating on the stairs and wondered if she should just keep going down or go back up to the floor above and take the lift. Just as she reached into her pocket, to feel for her phone she felt a hand on her shoulder. She was too terrified to scream.

42

Megan grasped at the roof which was just inches above her nose, her nails scratching at the metal surface. But it made no difference and she tried desperately to kick her feet up and down, despite the rope that bound them. She blinked manically, her eyes unable to focus in the darkness. The smell of diesel crept up her nose and the dirty rag in her mouth gagged her screams.

What had happened? She desperately tried to clutch to foggy shreds of memory. But her head throbbed and she choked as she felt a sob rise in her throat.

She could hear men talking nearby. Low, urgent murmurs. Then staccato shouts and rapid accusations. Where was she? Then she remembered the stairwell and the fear and the hand on her shoulder. She heard a hum, then the click of an ignition and she lurched forward again as the car began to move. Megan was terrified, lying there in the dark wondering when the car would stop and where it was going.

Ten minutes later, the car rolled to a stop. She waited nervously, her body rigid and her mouth flooded with saliva. Then there was a creak, a scrape from above and all of a sudden the boot was flooded with icy air.

She winced at the sudden plunge in temperature and the glaring lights. Bracing herself, her eyes widened as she caught sight of a face she knew. Trying to arch her trussed-up body away from the hands reaching towards her, she started to shake. How could this be happening? Jamie stared at her, locking his eyes onto hers. Slowly, he put his finger to his mouth and shook his head. Nobody could help her now. She knew then there was no going back. This was it. Then there was a bang.

Jamie jumped back, startled, and more nerves started to swirl around Megan's stomach. She tried to steady herself yet couldn't believe what was happening. Had Jamie lied to her all this time? Was he really a cop? And had she been stupid to fall for his chat? She wanted to bawl when she realised what this meant. He knew almost everything about her, he knew where she lived and where Joanna and George were. She choked another sob back as she realised she probably would never see them again. Was this it? She heard some more shouting and she thought Jamie said, 'It's okay. It's just needs mucking about. You're okay.'

Then he was there again, reaching towards her. She tried to move away and out of his clutch, but she was exhausted and she slumped back.

'Sssh Megan. It's okay. It's okay. You're safe now,' he said, pulling out the gag.

She threw him a look of disdain. Her mouth was dry and it hurt to speak. 'Get off me.'

Jamie looked confused.

'I trusted you,' she said, weakly. The pain at the back of her head had eased a little and was tender when she touched it.

Jamie's mouth was in a tight line as he reached in to untie her feet and hands. He pulled her up and towards him, helping her out of the boot. Megan's legs trembled as she looked around. It was dark. When her eyes adjusted to the dark she saw they were in a supermarket carpark. She glanced back at Jamie whose face was a mask of concern.

'What the hell is going on?'

'Believe it or not, I was trying to look after you,' he said, a tortured expression on his face when he saw her touch her head again.

Megan exhaled loudly.

'I saw you, Megan. I was at the flats and saw you being hauled out of the stairwell.'

'But why were you there?' she asked.

'Warren had asked me to check the premises and collect some cash for him . . . he has brothels like that all over the city.' Jamie paused for a minute. 'That was just one of many.'

'So when did you see me?' Megan's mind was still clouded and her heart racing.

'When that big ape hauled you out of the stairwell. He'd thumped you and you must have lost consciousness. It was my idea to get you in the boot of the car. I said I would deal with you later.' He paused, unsure what to say next.

Megan stared at him, her cheeks wet with tears.

'It was the only way I could think to protect you,' said Jamie, his voice gentle. 'At least if you were in there with me then I knew you would be safe.'

Megan allowed him to put a comforting arm round her. She shook as she said, 'So are you supposed to murder me now then? And get rid of my body?' She looked around.

'Megan, the best thing you can do is get home and not mention this to anyone. I'll be in so much shit if anyone finds out what's been happening.'

For a moment, Megan felt sorry for him. He looked vulnerable standing there, his face a mask of concern. 'But what you going to do now? What happens next?'

He cleared his throat. 'We're planning a raid.'

Megan's eyes widened. 'When?'

'Soon.'

'I want to be there to cover it,' she said. 'It's the least you can do.'

Jamie wagged a finger at her. 'You don't ask much, do you? And how do you suggest I drop that into the conversation with my boss?'

Megan touched her sore head and winced. 'I'm sure you'll think of something,' she said. 'Won't you? I mean I've got that dossier I can hand to you which may help you with your enquiries. It basically hands you some of the culprits on a plate. Anyway, having me there to cover it, exclusively mind, is all good PR for the police. You're not exactly covering yourself in glory these days, are you? Now if you don't mind, I'd really like to go home.'

'Do you think you should get your head checked out first?' he said, resting his hand on her back.

'No. It's fine. I just want to go home.'

43

Megan sat by the window looking down at the world below. The late morning sunshine bathed the street in an oily light. A bus hissed past, a couple of children skipped by and an old man struggled with his swollen carrier bags from Morrisons. She'd heard from Jamie only briefly since the other night, when he called to check she was okay, and now she was growing restless. She flicked on the television and zapped through the channels, then switched it off. The feelings of anxiety and dread descended down upon her like a heavy weight. Eventually, last night, she had spoken to Richard and told him what had happened. He'd been furious that she'd taken such a risk but then she saw the flash of excitement in his eyes. Maybe he'd remembered that he loved breaking news stories. She knew he found the pace of a Sunday newspaper frustrating at times. He'd worked in London for years at the Daily Mail and had seen it all and reported on some of the biggest news stories including Lockerbie, the IRA's ceaseless reign of terror, Dunblane and 9/11.

'This is brilliant,' he said. 'I knew the lawyers wouldn't let us run anything yet. It's just not strong enough. But if we get exclusive coverage of the raid and can bargain with them and promise to show them what we've got . . . then we've got ourselves a splash.' He scratched his head. 'Leave it with me Megan. I'll make some calls and see what I can sort. Go home. And start writing up what you can.'

Megan felt a frisson of excitement race through her. 'Okay . . . though what about Sam?'

'Still no word from him?'

Megan shook her head.

'Okay. Just you crack on with it in the meantime and keep trying his number.'

She nodded. 'Sure, I'll get onto it.'

She'd been up until late, writing copy, and had fallen asleep in the early hours. She didn't hear Joanna and George leave. She stood up and stretched and was about to go for a shower when her phone rang.

'There's been a development,' said Jamie.

'What kind of development?'

'The shit has hit the fan here. We've all been hauled in and accused of leaking stuff to the press.'

Megan's face flushed. 'What do you mean?'

'Just what I said,' his voice was curt.

'What happens now?'

'Looks like you're getting your own way with the raid.'

Megan's pulse quickened.

'Aye. Remember you don't know who I am. You've never seen me in your life.' He hung up.

She saw the incoming call from Richard and immediately answered.

'We're on,' he said, his voice high with excitement. 'It's happening. Just you and the snapper. Exclusive coverage.'

'When's it happening?' said Megan, trying to maintain her composure.

'The early hours of tomorrow. They'll brief you beforehand and I'll phone you later to make sure you're up to speed.'

'Okay Richard. Don't worry. I've done it before.'

'What — a police raid?' he said, sounding surprised.

'Yes, when I worked in Aberdeen. Mind you it was for drugs,' she said, thinking about that cold, damp morning near the harbour. Her teeth started to chatter.

'Right, well, you know what you're doing then. Stay back, let Craig take the pictures and try and get some footage . . . we'll need that for the website.'

Her heart sank at the mention of Craig. 'Craig?'

'Yes. He's the best man for the job. He's discreet and he'll get the pictures. I'm not letting any of the others fuck this up.'

She half-smiled as she pictured Richard sitting back on his chair, a hand behind his head. He was, of course, right.

'Keep in touch and let me know as soon as it's done. And remember, not a word to anyone. We don't want anyone getting wind of what we're up to.'

'Do you want me to come into the office?' she said.

'No. Stay away from the office just now. The fewer people who know about this the better.'

'Okay,' she said, walking back over to the window and looking out.

'Speak later,' he said and hung up.

Megan stood for a moment thinking. This was her chance to break a huge story and get a scoop. She couldn't afford to muck it up.

44

Craig picked her up early the next morning. It was still dark as they drove along the rain-splattered streets. The radio was on and Megan was grateful for the chatter and music. She wasn't in the mood to talk. Looking out the window, she stared at the reflection of the orange streetlights in the puddles. Craig parked, as instructed, well away from the block of flats and sighed as he turned off the engine. 'Trust it to be raining, eh?'

'It adds to the atmosphere,' said Megan. 'And it means we can keep our hoods up without looking suspicious.'

Craig chuckled. 'I suppose so.'

'So,' she said, glancing at her watch. 'You okay with the plan?'

He nodded his head. 'Aye. Keep our distance and get as many shots as possible.'

Megan reached in her pocket for the small camera she had. 'And I'll try get some footage.'

'You'd better. Richard'll kill you if you don't. Can you imagine?' He tried to smile.

Megan knew he was trying to lighten the mood but her heart was thudding and her mouth dry.

'Wonder if these bastards have any idea what's coming to them.' He reached to open the door. 'You ready?'

Megan paused for a minute and took a deep breathe.

'Take it it's been a while since you last did a stake-out or anything like this?' he said.

'No,' she lied, trying to remember the last time she'd done a story like this. It *had* been a while. Though she wasn't going to admit that to Craig. 'Right okay. Let's do this.'

'Afterwards you can treat me to a nice coffee and a bacon roll,' he said.

She rolled her eyes at him. They walked quietly and without speaking as they made their way towards the block of flats Megan had been at the other night. They'd been instructed to wait well away from the door of the building, until the police came out. Craig had driven past the night before and done a recce. He'd identified a skip they could hide behind. Megan noticed the unmarked police cars dotted around the car park. She wondered when the police vans would arrive with reinforcements. She knelt down beside Craig, her face close to his as they trained their eyes on the door.

'Like your perfume,' he said. 'Did you put that on just for me?'

'Oh, piss off Craig,' she said, more sharply than she'd intended.

He raised an eyebrow at her and shrugged. 'Just joking.'

Megan's eyes were stinging from the biting wind that was howling past them. Her legs ached as she crouched down on the wet tarmac. Come on, she said. Come on, let's get this started. Glancing at her watch, she bit her lip. Any minute now. That was what she'd been told. Unless there had been a change of plan. She reached into her pocket for her phone. No messages. Nothing. She thought about Jamie and wondered if he was in one of the unmarked cars. Or if he was keeping well away. She would get in touch with him after all of this, she thought, and thank him for his help. That's if it all worked out. Why was she even thinking about him right now? She needed to concentrate.

Craig leaned forward. 'Here we go.'

She peeked round the side of the skip and saw a convoy of police vans pulling into the car park and stopped outside the building.

'We're on, Megan,' said Craig, smiling at her.

She held her breath and watched while several police officers wearing helmets, and armed with batons, quickly moved towards the door. Then they disappeared inside.

'Come on,' whispered Megan. 'Can we get closer?'

Craig chewed his lip. 'Aye. Over there,' he said, pointing to a car.

Just as they got behind it they heard banging from inside the building and shouts of 'Police. Police. Stay where you are.'

Craig's eyes were focused straight ahead on the door and Megan was trying to mentally record as much of it as possible, to add colour to the piece. It had started to grow light but the constant drizzle created a gloomy effect. Then she jumped back as she heard the smashing of glass, then a gut-wrenching scream. Then there was a sickening thud on the ground, beside one of the vans.

'Fuck me,' said Craig as he looked ahead.

Megan felt the bile rise from her stomach as she followed Craig's gaze and two cops jumped from the van and crouched to the ground. Her eyes almost popped from her head when she saw the crumpled body of a woman, lying spread-eagled on the ground.

45

The silence was deafening as the realisation of what had happened took hold.

Megan watched as one of the policeman stood up, ashen faced, and spoke into a radio. The other one walked behind the van and she heard him being sick. Then another appeared with a blanket and placed it over the body. Megan's head was spinning. How could that have just happened?

'Look,' said Craig, 'here they come.' There was a clatter through the door and he moved closer.

The sounds of the constant whirring and clicking of Craig's camera was all that could be heard as the police came out onto the pavement holding three handcuffed men by the elbows. Megan stood close to Craig with her camera trained on the scene ahead. Two of the men were dressed in tracksuit bottoms and T-shirts. One was bald, with tattoos all over his arms. The other had cropped hair, a sallow face and he was smirking. The third man wore a suit and hung his head in shame. Megan wondered if he was perhaps a client. Each was put into the back of a van, the doors slammed shut.

Then Megan looked as the door of the building opened again and four women were led out.

'Jesus Christ,' said Craig. 'Gets even better.'

For a moment, Megan stopped filming. She was unable to take her eyes off them. Were they even women? They looked like young girls, teenagers with haunted eyes who'd lived through far more than anyone of their age should have had to. They were all scantily dressed, wearing an assortment of mini-skirts and shorts. Two wore high heels and the other two had no shoes on. Their faces were pale and they looked confused as they glanced around. Megan's eyes were drawn to the scabs on one of woman's bare legs. She was crying and agitated. Then when another of the girls spotted the heap on the ground, she began to wail. The policewomen flanking them quietly led them to another van.

Megan rubbed her eyes. Something wasn't right. These girls were all white. Sam had definitely sent her pictures of a young black girl. Where was *she*?

'Craig,' she said, quietly. 'Did you notice anything about the girl who jumped?'

'No . . . just that she's dead,' he said, drily.

She was too numb to respond. She looked up at the window from which the woman had jumped. The police would be up there now, sealing it off as a crime scene.

'Don't even think about it,' said Craig who noticed where she was looking. 'We'd be in the shit if we even tried to go anywhere near it.' He pointed a finger at her. 'I like your thinking though.'

'They can't stop us from going inside,' she said.

Craig flicked his eyes around. 'I think it would be obvious though, don't you? We are being watched, you know. And don't be surprised if Richard gets a call telling us not to mention the jumper.'

Megan's cheeks flushed. 'But why?' she said defensively.

'Well then it comes across as being a bit of a cocked-up raid doesn't it?'

Megan had to agree. 'They were meant to bring people out alive. Not corpses.'

'Looks like someone is coming over now,' said Craig, narrowing his eyes. 'Flaming 'eck, it's the boss.'

Megan looked across at the man striding towards them. She recognised him from the press conference. He didn't look very happy.

'Megan Ross? I'm DS Smith,' he said, reaching out to shake Megan's hand. He gave a curt nod to Craig. 'Thanks for coming,' he said crisply. 'I trust that you have plenty of material now. I'll be in touch with your editor shortly. I don't need to tell you not to be mentioning *this* to anyone. ' He flicked his eyes towards the body, then glared at Megan, who tried not to gulp.

'I think now it's time you were on your way.' Then he turned and walked away.

'You okay?' said Craig as they walked back to the car.

Megan nodded. She was numb, shocked and too exhausted to enjoy the moment of their exclusive. She couldn't stop thinking about the girls. Where had they been taken to? What were they thinking? And what would happen to them?

Craig started the ignition and this time when the radio came on, she asked him to switch it off. Listening to the jaunty tunes just felt wrong.

'Shall we head straight to the office?' he said. 'Or do you want to get me that coffee and bacon roll?'

Megan glared at him. 'How can you even think about food after that?'

'I need to eat to keep up my strength,' he said. 'If I stopped eating every time I saw something like that then I'd be as thin as a rake.'

'What — do you often see bodies falling from the sky?' she said, staring at him in disbelief.

He smirked at her. 'You'd be horrified if I told you all the things I'd seen.'

She turned away. 'I'll call Richard and give him a debrief.'

46

Megan pushed back her chair, stood up and stretched. She'd written up the copy from earlier and was waiting on further instruction from Richard. As expected, they'd been given strict police orders not to mention details of the woman who had jumped. The police said they would deal with that separately.

'When do we go and front them all up then?' she said to Richard who had just walked out of his office.

'We don't,' he said, his face clouding over.

'What do you mean?'

'I mean that at the moment our hands are tied. We don't have enough to name and shame them. It's a live investigation. And until there's some co-operation from the witnesses then we can't prove anything.'

Megan threw her hands in the air. 'All we can write about is the raid then?'

'Well, yes. But you can stitch in your other lines about the links between the two bodies.'

Megan hit her hand against the desk. 'But there's so much more to say, Richard! The story is much bigger than that. There's a judge and a politician and a football chairman involved.'

'Yes, I know. But the lawyers won't let us name them or use their pictures.'

Just then Megan's phone rang.

'I'll let you take that,' he said, using the opportunity to escape.

It was Natasha. 'How are you, lovely?'

'Em, okay,' said Megan, desperate to tell her what had happened and frustrated by Richard's reaction.

'How's your week been?'

'Okay,' she said, drumming her fingers on the desk. 'You can read all about it at the weekend. Actually, Natasha . . . can I just run a hypothetical question past you?'

'Of course you can. Oh, and by the way, I found out who stole my memory stick.'

'You did?' said Megan. She'd forgotten all about that.

'Yes. It was the lovely assistant. Peter. Thought he would make a wee bit extra cash from selling a story to the *News*.' She paused. 'I'm sorry that I blamed you.'

Megan waved a hand, forgetting that Natasha couldn't see it. 'Forget about it. Just sorry that you had such a wee tosser working with you.'

'Yes, well. He's been given his marching orders. He's gone. So, tell me, what did you want to ask?'

'Okay, so say police raided a bar or a brothel. And they made some arrests and also managed to bring the girls out. What would happen to them?'

'Wow. That's some question,' she said. 'But that's where this new legislation comes in. Don't you listen to *anything* I say?' She laughed.

'I do. But the new legislation isn't yet in force. What happens now? Are they still protected by the law?'

Natasha clicked her teeth together. 'Yes. I would say they are. I mean it's not their fault the law's not yet in place.'

'Definitely?' asked Megan.

'Let me check and call you back.' She hung up abruptly.

Megan sat mulling over what she'd said. She automatically scrolled through the news wires checking for any new stories.

Nothing that caught her immediate attention. She felt agitated and worried. Something wasn't right. Where was Sam when she needed him? She called his number yet again. This time it rang and she knew, from the long, spaced out rings, that he was abroad.

'Hello,' said a cautious voice.

'Sam? It's me, Megan. Where have you been?'

'Just been keeping out the way.'

She thought she heard a splash in the background. 'Could you not have returned at least one of my calls?'

'Actually no,' he said and chuckled. 'I left my phone by the pool and, well, it got a bit wet. It's been in a bag of rice for the last week. Only got it working again this morning.'

Megan thumped her desk in frustration. 'You could have emailed me back or replied to the messages?'

'Sorry,' he said, sounding sheepish. 'But, well, I'd kind of done my bit. We thought it best if I laid low. Left the rest to you.'

'We?' she said, confused.

'Yes. Me and Richard.'

Megan wanted to scream. 'Why didn't he tell me where you were and what you were doing?'

'Och you know what he's like. He gives nothing away. And I was sworn to secrecy. Anyway how's it going?'

'It's okay,' said Megan, suddenly weary again. 'But she wasn't there, Sam.'

'Who?'

'The girl you mentioned.'

Silence.

'Right. Well . . . maybe she was moved on. Or somewhere else?'

Megan's heart sank. 'Maybe,' she said. 'Anyway, I'd better go. Keep in touch.'

She placed her phone on the desk next to her and dropped her head into her hands. She wondered if the girl was dead, and that's why she never came out of the flats.

47

The following day, Megan was subdued even though her byline was on the splash and her story had been picked up by all the other papers. She lay in bed for a while, too exhausted to think, and drifted in and out of sleep. Eventually she'd woken up, rolled over and picked up her phone scrolling through the messages. She gasped when she saw one from Sam. The politician in the pictures had quit. She opened up the BBC's news page.

Breaking News: Tory MSP Thomas David has announced he is to quit Holyrood with immediate effect. He said he wishes to spend more time with his family.

'Ha,' she snorted. 'The usual, lame old excuse.' Megan sat up and reached for her tablet so she could have a look at the other papers.

Sunday Post, 2 May, 2016

Arrest at Brothel in Police Anti-Trafficking Crackdown

A 38-year-old man has been arrested in connection with brothel keeping following police raids in Glasgow. It comes as part of a wider investigation into human trafficking and serious and organised crime.

The raid targeted an address in Partick in Glasgow, and also involved

Europol officers. Police Scotland confirmed one man was arrested in connection with brothel-keeping and serious and organised crime. He is expected to appear in court tomorrow.

THE SUN ON SUNDAY, *2 May, 2016*

Assets Seized in Lap-Dancing Club Raid

One of Scotland's top lap-dancing clubs was raided yesterday in a major proceeds-of-crime probe. Police swooped on the Tinkle Club in Glasgow city centre where they seized £20,000 in cash. They later raided owner Warren McGregor's home in the Bearsden suburb of the city, where they seized a further £10,000 in cash along with jewellery.

McGregor spent most of the day being quizzed by cops but was later released.

A report will now be submitted to the Procurator Fiscal. The club has been closed since the raid. It is a popular venue which has previously been visited by a number of high-profile celebrities and businessmen. For legal reasons we are not able to identify patrons of the club.

MEGAN TUTTED TO HERSELF. None of them had any new lines. They'd just recycled her story but, of course, hadn't credited her paper for any of it. Then she opened her Twitter account.

TWITTER

@nosyparker who are the celebrities who've been going for a tinkle at the club? #gaggingorder

@tellingthetruth read all about it here! household names! politicians! media luvvies! coming soon! #gaggingorder

@jammydonut why the news blackout? #gaggingorder

@tellingthetruth cos they're not just tinkling at the club. more and worse to come #gaggingorder #truthwillberevealed

. . .

She was so relieved she couldn't help smiling. At least people were fired up enough to actually talk about. If she had to use social media to spark the debate and engage people with who the names were then so be it. Of course she'd chosen an anonymous username. Richard would hit the roof if he knew what she'd done. She'd been so incensed though that the paper couldn't name and shame any of those involved, that she'd decided to move things along herself. Now she had lit the fuse and the fire would take hold without any more help from her.

She was desperate for a drink, so pulled on an old sweatshirt and padded through to the kitchen.

'Morning Auntie Megan,' said George. He was pouring Cheerios into a bowl and had his football gear on.

'Hi sweetie,' she said. 'How are you? Feels like I haven't seen you for ages.'

He looked at her solemnly. 'I've a busy life, Auntie Megan.'

She giggled. 'Yes George, you do.'

'Well done Megan,' said Joanna, walking into the kitchen. 'Great story. You must be delighted.'

Megan half-shrugged. 'I suppose so.'

'I'm going to make a cuppa. Do you want one?' said Joanna. She turned on the radio before looking around for a mug.

'Here, let me dry some,' said Megan, walking to the rack. She looked across at her sister, who seemed distracted. Megan started to dry the crockery and then stopped for a moment to listen to the news.

'Police in Glasgow are appealing for help to identify the victim of a traffic accident. A young woman who was knocked down in a Glasgow street last month remains in a serious condition in hospital. The woman was spotted running towards cars in a distressed state on the 30th April in Dumbarton Road. She was thought to be aged 16 or 17, of Nigerian descent, and police have appealed to the public for more information to try to identify her. Police sources claim she could be a victim of human trafficking. A spokeswoman for Police Scotland appealed to the public for information . . .'

In Megan's mind she could hear the thud and squeal of brakes.

She could see the girl's body somersaulting in the air. It all made sense now. She had actually been there and seen it happen.

She dropped the mug and it crashed onto the floor. George jumped in surprise, dropping his spoon with a clatter on the floor. Joanna gasped when she saw the shards of ceramic scattered across the tiles.

'What's the matter?' She bent down to pick up a piece.

'I know who she is. The girl. The girl on the news a minute ago. I saw her.'

'What are you talking about?'

'The one who was knocked down. She's in hospital.'

'Slow down, Megan. You're making no sense. What are you talking about?'

'The Nigerian girl who was knocked down. I was there.'

'Oh.'

'I saw her. I saw her being knocked down that morning I was out running. It all makes sense now.'

'You're making no sense to me, Megan.'

'I know who she is. She had a name. Sam told me.'

Joanna looked confused. '

Megan ran through to her bedroom and reached for the bundle of pictures Sam had sent. She looked for the image of the girl. Megan knew it was the girl on the news. It had to be. She handed a picture to Joanna. 'She's called Mercy. Itohan in Nigeria.' Megan wiped away a tear. 'That girl is somebody's child.'

'And now she has a name. You can give her a name.'

Megan nodded. 'Yes,' she said softly. 'Itohan. Mercy. I'm glad we can give you a name. I'd better let the police know.'

48

There was a knock at the door and Megan paused for a moment before answering.

When the person knocked again and coughed, she opened the door, holding it slightly ajar. It was Jamie.

'Hi,' he said, lingering on the doorstep.

'Come on in,' she said.

He leant down to kiss her and gently touched the faded bruise on her head. The hallway was stacked with packing-boxes. 'What's all this?' he asked in surprise.

'Just a few more of my things from Edinburgh.'

He raised an eyebrow. 'So he sent them on after all?'

She nodded, rolling her eyes. 'Yes. I wasn't that bothered if I didn't get everything. But I had started to miss my books and CDs,' she said. 'Anyway it's over. That's the lot. Mind you, I'm not quite sure what happened to make him change his mind. The last I heard he was threatening to chuck it all in the bin.'

Jamie smiled.

'So,' she said, 'What happens now?'

'Well we've had McGregor in for questioning. And there's more to come . . .'

'That's great.' Her voice was flat. 'But they're not the main players, are they, Jamie? They're just the pawns.'

'But it all helps. These are all steps to landing the big ones. And look at the girls who have been freed. Thanks to you, we were able to raid the brothel and get them out. We just need to be patient. Hopefully some of them will testify.'

'It doesn't help the dead girls, though, does it? It won't bring them back. Will anyone ever get charged with their murders?' Megan leaned against the wall, flicking her eyes over Jamie. She was tempted to allow herself to crumple into his arms but she knew it would be pointless. 'And the men in the pictures? The judge? He just walks away because of who he is.'

Jamie frowned. 'Look, just because his sister is the chief it doesn't mean he will get away with anything. But at the moment, without witnesses, then there's not a lot we can do. We *will* get him, though. And in the meantime he's resigned from his position.'

'How? From where I'm standing it appears he can get away with what he wants.'

'We've got forensic accountants examining his business interests. Seems he has links which tie him to the company which owned the flat where it was all happening. It's just a case of joining up the dots. I'm confident he'll get what's coming to him regardless of his links to the chief. The others will too.'

'And what about Paul?'

Jamie cocked his head to the side. 'I was wondering when you would work out he was involved.'

'I worked it out from the pictures. I mean it took me a while to figure out it was Paul. He was obviously wearing a disguise. That hat and those glasses. Not exactly original or effective. But, well, I got Ronnie in the office to zoom in and it all just clicked. I just wondered if he would have claimed to be working undercover,' Megan retorted.

Jamie snorted in disgust. 'He was very much a service user. And I suspect he knew more than he should. Which is perhaps why he was pushed.' He looked pensive.

'What is it?' said Megan, waiting for him to continue.

'This is definitely and completely off the record. Okay?'

'Yes. I'm too knackered to do anything anyway.'

'Remember the business guy we talked about. Murray McVey?'

Megan's eyes widened. 'The *Heartbeat* App guy?'

'Exactly. Well his body has just been found. Washed up on a beach in Ayr.'

Megan looked enquiringly at him. 'What happened?'

'We think suicide. He sent police a letter confessing to his role in the trafficking ring. Looks like he was behind an App designed for an online service with girls going to the highest bidder. Guilt got the better of him and he wanted to come clean. Claims he didn't know that was what it would be used for.'

'Good God,' said Megan. 'The story just gets bigger and bigger.'

'Aye but that's not for printing,' he said in alarm. 'I'd get the sack for sure.'

Look,' said Megan, 'thanks for coming to tell me, and thanks for all your help. I'm sorry if I got you in trouble.'

He stepped towards her and brushed his hand against her arm. 'It's okay. Nobody worked it out.'

She sighed in relief. 'So, you can keep feeding me lines then?'

He chuckled and crossed his arms.

'Fancy a cuppa?' she said, turning and waving him through to the kitchen. 'I was just about to stick the kettle on.'

'Where's your sister and George?' he asked.

'They're not far away. They just nipped to the shops.' A faint frown crossed Megan's face. She needed to speak to her sister. Joanna was clearly worrying about something. She wasn't herself.

'I must sort tickets out for Firhill. A promise is a promise,' he said, sitting down at the table. Megan could feel his gaze on her. Despite the flicker of attraction she felt being near him, she had to try and ignore it.

'So,' she said. 'What are you going to do when this investigation is over?'

He sat with his chin in his hand. 'Maybe try and get a life. Not work so much.'

She looked at him pensively, wondering if work had caused his marriage to break down. 'Yes, work can kind of take over everything, can't it? I mean I used to make loads of New Year resolutions about not working so much, you know. Things I would like to do.'

'That sounds exactly like me,' he said, taking the mug she'd handed to him. 'What sort of things were on your list?'

Megan chewed her bottom lip and thought. 'To leave work behind and go surfing more often. To take up running properly and maybe even train for a half marathon. Or do one of those Tough Mudder events.' She sat down next to him. 'I also wanted to spend more time with my sister and George.'

'Well at least you're doing that. He's a good lad.'

'I know. It's been great getting to know him. I promised to take him surfing too.' Megan paused. 'How about you? What's on your list of things to do outside work?'

He looked down at his hands which were clasped on the table. Taking a big sigh, he said, 'For the past year I've worked non-stop . . . it's how I coped.'

'Coped with your marriage break-up?' asked Megan gently.

His cracked voice gave his emotion away. 'My marriage didn't break up, Megan. My wife . . . well, she died. Last year, she died.'

Megan hadn't been expecting that. She reached across and awkwardly patted his arm. 'I'm so sorry Jamie. I'm so sorry to hear that.'

He took a sip of tea to mask the silence which now filled the room. Then he looked up, trying to smile. 'Bit of a conversation stopper isn't it?'

'Do you want to talk about what happened?'

He shook his head. 'No. Maybe another time.' Standing up, he walked to the sink with his mug. 'Look, I'd better go. Leave you to it. But thanks for the tea.'

'You're welcome. Any time,' she said. 'And I mean that, Jamie.' She reached up to kiss his cheek.

Jamie flushed. 'Watch yourself with those boxes now,' he said, walking to the door.

She looked at him pensively. 'Jamie, I don't suppose you had something to do with all of this?' She gestured at the boxes.

He chuckled nervously. 'Em, not really . . .'

'Oh dear. Why do I not like the sound of this?' Her shoulders slumped.

'It was nothing to do with me. Honestly. However, a wee birdie may have told me that he and his posh lawyer friends were caught coming out of a male only dinner, all dressed in their tartan trews, at some venue on Princes Street.'

Megan narrowed her eyes, her arms crossed. She could just see them all, completely drunk and acting like pricks. 'Oh dear. I can imagine it was messy?'

'Well, apparently your ex was caught urinating in the window of Russell and Bromley. A mate of mine lifted him.'

Megan's eyes widened.

'He got off with a warning. He's a lawyer isn't he? Can't afford to have *any* blemishes on his record.'

Megan started to laugh. 'That's the best news I've had in a long time.'

'Let's just say that I don't think he'll bother you anymore.' A faint smile passed over Jamie's face.

Megan heard a key in the lock. 'That'll be them back.'

'Okay. Well I'll be in touch . . . maybe we could have a drink sometime?'

'And not talk about work?'

Jamie shrugged. 'Well, we could try.' He ruffled George's head as he ran in and said bye to Joanna who had carrier bags on each hand. 'I'd like that Megan. See you later.'

'Here let me help you,' said Megan, her eyes flicking back to Jamie as he turned and left. Reaching out she took a couple of bags from her sister and carried them into the kitchen.

'Thanks,' said Joanna.

'Is everything okay?' asked Megan.

'No,' she whispered. 'No. It's not.'

Megan felt her stomach lurch in anticipation of what was coming next.

'It's George's dad. He's been in touch.' Joanna didn't look at all pleased. 'Megan. He's been in prison. And he's due for release . . .' she looked over her shoulder. 'What on earth do I do? And what do I say to George?'

Megan had no idea what to say. 'I think . . .' she said, her voice trailing away, 'I think we deal with it as and when we need to.' She walked over to Joanna and reached down to hug her. 'It will all be okay. Don't worry,' she said, sounding more confident than she felt.

49

Megan was in Govan, in the south-west of the city. Craig had accompanied her just in case pictures were needed. Megan thought it was highly unlikely. She was lucky enough even to be getting the words.

She looked up at the building in front of her. The Queen Elizabeth University Hospital which had recently opened. It still looked brand new and unblemished. It was heralded as one of the largest acute hospitals in the UK with state of the art services and care. Yet she and her colleagues associated it with where all the stabbing victims in the city were taken.

'All the neds end up in there,' Ronnie had told her, brightly. 'Cause all sorts of trouble for the staff.'

She and Craig walked through the atrium and past the Marks and Spencer food shop.

'I can maybe get some food on the way out,' he said, scratching his head. 'Sunita's coming over for dinner.'

Megan rolled her eyes. 'What, so you're going to get her a ready meal from a hospital shop?'

'It's not just *any* hospital shop though is it?'

'No Craig. You're right. It's not. You got me there.' She smiled and looked ahead. Gina, her friend from police communications, was walking towards her.

'Hi Gina,' she said. 'Good to see you.' She turned to introduce Craig.

'Hi Gina. How are you. It's been a while.'

'Yes, it has,' she said, crisply.

Megan noticed Craig blush. Honestly, she thought. Has he been out with her as well? She threw him a look and he shrugged. 'Thanks for letting us come in, Gina.'

Gina turned to walk back the way she had come, gesturing at them to follow. 'No problem. I have to admit it wasn't my idea though. It was hers. She wants someone to hear her story . . . I would say that there's zero chance of pictures though.'

'Does she know about the other girls?'

'Yes. Though we're still trying to establish how many of them she had met. It seems like different girls came and went . . . obviously we don't know where to.'

Megan sighed as she thought of the frustrating and futile attempts police were making at tracing all the girls from The Tinkle Club. Jamie had confirmed it was a slow and laborious process, especially when the girls were too terrified to talk or admit anything. 'How is she?'

'Getting better. Hopefully she will get out of hospital soon.'

Megan nodded. 'And you're sure she's happy to talk about this? She's not scared?'

'Honestly, Megan. I think she is terrified. That's why you need to change her name, to protect her. But she wants to help. She spoke of a friend she had in the brothel, who disappeared . . . she saw your story in the paper. It was her idea to talk to you . . . I'm just not sure how much she will say.'

Megan wasn't expecting her to say a lot. She was more than happy to play it by ear and take the girl's lead. Megan knew she would be severely traumatised from what had happened to her. She could only begin to imagine it, and that was horrific enough. She felt a surge of anger flash through her when she thought about what had happened and what was still happening to girls like her.

Natasha had already confirmed to Megan that all of the girls were being kept in a safe house and being looked after as victims, in line with the new legislation. The girl would also be protected and treated as a victim. They had done *nothing* wrong. 'She'll get help and support, Megan. I'll make sure of that. We're hoping to get her home. But only if that is what she wants.'

They followed Gina into the lift and waited in silence. The door pinged open and they walked down another corridor, through a set of double doors and to another set of doors where they had to wait until they were allowed through. The smell of antiseptic mixed with over-cooked food flooded her nostrils. Megan had never felt comfortable in hospitals. They triggered too many unhappy memories.

'She's down here,' said Gina, pointing to a door at the far end of the corridor. A lone policewoman sat outside, looking at her phone. She stood up as Gina approached and checked Megan and Craig's ID. Craig was instructed to wait with the policewoman. He would only be allowed into the room with the girl's permission. Even then, any shots would most likely obscure the girl's face so that she couldn't be identified.

Slowly, Gina opened the door. Megan felt butterflies flutter across her stomach as she was shown into the room. There, on the bed, was the girl. She was small and delicate, resting against the pillows which were propping her up. Her face was still swollen and there were deep cuts on her face. Her hair was fanned out around her, like a halo. There was still a bandage on her wrist. She didn't take her eyes off Megan as she walked towards her. Smiling, to try and reassure her, Megan glanced around the room while Gina made the introductions then sat down at the side of the room.

Megan stood by the side of the girl's bed and gently took her hand in hers. 'Idato,' she said. 'Hello. My name is Megan . . . and I want to help you.' She felt Idato squeeze her hand.

'Thank you for coming,' she whispered, her eyes moist with tears.

'I want to help,' said Megan. 'I want to tell everyone what you have been through, Idato. This shouldn't have happened.' She paused. Megan knew there really were no adequate words of comfort she could offer. 'I am so sorry for what has happened to you . . . it's not fair and it is wrong.'

The girl coughed. 'I want to tell you,' she said softly. She glanced around nervously. 'Please. Please, believe what I say.'

Megan moved closer and sat down at the side of the bed. 'Of course. Just start at the beginning, Idato,' she said gently, brushing her fingers against the girl's. 'And, please, just take your time.'

The girl reached for her glass of water and took a sip. She sighed and closed her eyes for a moment. Then she opened them and slowly she began to speak.

AUTHOR'S NOTE

Thank you for choosing to buy and read *The Invisible Chains.*

I began researching and writing a version of this book in 2014 as part of a creative doctoral research project at Stirling University. My unwavering focus has always been about raising awareness of human trafficking, an appalling abuse of human rights which is the world's fastest growing crime. It is a hidden crime, which traps people through the use of violence, coercion and deception, and exploits them for financial gain.

Modern-day slavery is found in almost every country in the world. People are being held against their will and forced to work in areas such as domestic settings, agriculture, fishing and nail bars as well as being forced into prostitution and marriage. At any given time in 2016, an estimated 40.3 million people were in modern slavery, including 24.9 million in forced labour and 15.4 million in forced marriage. (Source: Global Estimates of Modern Slavery: Forced Labour and Forced Marriage,Geneva, September 2017.) According to The Centre for Social Justice (CSJ) and Justice and Care report, in 2020, there are at least 100,000 victims in the UK. It also warned of a "serious risk" that coronavirus could result in a rise in modern slavery and human trafficking. (Source: The Centre for Social Justice, It Still Happens Here: Fighting UK Slavery in the 2020s)

All profits raised from the sales of this book will go to the Trafficking Awareness Raising Alliance (TARA) a support service in Glasgow for trafficking survivors, to help identify and support women who may have been trafficked for the purpose of commercial sexual exploitation, and to Survivors of Human Trafficking in Scotland (SOHTIS). For more information visit www.sohtis.org and www.glasgow.gov.uk/TARA

Over the past 20 years, I have worked closely with survivors of abuse, asylum seekers, people traumatised by war crimes and those affected by gender violence. The importance of sharing stories, no matter how difficult and complex they are, is something that will always be at the heart of my work.

ACKNOWLEDGEMENTS

This book, and my PhD research project, would not have been possible without the support and help of many.

Significant thanks are due to the Arts and Humanities Research Council for funding my doctoral research and to all the staff at the Scottish Graduate School of Arts and Humanities.

I would like to thank my supervisor Dr Liam Murray Bell, at Stirling University, for his constant support, advice and encouragement during this research project. I was extremely lucky to have his input and wise counsel throughout. I would also like to express my gratitude to Professor Claire Squires who was a superb secondary supervisor for the same reasons. Thanks are due to Professor Karen Boyle for her input and help, to Professor Kathleen Jamie for her encouragement right from the start, and thanks to Dr Chris Powici and Kevin MacNeil for advice and support. Thanks also must go to Professor Louise Welsh and Dr Cristina Johnston for their input and feedback, and to Dr Charlotte Beyer for her interest and support.

I am also indebted to Julie Watson and her colleagues at Women's Aid East and Midlothian and Nel Whiting. I would like to thank Bronagh Andrew at the TARA Project in Glasgow, Christina

McKelvie MSP, Adrian Searle, Magi Gibson, Matt Patrick, Ross Dow, Neill Thomson and Dr Pete Armstrong.

Thanks are also due to Lin Anderson, Anna Smith and Kati Hiekkapelto for agreeing to be interviewed for the research project. I would also like to express my gratitude to Val McDermid who has been particularly generous with her time, encouragement and help. Hanif Kureishi is another writer, and mentor, whose advice over the years has been appreciated.

Dr Emmet McIntyre, I want to express my gratitude to you, for so enthusiastically encouraging me to believe I could do this and for designing another amazing book cover! Thanks to Jenny B. Lovatt for introducing me to Liza Marklund's books. Thanks to Kiran Kataria and to Alison Rae, my book fairy, for her immense editorial help, and to Lynne Hill, Elaine Bissett and Frances Wells for reading in advance. An extra special thanks must go to Louise Welsh, for providing the book's cover quote.

Finally, I would like to thank my family and friends for their patience and support, which has been constant and much needed throughout this whole process.

THE GIRL I LEFT BEHIND

If you enjoyed this book, then don't miss this other gripping thriller by LE Hill

THE GIRL I LEFT BEHIND

What if all you thought was true was the most terrifying lie imaginable?

Sophie Lewis knows what it's like to live with secrets. The arrival of her daughter has triggered memories from her own childhood which she would rather leave buried firmly in the past.

Ten years ago she left the UK to start a new life in Sydney. Now, her husband's job offer of a year's work in London forces her to make a decision whether to come home. For Sophie, it could finally be time to confront her demons. Her unsuspecting husband knows nothing about her past or of her plans to seek revenge.

When Sophie comes face to face with her abusive step-father, it triggers a chain of events so catastrophic they'll both wish she'd left the past where it belongs – dead and buried. And she is forced to question whether her whole life has been built on a lie.

This twisty and gripping psychological thriller will keep you guessing until the very last page.

Available now to buy here: https://amzn.to/3jo7Qra

PRAISE FOR THE GIRL I LEFT BEHIND

'A gripping read that moves between the past and present and keeps you hooked right until the last sentence. I couldn't put this down once I started it!' Goodreads

'Perfectly paced plot with depth and twists. Page turner that had me hooked from the start.' Goodreads

'The sign of a great thriller is when you're always itching to get back to it, and *The Girl I Left Behind* captured me completely over the course of two to three days. The format of short chapters and alternating past/present timeframe keeps momentum and the compelling story keeps you hooked in right to the last page. The material is quite dark but skilfully handled with insight and care by the author.' Amazon

'A real page turner with an unexpected twist at the end. Stayed up far too late on a few nights reading this book. It totally draws you in. I loved the language the author used.' Amazon

ABOUT THE AUTHOR

LE Hill began her writing career as a journalist and spent much of her working life in Glasgow, Edinburgh and London. She has also worked in marketing, communications, research and teaching. She is particularly interested in creative writing for health and well-being and runs a small social enterprise using shared reading and creative writing to reduce social isolation.

She has an MA in Creative Writing (Distinction) from Kingston University and in 2014 was awarded a Scottish Graduate School of Arts and Humanities doctoral grant for PhD research at Stirling University. This project focused on the role of women in Scottish and Nordic crime fiction. Her work has appeared in various anthologies and books and has been shortlisted in national writing competitions. She has been a writer in residence with Women's Aid East and Midlothian. This work has twice been nominated in the Write to End Violence Against Women Awards. Her debut novel, *The Girl I Left Behind*, was published in 2020. For more information visit: www.lornaehill.co.uk

If you enjoyed *The Invisible Chains,* please consider leaving a review online:

Amazon UK: https://amzn.to/2HT36Wo
Amazon Canada: https://amzn.to/37ZdbM8
Amazon US: https://amzn.to/34K29sr
Amazon Australia: https://amzn.to/2TK785K

Printed in Great Britain
by Amazon